Accidentally FOREVER

CARRIE ANN

NEW YORK TIMES BESTSELLING AUTHOR

RYAN

Accidentally Forever

Special Edition

Montgomery Ink Legacy
Book 8

Carrie Ann Ryan

Author Note

Aria's father, Alexander, is a fan favorite from the book Ink Exposed. His story dealt with alcoholism, addiction, and the pain they endure within and what happens to their family.

Aria is not an addict, nor is Crew. But Travis, Aria's best friend is. I took delicate care in this story as I always try to do. But Travis is not the hero of this book. He is in pain. And Aria's strength in trying to provide help shows that.

There is no self-termination in this book. However there are thoughts of self harm by side characters—not by Aria or Crew so it will never be in their POV.

All content warnings are listed on the book page for this book on my website.

If you or someone you know is struggling with mental health, there are many resources available, including:

In the US: 988 Suicide & Crisis Lifeline: Call or text 988 to connect with a trained crisis counselor 24 hours a day, 7 days a week. You can also chat online with a counselor.

In the UK you can call 1 1 1, 24 hours a day.

In Australia, you can call 13 1 1 14.

And many more in other countries.

Accidentally Forever
By: Carrie Ann Ryan
© 2025 Carrie Ann Ryan

Cover Art by Sweet N Spicy Designs

All content warnings are listed on the book page for this book on my website.

Praise for Carrie Ann Ryan

"Count on Carrie Ann Ryan for emotional, sexy, character driven stories that capture your heart!" – Carly Phillips, NY Times bestselling author

"Carrie Ann Ryan's romances are my newest addiction! The emotion in her books captures me from the very beginning. The hope and healing hold me close until the end. These love stories will simply sweep you away." ~ NYT Bestselling Author Deveny Perry

"Carrie Ann Ryan writes the perfect balance of sweet and heat ensuring every story feeds the soul." - Audrey Carlan, #1 New York Times Bestselling Author

"Carrie Ann Ryan never fails to draw readers in with passion, raw sensuality, and characters that pop off the page. Any book by Carrie Ann is an absolute treat." – New York Times Bestselling Author J. Kenner

"Carrie Ann Ryan knows how to pull your heart-strings and make your pulse pound! Her wonderful Redwood Pack series will draw you in and keep you reading long into the night. I can't wait to see what comes next with the new generation, the Talons. Keep them coming, Carrie Ann!" –Lara Adrian, New York Times bestselling author of CRAVE THE NIGHT

"With snarky humor, sizzling love scenes, and brilliant, imaginative worldbuilding, The Dante's Circle series reads as if Carrie Ann Ryan peeked at my personal wish list!" – NYT Bestselling Author, Larissa Ione

"Carrie Ann Ryan writes sexy shifters in a world full of passionate happily-ever-afters." – *New York Times* Bestselling Author Vivian Arend

"Carrie Ann's books are sexy with characters you can't help but love from page one. They are heat and heart blended to perfection." *New York Times* Bestselling Author Jayne Rylon

Carrie Ann Ryan's books are wickedly funny and deliciously hot, with plenty of twists to keep you guessing. They'll keep you up all night!" USA Today Bestselling Author Cari Quinn

"Once again, Carrie Ann Ryan knocks the Dante's Circle series out of the park. The queen of hot, sexy, enthralling paranormal romance, Carrie Ann is an author not to miss!" *New York Times* bestselling Author Marie Harte

Dedication

To Team Carrie Ann.
Thank you for showing me I can rely on others.
Aria found that out the hard way and I'm grateful I
didn't have to.

Prologue

Crew

I could have sworn the sheet rock rumbled as the pictures on the wall shuddered.

"Please. I can't...please."

I shut her up with my mouth, one hand sliding up her thigh, pushing her dress out of the way so I could get more of her skin. The other hand slid up her arm and pinned it above her head, fingers tangling with one another.

My mouth crushed down on hers, both of us fighting for control, driving deep within one another.

My hand slid between her legs, over her panties, and cupped her.

"Oh," she moaned, and I continued to kiss her, trailing my mouth down her jaw, over her neck. When my fingers tugged her panties to the side, my palm went slick just by a bare brush.

"So fucking wet for me. You want this. You're a dirty girl, aren't you?"

"Stop talking and make me come."

I let go of her hand and slid that hand right over her throat, my thumb sliding along her neck. "Oh, it's like that, is it?"

Those piercing blue eyes narrowed. "Always."

I ignored the barb, and then with my gaze on hers, speared her with two fingers. She drenched my hand, my thumb pressing along her clit as she rocked her hips.

"That's it, be a good little girl and ride my hand."

"Don't call me that," she bit out before I slid my thumb into her mouth, forcing her to lick and suck.

"Fine."

And that was right anyway. Because she knew I only said the words to get a rise out of her. I never knew what I was saying when it came to her. No. We would keep this distance, as I finger fucked her, and she drenched my hand as if she couldn't hold back any longer.

And when she came, clamping down on my fingers,

I kept moving, the sounds of sex filling the hallway. There was nothing more I could do, nothing more that I could say. So I pulled my fingers out of her, and then used both hands to grip her hips.

"More?" I asked.

No matter how much I wanted to pretend that this meant nothing, something told me this was a lie. But no, this had to be just sex. A quick fuck, a hard one. She could debase me, call me names, and I would do just the same for her.

Because it didn't matter.

Nothing mattered.

"I just...I don't want to think." She stared up at me with wide eyes and I knew what she needed—what she refused to or couldn't voice.

I nodded, understanding, then undid my jeans with one hand, keeping my mouth on hers. When we pulled away, and I slid the condom over my length, I couldn't help but take a moment to step back and stare at the beauty of her.

I had already pulled down her dress so her breasts were bare, her nipples hard little points already swollen from my mouth from before. Half of her dress had scrunched to the side, the other half pushed up. Her panties were a damp mess shoved to the side, and I wanted her. *Needed* her.

I kissed her again, hating myself. And then I slammed deep inside her. One thrust, one motion, and she was screaming my name, pulsating around my cock as she came, and I *moved*.

The picture frames continued to bash against the wall as I fucked her hard against it. There was nothing more I could do, just *this*.

I needed her. Needed her more than the air I breathed. But I knew it had to be only for sex. It was what we were good for.

It wasn't as if I really wanted more.

And when I finally came, pinning her to the wall, her fingernails dug into my shoulders, and I kept her to me, hips against hips, buried balls deep. Both of our breaths came in pants as we tried to calm our hearts, but there was nothing more I could do. Nothing more I could say.

I pulled out of her and ditched the condom in the trash nearby. She righted herself, not meeting my gaze, and I ignored it.

Because this was just a mistake.

Just like it had been before.

"So, are we going to talk about it?" I asked, my voice a growl. I didn't mean for the biting tone. I didn't *mean* to say anything. But I was so damn tired.

Aria Montgomery shook her head and wiped a tear from her cheek.

I cursed under my breath and moved closer, wiping the second tear with my thumb. Nothing made sense anymore. It couldn't. I had done that. Doing what both of us had wanted. Playing a game. And I had left that tear. I hated the names. But the names were doing what we were good at. Playing a game.

"I can't," she whispered, her voice breaking.

I tucked myself back into my pants and swallowed hard. "Because you love him. Even with all he's done, you love him."

She met my gaze again, those blue Montgomery eyes staring daggers into my soul. "No, I... I know I can't love him. And I don't really."

"Aria. You can lie to yourself every day. But you don't get to lie to me. Not when we play games here. We can play games when I'm deep inside you, but you don't get to play games *here*."

"I loved the idea of him...but with this..." Her voice trailed off and she didn't look at me. I knew there was more going on in that brilliant mind of hers than this moment. And I wasn't part of it. We'd both taken advantage. Just like always. "This can't happen again."

I nodded tightly, knowing that all good things, even

how dirty and manipulative they could be, had to come to an end.

"Fine."

"You were with Daisy. My best friend. My cousin."

And here it came—the rationalization. It surprised me it had taken her this long to find the road she wanted to go down when it came to pushing me away. Too bad I'd be the one walking—even if she didn't realize it. "Well, Daisy's not my cousin because that would have been wrong, but she is my best friend. I'm allowed to fuck other people you know."

Aria looked like I had hit her, and I could have rightly hit myself.

"Aria..."

She shook her head. "I have to go."

I looked down at her disheveled dress and hair and didn't bother to tell her that she should get cleaned up. Because if she stayed, we'd fuck again, and then she would do the worst thing ever and fall asleep in my arms.

And that's not what we did.

"Fine. Go. But we're done—you and me. I'm done being the one that you run to when things get hard because you know I don't ask questions."

Aria lifted her chin then, looking like the Montgomery I knew. So fierce, so passionate. So not mine.

"All you do is ask questions, Crew. I'm the one that never has the answers. And you're the one that never lets me ask *mine*." And when another tear fell, and another, I didn't bother to wipe them away. Instead, she turned and left, picking up her purse and closing the door quietly behind her.

Aria Montgomery didn't want to cause a scene. She wouldn't slam the door. Instead, she would leave, and once again I watched the woman that I pretended not to love run away.

Chapter One

Crew

"**D**on't worry, Crew. One day your Prince or Princess will come." Lexington paused, his eyes dancing with laughter. "Of course, the goal is to make them come more than once, I would think."

I stared at my best friend and took a step back. "Really? After all our time together, all the issues that surround us day in and day out, you go with *that* joke?"

Lex widened his eyes comically. "It's a good joke. A great joke even. You are just one ballad away from becoming a Disney prince this point."

Dash frowned. "Do princes get ballads? Usually it's the princess who gets to sing about how her life is in shambles, or whatever dreams she has, or the fact that she's falling in love. Do the guys even get a song of their own that's not about how big their muscles are?"

Lex shook his head. "In *Frozen 2*, the guy who talks to reindeer gets his own boy band song. It's quite astounding because they didn't let Jonathan Groff sing in the first movie beyond that weird reindeer song. And he is a Tony award winning singer. It was a disservice."

I pinched the bridge of my nose, wondering exactly how Lexington had not only become my best friend, but had also started to bring every single one of his family members into my circle. That was how Dash had joined in on our dinner for the evening.

"First, don't call that song weird. We both know that most animals are better than people."

Lex tilted his beer at me in acknowledgment.

"Second, he technically won the Tony *after* both movies were out."

"I'm not worried but pleased that you know so much about Jonathan Groff. Is there anything else I should know?" Dash asked, a smile playing on his face before he took a sip of his beer.

"I had a crush on him and his costar from that serial killer show. She was hot. So of course I know things. I'm a fountain of useless knowledge. Get me on *Jeopardy*, and I could kick ass." I winked before stealing one of Lex's onion rings.

Lex narrowed his gaze at me. "You didn't want onion rings. You wanted sweet potato fries. Why are you stealing mine?"

"Because they don't taste good cold, and you're letting them go to waste. I am just allowing the onion ring to fulfill its life's purpose." I crunched down on the greasy yet crispy perfection and took another sip of my beer.

"Now that I have learned far too much about you..." Dash continued, smiling, "let's circle back to the original point of this conversation. Are you searching for your one and only? Because if you haven't noticed, our family is starting to fall like flies. One after another. Quite frankly, I'm getting tired of weddings. I know everybody tries to have their ceremony slightly different, but in the end, it's cake and flowers. Flowers and cake."

Lexington gave me a look before rolling his eyes at his cousin. "Please do not tell any of our other family members—who happen to be in love—how you feel about weddings. Or you'll have to deal with the wrath of the mothers."

Dash didn't back down. "You know I'm not wrong here."

Lex shrugged, absently playing with the lettuce on his burger. "I don't really care. Everybody does what they want and with all the crap our family has gone through over the past few years, they deserve cake and flowers."

"I'd rather just have the cake."

I held back a grin at the two of them as they continued to discuss the various family members that were either getting married, already married, or having babies. It was only because I knew the Montgomerys so well that I could keep up with the conversation.

Lex and Dash were first cousins, as their fathers were brothers. However, the rest of the Montgomerys called themselves cousins regardless of the connections. With so many children in their generation, it was just easier for everybody to go by the same moniker, that way they didn't have to guess as to who the aunt, second aunt twice removed, or neighbor was.

As I had come from a single child household, with no cousins to speak of, my best friend's family seemed a little ridiculous. They were loud, sometimes rowdy, but always there for you.

I knew they would lay down everything, including their own lives, to protect their family. I had seen it in action multiple times when danger came at them without warning.

And while part of me could be jealous over their

closeness, in the end I knew they would do the same for me.

Because it had been Lex's house that I had slept at when I was a kid and needed to get out from under my parents' thumb.

When my mother's fists had been sharper than her barbs. And when my father had stood back and allowed her to do so, before sending his own vitriol down the line. Sometimes the math of families didn't add up to me. I was one. With two parents, and I'd been the statistic.

The one kid who'd been forced to hide his bruises, to pretend that I had just forgotten my lunch. Instead it had been a way for my father to lash out at me by throwing away the lunch I had made for myself. And neither one of my parents would've ever given me money in order to eat. Their little way to punish me even though they had more money than most knew what to do with.

It had been Lex and his cousins who had taken me in.

And yet with the multitudes of siblings and cousins that my best friend had, all of them had loving and caring parents. There might be secrets and fights, but that came with any family. No matter what, they knew they were loved and always had a place to run home to.

And in the end, I'd had a place to do the same. Even if my parents had done all they could to make sure it wasn't a possibility.

"Earth to Crew, are you okay?"

I pulled myself out of my far too reflective thoughts and stole another onion ring. The fact that Lex didn't say anything told me he was worried about me. He didn't need to be. Nobody did. I was the sane one, the calm one out of all our friends. And if I kept telling myself that, I would one day believe it.

"I'm fine. And no, I'm not on the hunt for my one and only."

Because I already found her.

Pain lashed against my soul one more time, and I ignored the sting. It was getting easier to do as time moved on. There was probably some semblance of peace or horror at that.

Maybe I didn't love her. Maybe it was just need or an infatuation. But she didn't love me back, and I wasn't a man to beg.

I knew once I did, there would be no going back. *She wasn't ready.*

And probably never would be.

"Does hunting for your one and only mean you're on the hunt for many and everyone?" Dash asked, a grin on his face.

I rolled my eyes before taking another bite of my burger. I had gone with mushroom Swiss, but with the direction of this conversation, it tasted like sawdust.

I liked this bar and grill. It was a place we came too often. Maybe because we ate here as much as we did, it was starting to feel a little closed in. Everybody thought they knew us and what our situations were. Therefore I knew that there were gazes on us as they were trying to listen to our conversation. And I wasn't a fan of that in any sense of the word.

"You know it," I finally answered. "Why settle for one when you can have more?"

"I would ask if that was at the same time, but I don't want to know the answer," Lex said dryly. "Considering some of our family members are in triads."

"I honestly don't know how they do that," I said with a shake of my head. "Dealing with just one other person for more than a few weeks is exhausting. I couldn't imagine having to deal with two."

"Noah, Ford, and Greer make it work," Dash said with a shrug. "But you're right. I don't know if it's for me."

"You would actually have to get more than one person to want to be with you, and that's asking a lot," Lex said before he ducked Dash's French fry.

"Stop throwing food," Margaret the owner of

Mastermind Bar and Grill said as she came forward. "Aren't you going to protect your boyfriend?" she asked me, giving me a wink.

I rolled my eyes and handed Lex a napkin. "There you go, dear. Let me know if you need me to beat up your cousin."

"You're the sweetest, darling," Lexington drawled.

Dash smirked before finishing his beer.

Margaret just looked between us, sighing. "The two of you are seriously the sweetest. Although I did like it when you were with Daisy. You two had chemistry. But I suppose you're working your way through the Montgomerys," Margaret tittered.

I fisted my hand, trying to keep the smile on my face pleasant. I liked coming here. The food was good, the atmosphere was fine, but it was getting a little too cloying for my tastes. "You know me. Once I'm done with Lex here, I'll find my next one. What do you say, Dash?"

Dash held up both hands. "Sorry, as much as I think you're hot, Lex would kill me if I stepped on his toes."

"Damn straight. Don't break us up before we're even finished."

Margaret sighed. "I don't know if you two are kidding or not."

"And you were doing a very good job about prodding," I said dryly, only letting a hint of the anger slide into my gaze.

Margaret paled ever so slightly, before giving us a tight nod and heading back to the bar.

"Well then, it looks like we're not getting another round," Lex said with a sigh. "You want to head to another place?"

Feeling a little ashamed of my reaction, I shrugged. "I don't need to go home, so sure. One more beer sounds like a plan."

Dash drained his drink. "Sounds good to me. Although you need to teach me that the growly look of yours."

I shook my head at Dash. "It's genetics. Sorry, bub. "

Both Montgomerys gave each other a glance before trying to look nonchalant. Once again, I had gotten far too close to the truth. Because of course meanness and arrogance were in my genetics. I was my parents' child after all. Only I didn't use it to harm anyone. Nor did I use it to beat the shit out of people who constantly questioned me. Or tried to put me in a box that made no sense.

Lex and I weren't dating. We never even tried. I had only dated Daisy, another Montgomery cousin. Technically I had been friends with Lex first, but in the end, I had grown closer to the Montgomerys because I had dated Daisy for a little while.

Now she was happily married, a mom, and had found herself a perfect, ready-made family. We were better off as friends.

Just as Lex and I were only friends.

No, there was only one Montgomery my damn heart craved, and she was the one Montgomery I couldn't have again.

Been there. Done that. Punched a hole in the wall.

Without words we paid our check and headed to the bar next door. I had my two drink limit and didn't want to go home. Because going home meant sitting alone in my house with the TV going, or a book in my hand. Or maybe countless files of paperwork I had on my desk. Between the gym, various other businesses I owned, and upcoming fights, I always had work to do.

The fact that somehow investing in real estate was only my side job helped me when I knew I wouldn't be getting any sleep.

It was hard to sleep when I only had thoughts of the one woman I couldn't help. Because she never wanted my help.

The three of us took a high top in the corner, the bartender getting us three beers on draft without even asking what we wanted. Either he remembered us or was in the mood to guess. I didn't care at the moment. My mind was in a thousand different directions, and I needed to focus.

I had a project I was itching to complete—a painting I knew I needed to focus on. So many things that weren't going to happen.

Not when Aria hadn't texted me back.

My jaw tightened as I checked my phone once again, waiting for an acknowledgment. She had promised me she would text when she got home. Promised that she would let me know she was safe.

It didn't matter that we hated each other. It didn't matter that sometimes we wanted each other. And it sure as fuck didn't matter that I loved her.

She had gone out into the state park by herself for a project and had promised to text when she got home.

And now it was dark, and she hadn't done so.

If she didn't text in the next thirty minutes, I'd call. I'd stop by her house. Just like the stalker I was.

I hated her just as much as I loved her, and I needed to make sure she was safe.

"Since we can't talk about your love life, can we talk about your upcoming project?" Lex asked, and I pulled myself out of my worries.

"You know I don't like talking about that shit."

"Don't call your work shit," Dash prodded.

"It's always shit until I'm done. You know how it is."

Dash rolled his eyes. "With the number of artists in our family, yes, I do. You and Aria are the exact same. You never like your things until it's finally on the wall. And even then, you both growl about it."

I did my best not to react at the sound of her name, but with the way that Lex looked at me, I had a feeling I hadn't been as nonchalant as possible. Nobody knew how I felt about Aria. Not even Aria herself. I'd barely allowed my own faults to penetrate my mind. But Lex was not allowed to know what I felt about her. It would just fuck up everything that we already had. There was no future with her. It had taken me far too long to realize that. I was not about to ruin the one good thing I had in my life— the Montgomery family.

If they knew what Aria and I had done, how dirty and disrespectful we were to each other when I fucked her raw against every surface in my house, they'd never let me back in again.

"You should be ecstatic with the fact that Hunting Memories ended up in New York? That's a great accomplishment. I'm proud of you."

I shrugged at Dash's words. "It is what it is. There're countless other people out there that are better than me."

"Where is the arrogant asshole of an artist that I know and love?" Lex asked, and I flipped him off.

"I'm in a mood. Get over it."

"You just need to get laid." Dash raised a finger. "But I'm not doing it. Sorry, I'm not going to be the next Montgomery Prince."

I burst out laughing and flipped him off as well. "You'd be the frog, not the prince. Everybody keeps calling me the Montgomery hanger-on, but I'm just trying to join the family the old-fashioned way. Marriage. I'll sleep my way into the family rather than having them adopt me as an adult. It makes sense."

They both rolled their eyes, and I drank my beer.

Because the joke was on me.

Aria Montgomery had already latched her claws into my heart, and there was no coming back from that scarring.

The problem was, she hadn't even done it on purpose. She was just herself.

Fiery, sexy, sometimes insecure, and always doing things for others.

And definitely in love with someone else.

It wasn't her fault that I loved her. But I was sure as hell going to blame her.

"I'm sure we can find one free to marry. If not, Mom and Dad will adopt you," Lex explained.

"And if they don't, my dads will," Dash put in.

Lex beamed. "That's all that matters."

Thankfully we moved on to other subjects since the other two worked together. They owned Montgomery Construction, the offshoot of the original construction company the Montgomerys owned. It shouldn't surprise me that their family worked so well together. Yes, they sometimes fought, but they were damn good at their jobs. One day soon they would build my dream home. I owned enough land to make that happen. Only a select few knew exactly how much.

Nobody else needed to know my business.

I looked at my phone again, and she still hadn't texted.

Worry clawed at my gut, but I had a feeling she wasn't going to text me anyway. Because the last time we had seen each other, I'd said such cruel things to her trying to protect my heart *and hers*, that I regretted them.

I needed to do the one thing that I hated.

Apologize.

"I'm going to head out. I have a lot of work to do."

"You good to drive?" Lex asked.

"I've had two beers in three hours and four glasses of water. I'm fine. You guys okay?" I asked.

"We're on the same beverage count as you," Lex

answered. "Have fun with your painting. Let us know if you need anything."

"Like being a model," Dash said.

I snorted and lifted my chin in goodbye. I didn't bother texting or calling Aria before heading to her place. I needed time to figure out what I was going to say, and frankly just to see her.

I was addicted, and I knew I needed to stop whatever this madness was. Only I didn't think there were any easy answers. I hated feeling like I wasn't enough. Yet I knew I wasn't. My family didn't deserve whatever goodness Montgomerys gave out.

And one day everybody would realize that.

I parked in front of Aria's house, only slightly annoyed when I realized all the lights were on.

It seemed she was home and hadn't bothered to text.

Anger coursing through my veins, I stomped up the pathway and nearly barged in when I noticed the door was partly open. Raised voices echoed through the house, and I was already running inside before I thought better of it.

"You fucking bitch! You think you can do this to me? I'll show you how strong you think you are."

Aria's back was to the wall, but instead of need and desire on her face like I saw the last time I'd had her pinned, there was only pure terror.

Her so-called best friend, the man the world thought she was in love with held her by her neck and used his other hand to punch her in the face.

Aria kicked out, screamed, and then I was moving— not caring if I killed the man who dared touch my woman.

Chapter Two

Aria

My head slammed into the wall, a ringing sound vibrating in my ears as I pushed at Travis's shoulders. Panic doing its best to override all reasonable thought, I tried to move my knee so I could hurt him like Crew had taught me. But in that moment, nothing seemed to work, and my brain threatened to go blank. It was as if all the lessons I had been taught over my life were gone. And I could not get out of this.

"You think you're so much better than me. But you're not. You're nothing. You follow me around like a dog begging for scraps. And you've done nothing for me. You want to fix me? I'm not your daddy. You can't fix me." Travis pressed his forearm to my throat.

I gasped for breath, my fingernails clawing at his skin as I tried to break free of his hold.

None of this made sense and honestly, it had all happened far too quickly. Travis had come over because he had wanted money.

Of course he had wanted money.

How was he supposed to pay for his pills and alcohol if he didn't have any income? It didn't matter that at one point Travis had been a beautiful sculptor. He could create magic and life from clay. When he was on his game, the world would weep at his artistry. I could never understand how he could bring so much life and talent with his hands.

And then he picked up a bottle. Then another. And he had drowned himself until the pickled remnants of the man who had once been my friend stood in his place.

When I had refused to give him money, he hit me.

It hadn't been the first time he'd hit me, and I'd walked away from him that time as well.

The first time had been a mistake.

The second time had been an elbow to my face when trying to talk him out of driving.

But there would be no calling this an accident. Not when he met my gaze, and I saw nothing but hatred. The man who had been my best friend. The man who I tried to keep safe was trying to kill me. I gasped, my body shaking as I tried to hold on to those thoughts. I wasn't strong enough.

"Trav—" He didn't even let me finish saying his name before he thrust down on my neck even harder. I fought for breath, stars beginning to dim in my vision.

"You call yourself my friend and yet you won't even help me. You know I'm in pain, Aria. You know I need help. And yet you hide everything from me. I don't think you know how hard it is for me. But you don't hide things from *him*. That no name asshole that has no talent and nothing. He clings on to your family as if he matters. And yet nobody in your precious bloodline really wants him. All he is is your second and third left-overs. And yet I bet you want to fuck him and he would probably let you. And frankly, he is the only *thing* you deserve."

Tears slid down my cheeks as I was finally able to take a deep breath, trying to shove him away. "Get out. Get out and don't come back."

"Oh, you're finally giving up on me? I thought you loved me," he whined. "I thought I was your best friend. But you're useless as always. Where is the money, Aria?"

"Go."

"No. You stupid bitch."

And when the fist came at my face, I tried to duck, but I couldn't quite believe he would hit me. It was as if everything happened in slow motion, and I was trying to catch up.

Pain radiated in my face, and I nearly slid to the floor, trying to get away from the next blow.

Only it never came.

Before I could blink, Crew was there.

I hadn't even known he was in my house.

By then I was sitting on the ground, my back to the wall, trying to catch my breath as Crew slammed his fist into Travis's jaw.

And then he hit him again.

And again.

"If you *ever* touch her, I will kill you. Do you understand me, you worthless piece of shit? I will end you. And they won't even be able to begin to search for your useless body."

"Fuck you," Travis spat, spittle hitting Crew's face.

I staggered up, trying to get my thoughts in order. But my head hurt, and I felt like I was going to throw up. I didn't know if I was bleeding, or where my other shoe was. I had lost it somehow when Travis pushed me to the wall.

"Crew," I whispered.

But he didn't hear me. Or at least he pretended not

to. Instead he hit Travis over and over again, and I finally moved closer.

"Don't kill him," I whispered. And without thinking I put my hand on Crew's shoulder. I didn't even hide the flinch as he turned to me, his gaze dark.

Horror crossed his face as he realized I had been afraid he would hit me in that moment. Even though I knew deep down that he would never lay a hand on me —not like there had been beneath Travis's motivations. Crew might hate me in this moment. Hate me for who we were to each other, but he would never hurt me. At least not physically.

After all, I was the one who hurt him.

"You're bleeding," Crew growled.

I put my hand on my face, my fingers shaking as I realized that the corner of my lip had a tiny cut.

"Just don't kill him."

I wanted to tell him that it wasn't that I loved Travis. I didn't want Crew to kill him because I didn't want Crew to end up in prison for life. But I couldn't say those words. Everything tightened in my chest, and I tried to suck in air but nothing would come.

Crew looked like he wanted to help, but then Travis lunged, not coming for him, but for me. So Crew tilted to the side, took the punch, and went back at it.

I needed to stop this, needed for everything to go

back to normal. Only I didn't know what normal was, and the lights hurt my eyes, and I was seeing double.

Did I have a concussion? Was that why I needed to throw up?

Before I could even formulate my thoughts, red and blue flashing lights filled my vision, making me even more nauseous. I couldn't track the events, my line of sight going blurry. And then I couldn't focus as I was on my hands and knees, heaving the contents of my stomach on the floor.

Crew moved toward me, but then he was face down on the ground, his arms handcuffed behind him.

It wasn't him.

Crew saved me.

But I couldn't say the words, my vision going dark.

And as I passed out, my gaze on Crew's, I couldn't read his face.

This was the man who I knew should hate me.

And the cops were taking him away.

And it was all my fault.

"YOU SHOULD BE AT HOME RESTING," SEBASTIAN growled, my twin's fists tight at his sides. My brother was always so good about keeping his emotions intact. He had been forced to because of so much loss at an early age, and because he'd been forced to raise his daughter alone for so long. But now he wasn't hiding anything.

"I will rest after we get him out of jail."

"Travis isn't pressing charges. Not that he had a leg to stand on. Crew didn't even get fully booked. Lex said he would go pick him up and take him home. We don't need to be there."

Translation: Crew didn't want me there.

"He had to spend the night in a holding cell because of me." I rubbed my throat, ignoring the burn that came from the bruises. "I just want to make sure he gets out fully."

"It wasn't your fault." Sebastian let out a breath. "He was in a holding cell because the cops couldn't figure out what was going on, and they took them both in until they found answers."

I flinched at his tone, hating myself for doing so. I was not weak. I had a loving family, and people cared about me. All I had done was try to show Travis how much I cared. To try to keep him safe.

And I had failed so dramatically that I was hurting everybody in my life.

"Aria. Let me just take you home."

I shook my head, and then winced. "No. I don't want to go home."

"Then let's go to my home. We won't go to Mom and Dad's. But you know they're going to find out soon. You need to tell them what happened."

"I will. I just need to see Crew."

I had woken up as soon as my eyes had closed, but the paramedics had still taken me to the hospital. Sebastian was my emergency contact, because he was my twin, and we didn't hide things from each other. And I had made him vow not to call anyone else.

Only everybody in our family was going to find out what happened soon. And there would be no hiding from this.

The whispers, and the concerned looks, and the deep talks about my friendship with Travis would continue. And I knew I deserved every minute of it. Everybody had been so worried that he would hurt me because they thought I loved him. It truly wasn't the case. Not really. It was because I was worried for him. I had thought maybe, just maybe, I might be able to fix him. And how stupid was that? There was no fixing him. But somebody needed to be in his corner. Because he had no one else. He had hurt and pushed away everyone else, so I had thought maybe I could be the strong one. But I had been wrong. So wrong. And now

Crew had had to spend a night in a cell because of my poor decision-making.

Sebastian studied my face, and I wasn't sure what he saw there. Frankly I wasn't sure what I wanted him to see.

"Go inside. He should be coming soon."

I swallowed hard and looked toward the station, knowing Crew was in there. I had done this. Crew had every right to scorn me for who we were to each other before this. Now he would have just that much more ammunition.

Before we could open the door Crew walked out, his gaze dark, his fists bruised.

I studied his face, wondering why it felt as if I had lost something special. It wasn't as if I ever had it.

Crew McTavish had been part of our family since he had first become friends with my cousin Lexington. He was practically family, at least that's what everyone said.

He had dated Daisy, another cousin of mine, and when that hadn't worked out, he had still stayed in our circles.

He was always there for us, no matter what. As was evidenced by what he had done for me last night.

And there was no way I would ever be able to repay him. Not that he would ever let me to begin with.

He had dark hair, longer on the top than on the sides, a square jaw, and a two-week-old beard. His hazel eyes changed colors depending on the light and his mood, and the small part of me that I tried to keep hidden always tried to guess what color his eyes would be the next time I saw him.

Today however, they were a dark gray. No color, no light. Just pure anger and disappointment.

Crew was bigger than Sebastian, broader shoulders, a few inches taller, but they were both decently muscular. And while my brother was covered in tattoos as he was a tattoo artist, Crew was slowly working on his ink. I had seen every inch of that ink, as well as the piercings he had used often on me over the months.

I might know his body, but I hadn't let myself know anything else. Not that he would've let me to begin with.

"Why the hell are you here?" Crew asked, the ice in his tone matching his eyes.

"She wouldn't let me take her home," Sebastian answered, and I glared at my brother.

"I needed to make sure you were fine. Stop worrying about me."

"He has a right to worry about you."

I narrowed my eyes at Crew, my head pounding. "I'm sorry. I'm sorry I couldn't stop it."

"Stop him from hitting you? Or stop the cops from molesting me?" Crew asked, and Sebastian cursed under his breath.

"Come on, let's go to the parking lot before they arrest us again."

"Not funny, Sebastian."

"There's nothing funny about this, Aria."

Shoulders deflating and exhausted, I let them both lead me to the parking lot, and I tried not to let them see the tremor in my hands.

But Crew noticed.

He always saw everything about me.

We stood by Sebastian's car as Crew folded his arms over his chest.

"As you can see, I am fine. The cops didn't have anything on me, and whatever you said to them in the hospital was along the same lines as what I said. We didn't lie, we didn't cheat, but I'm still not ready to hash it out. I don't know where your little boyfriend is, but I am so fucking angry right now."

Sebastian sighed. "Crew. This isn't helping."

We both looked at Sebastian and I shook my head. "Will you please get in the car? We need to have this out."

Sebastian looked between us before throwing up his hands and eventually getting in the car. He would probably be able to hear us through the windows, but I didn't care.

I was just so tired. "Crew. I'm so sorry."

"Don't be." For an instant I saw the pure terror in his gaze, and I wanted to reach out. I wanted to hold him and tell him I was okay. And for him to tell me the same. But I didn't have that right. And nobody knew the connection we had anyway. Or at least the connection we *once* had. We had both destroyed whatever could've been long ago.

Only now wasn't the time to focus on that. "There won't be anything on your record, right?"

"No. No charges. They figured out what happened. Or at least, what happened after I got there." Crew ran his hands over his face, looking as exhausted as I felt in that moment. "You really should be in bed. He could've killed you, Aria. And I don't know what he would've done if I hadn't shown up when I did."

Tears began to fall down my cheeks, but I didn't brush them away. I didn't have the energy. "I tried to fight back. But it was like I forgot how to. I know you tried to make sure I knew what I was doing, same with my dad, but I couldn't think. I don't know what's wrong with me, Crew. I'm sorry you were in the middle of this."

He cursed under his breath again before reaching

out to wipe away my tears. That made me want to cry harder. To fall into his arms and pretend that everything was okay.

I wasn't sure if my touch would be welcomed—nor did I know if I was ready to show the world the scars of my soul with that single touch.

"I don't want you to see him anymore, Aria. I know we already fought about this. I am tired of fighting. I just can't look at the bruises on your neck and your cheek and not want to kill him. I know you hate me. But do it for yourself. Walk away. He's not worth it."

Each word was like a blow, but I understood them. How could I not when I knew the truth?

I had been friends with Travis since middle school. He hadn't been my first kiss, but he had been one of them. We had similar interests, and he'd always made me laugh. We had never dated, but the crush I'd had on him had waned years ago. So when he had fallen into his demons, for some reason I had thought I would be the one to pull him out of it.

I thought I had been enough for him, but I hadn't been. It hadn't been the love so many people thought it was. It had been my desire to fix everything. And I had failed. And I kept hurting everyone around me trying to protect the person I thought needed me.

"I *am* done." Crew's eyes widened, and I continued.

"I just wanted to make sure they didn't keep you. And I wanted to thank you."

I heard the lack of emotion in my voice, saw the worry on Crew's face. But he didn't need to save me anymore. He needed to move on. Because while the puppy love I felt for Travis hadn't been there for a long time, the deep and abiding need for the man in front of me scared me. But he didn't want me, didn't want my baggage, and I didn't want to be the one who drowned him.

"Stop thinking." He shook his head. "I'm so fucking angry, Aria."

I stiffened but didn't say anything.

"He could've killed you, and I could've been too late. Just go get some sleep. I just can't." And with that, he ran his thumb down my cheek once more, as if afraid to hurt me, before he turned and walked toward Lexington.

I hadn't even realized my cousin had shown up, but there he was, engine running, as Crew got in without another word. As I stood there, my brother coming up behind me, I couldn't help but wonder what else I could screw up for the day.

"Let's get you back to my guest room, put more ice on that cheek, and then you're going to let me feed you." My brother paused. "This wasn't your fault, Aria."

I didn't say anything, because I knew he was lying to both of us. But I got in the car and let him drive me to his home because I wasn't the only one in pain today.

Raven and Nora were out of the house, and I was grateful for the reprieve. I didn't want to have to explain my bruises to his wife or daughter, so instead I took the ice pack from Sebastian and went into the guest bathroom.

I ignored the photos on the walls, the artistic pieces my father and I had each done for him. My brother had made this part of his home an homage to his family's art. But all I could see was the lack of substance in mine. I turned on the shower and let the steam begin to billow through the room before I walked under the stream with my clothes on and sank to the ground.

This time I let the tears freely fall as I sobbed into my hands. My shoulders shook, and I had to hope that the water would drown out the sounds of my failure.

I had been so wrong. I couldn't fix Travis. He wasn't the boy that I had known. He wasn't even a man I could recognize now. I didn't know what was going to happen next with him, but I knew I needed to stop. I wasn't like my mother who had been able to show my father what a future could be. I wasn't like my friends who could be a touchstone.

Instead I was the one who couldn't see the darkness until the shadows had gripped me in their hold.

And along the way, I had hurt the one man who had ever tried to care for me.

I wasn't crying because I had lost Travis. Because I had lost him long ago.

I was crying because I lost myself.

And because I lost the man I told myself I wasn't allowed to love.

Chapter Three

Crew

With a gasp, I once again woke up after a dream with Aria as the center. It felt like it was the only thing that I did these days.

Go to sleep doing my best not to think about her.

And wake up drenched in sweat because she was the only thing on my mind.

This time it hadn't been with her screaming, begging me to help and I was too late and too weak to save her. The dream that I'd been forced to endure for the past week since walking in on Travis hurting her felt as if it would never go away. No, it had been another kind of dream.

The whole damn situation felt so unlike Aria. Because that woman was stubborn as hell and always pushed people away who wanted to help her. She had to be the one doing it herself. She had to be the one protecting herself. No matter what came at her, she was the one who changed things. The fact that I loved that she was so damn stubborn probably had more to do with my idiocy than her willingness to walk away. After all, we'd always promised no feelings. No promises beyond those.

I still remembered that first time we kissed. The two of us had been a little drunk, but not *that* drunk. My dad had said some shit the hour before, and I had nearly made my knuckles bleed against the punching bag. She had walked in from her self-defense class, shook her head, and dragged me to the pub. She'd had an issue with Travis that had nothing to do with drinking and everything to do with the man being a narcissistic asshole. The two of us had one too many beers and fell into one another.

In truth, I'd let myself finally have what I'd always wanted—if only for a night.

No promises, except to always be friends. And we had done a decent job of that. Not a single person knew we had slept together multiple times over the year.

And not a single person knew I was so fucking in love with her that it hurt to breathe if I thought about it too hard. It was my cross to bear. After all, we had promised each other not to catch feelings and that was the first thing that I had done.

It didn't help that she was a damn Montgomery. And I had already dated Daisy, and while that hadn't worked out, we had been better friends anyway. Plus I loved Daisy's husband. We got along, and there wasn't any awkwardness about the fact that Daisy and I used to sleep together. And contrary to popular belief, Lex and I had never dated. We were just friends, friends that like to fuck with people's minds because everybody outside of his family was way too judgmental and nosy.

Any feelings I had for Aria were always an issue. Because she clearly didn't feel what I felt. And after everything that happened with Travis, she was in no place to even want more.

Yet the dream I had shot up from had nothing to do with her being unable to fight back. For me not being fast enough.

No, we were once again in bed, my mouth on hers, her hands roaming slowly over my back.

I had sunk into her, slowly thrusting in and out in that way that teased and made her eyes roll into the back of her head. She loved it when I went slow, even though she begged me to go fast and hard.

We might have played rough, but I knew she liked it soft. So I usually never gave it to her soft. As that would be crossing a line, or would reveal far too much. Because while I knew that I loved her, I also knew I couldn't have her. She was way too damn good for me. Especially with what I had to deal with today.

I got out of bed and tried to get thoughts of Aria out of my mind. Except the erection currently tenting my boxer briefs said otherwise. My cock felt as if one touch would make me blow but I knew if I fucked my fist in this moment, I'd only be thinking of her..

I quickly turned on the shower, set it to ice cold, and stepped in, ignoring the pinpricks of sensation. Then I did the one thing I knew I would hit myself for later and gripped the base of my cock, stroking myself.

I squeezed hard, just on the edge of pain, imagining Aria's mouth wrapped around my dick as she sank to her knees, her eyes wide. She'd grip my hips, her nails digging in, and I would thrust harder before coming down that beautiful throat. Or maybe I'd paint her tits with my cum, knowing she'd glare at me for it.

And when I would crush my mouth to hers, tasting myself on her tongue, she would moan into me, and I would send her right over the edge with my fingers. I'd stretch her with two, then three fingers, loving the way her soft pussy would clench around me. I'd be rough at first, then gentle right when she was at the edge, before playing with her clit to send her over.

Imagining her body going weak, her nipples hard, her mouth parting as she came, finally brought me over. I came hard, spurting over the shower wall, my breath coming in pants. I lifted the handheld showerhead and washed off my shame.

I was a monster. A filthy, disgusting monster.

I knew I wasn't going to stop. There was something wrong with me, but I couldn't change it. I was far too gone by now.

Afterward, I quickly showered and stepped out of the walk-in monstrosity that Lexington and the others had built for me. I loved the damn thing, but it could easily fit eight people.

It helped having friends who called themselves family in the construction business. My dream home had been built and decorated to perfection because of the Montgomerys. They'd known exactly what I wanted without me having to think too hard on it. There were only a few times where we'd butted heads since budget hadn't mattered to me and they'd wanted to ensure I didn't spend my entire savings.

Not everybody knew that I had paid for everything in cash. Lexington did because Lexington knew most of everything. Except he didn't know about Aria, of course. Nobody needed to know about her.

There was a reason I kept my secrets. Namely why I

was in a fucking mood at the moment and it wasn't solely about the woman I couldn't get out of my head. I quickly dressed, and knew if I didn't get out of there quickly, I would be late.

I winced at those thoughts, before pouring myself coffee in a to go mug, and walked out of my chef's kitchen, through the garage, and into my favorite SUV.

The fact that I had six vehicles and two motorcycles probably showed I had a problem. But I didn't care. Yet spending money on things that would annoy the fuck out of my parents always gave me an adrenaline rush. Nobody needed to know the McTavish family. Especially when, if things went right, I would be the last of the line.

And with that morbid thought, I revved the engine and headed to where my dad expected me. I snorted at the idea my dad truly cared as I sped down the highway. I wasn't even sure Dad was going to remember who I was at this point.

Early on-set Alzheimer's was a terrible disease. I gripped the edge of the steering wheel tight and forced myself to take deep breaths before moving one hand to take a sip of my coffee. I had done countless hours of research into it and knew there was no going back after these moments. We were just taking our steps one day at a time until there would be nothing left.

The doctors always mentioned that he would sometimes have angry outbursts, or rage against me for no reason. And I had always given them a placid expression. Yes, his main doctor thought I was a jerk, someone who didn't even deserve to be there, and I didn't care.

Because rages, cruel names, and treating someone like shit was nothing new for the McTavish family.

Coffee sour in my stomach now, I set down the half-drunk thermos before parking in the memory care center. I bypassed the valet, because of course this place would have a valet, and steeled myself for what was to come.

I didn't even know why I was here anymore. It wasn't as if my father had ever visited me at school functions, sporting events, or during one of the countless times that woman had sent me to the hospital. The only times they'd ever showed up was to a graduation and medal ceremony so they could look good for their rich friends. When it came to art school, they'd rolled their eyes at me and hadn't bothered to ask about what I was doing or even my specialty.

When I had sold my first million-dollar piece, they had shown up to the showcase. Uninvited of course. They tried to use me for connections, even though they had countless ones of their own. But it didn't matter what the McTavishes had. They always needed to go higher on the social ladder. It was what they did after all.

Or perhaps I should say it's what *we* did.

I was a McTavish.

It was in my blood.

And would be etched on my gravestone when the time came.

On that morbid thought, I moved toward the welcome area. The nurse up front smiled at me with those widened doe eyes, and I lifted my chin.

"Mr. McTavish. We're expecting you. Your father is in the Great Room. If you just follow the path down the hall, you'll find the signs for the main space. Unless you'd like me to show you the way?" she asked, her voice breathy.

I shook my head and walked past her after signing in.

The woman was gorgeous, that was for sure. But every single person employed here was beautiful. It was as if you had to have stunning looks and a pouty mouth in order to be employed here.

It was the most elite memory care center in the state, if not in the region itself. Only the best for the McTavishes. But nothing was going to keep my father alive. Part of me knew I shouldn't care—not with what he'd done.

That part reminded me why I needed to keep my hands off Aria Montgomery. That part of me was the wretchedness that proved it was a good thing that she kept running away.

I shook myself out of that thought because I needed to be on my toes when it came to my father. His nurse came forward, a broad smile on his chiseled face. "Crew. It's good you're here. He's having a good day."

I gave the man a brittle smile before nodding. "Thanks."

"You just let us know if you need anything. Would you like sparkling water?"

I shook my head. "I'm good. Thanks."

The man said a few other things, but I ignored him, my gaze on my father as he stared out the window toward the Rocky Mountains.

It shocked me how he'd changed. At least physically. He wasn't the large mountain of a man he'd once been. I was a couple of inches taller than him and broader than he'd been in his heyday, but we'd always looked alike. Something my mother had boasted about to her friends and beaten me for later. I never understood why looking at my face, a practical mere image of the man she loved, would send her to the edge.

My mother never hit my dad—at least not when I had been around. Maybe she'd done so when they'd first been married before I'd come along and taken his place. I wasn't sure and I'd never asked. But she took her rage and anger out on me. Sometimes with a wooden spoon, sometimes with belts. She'd tied me up with that belt, and continued to beat me where bruises wouldn't show. She would scream and rage and tell me how horrible I was.

And then she would glare at my father and make him say the same things. She put the belt in his hands and ordered him to do the same as she did. Each lash deeper and harder than what she'd been able to do with her strength.

And he would go along with it. He was never the first to hit me. No, he had to be forced to do it—but he'd still relished it. The same strength I held today had been in his body. I worked out and learned to fight for many reasons, but it had always started with wanting to be anything but him.

I had friends in our circles who had come from broken homes. Where people had dealt with loss, hate, or abuse. The Montgomerys were the only family I knew who seemed to be healthy and whole. They communicated, loved each other, and there wasn't a hint of abuse or hatred. It was healthy, odd, and I had always been so damn jealous of them.

Our other friends though weren't always so lucky.

Only in their lives, it was the father who became the abuser. Always the father who railed and raged.

Never the mother.

My mother was the McTavish. And my father had changed his name to suit her. He had come from an equal amount of money, but not the same amount of prestige. And my mother was never going to lose her name anyway.

It was the first in a long history of my father capitulating for the woman who had tried to beat the snark and blood out of me. My father had gone along with it because he was scared of her—at first. Then he changed.

He savored it.

He loved being her blade.

And as I stared at the man who had resented me from the day I was born, I once again hadn't asked myself why I was here.

"You're late."

"Wasn't sure you would care," I said. I held back a curse for speaking up. Silence was usually better in these situations because my father hated it—even as he was now.

"Talking back. You're learning. It only took what, thirty years? That doesn't really matter though, does it? You're never going to be good enough, Crew. Are you still working with your paint by numbers?"

The words didn't cut like they usually did. "You know it. One day I will even learn how to make the color green. It's a little hard though."

"You always were a sarcastic little shit."

"Thank you for reminding me. I'd almost forgotten." I clenched my jaw, ignoring the pain in my raw knuckles as I forced my fists to relax.

"You should watch your tone with me. I might be in here, but the only reason you're even allowed to breathe is because of me. You're nothing. You always were nothing. Nobody wants you. Nobody in here, nobody out there. It's why you're spending your afternoon in this godforsaken place. And yet, why are you here? To lord over me with some ill placed sense of loyalty or need. No matter what happens to me, I'm still better than you. That woman will still be better than you."

I shook my head, ignoring the twinge between my shoulder blades. "Even the woman that left you?" I asked, tilting my head as I studied the man who only loved to belittle me.

"She didn't leave me. She left *you*. She loved me. And she never loved you. You were the slight. The accident. But you still have the McTavish name. You'd think with that and your little art, you could find someone to blow you. I know you are a mewling little weasel, but you need to do your duty and find yourself a wife.

Spawn a little brat or two. I don't care. But get it done. You know your duty."

"Sure. I can figure that out." I said it so dryly, that the man who called himself my father glared at me.

"You unrepentant waste of air." My father moved quickly, arm outstretched. I didn't duck the first blow. Why bother. It didn't hurt anymore. But when the second blow came, I moved out of the way, tired of this.

I had no idea why I came anymore. It wasn't as if he had ever loved me.

But watching this man who'd once been so big he made me quake in my shoes become this broken man felt as if it was my penance.

Or maybe my future.

The orderlies came to pull him away, and I turned without a second glance. The Montgomerys had this beautiful family who cared for each other, were always there for one another.

Yet it was *his* blood that ran through my veins.

I walked past the nurse with wide eyes and made my way to my SUV, cursing under my breath when I realized who leaned against it.

My mother crossed her arms over her chest and glared at me in her three-thousand-dollar suit. "You love to break a good man down, don't you?" my mom asked, her tone that same banal cruelty I was used to.

I shook my head, exhausted. It wasn't even lunchtime yet, and I was done with this bullshit.

"That's rich coming from the woman who left the man currently in there."

My mother waved that off as if leaving a broken man alone in memory care and never once visiting him was the norm. When the disease had finally been too much for my mother to handle, she dropped my father off without a second glance and filed separation papers. She hadn't finished the divorce, and I wasn't sure if it was because she still loved him, or the paperwork would be too difficult to finalize. I did not understand anything that came from my mother. But then again, I never had. When I had gotten big enough to fight back, she stopped hitting me. Then my father had tried to go in, but I had gotten bigger than him as well.

The verbal assault had never stopped until I could leave. They always found ways to get into my life and needled their way through.

The money that I had, the countless investments that'd piled on top of one another, had come from the trust my grandparents had set up. Nothing in my home, in my businesses, or in my life came from my parents. They wouldn't think of it that way, but I'd done my best to clear them from my life.

"You're supposed to visit him and make him feel safe. And yet all you do is make him angry."

"Which nurse tattled to you that I was here?" I asked.

"Does it matter? You're not doing what you're supposed to. You never did."

The nerve of this woman. "This is rote by this point. If you're not going to go in there and take care of him, why are you in the parking lot?" I didn't understand her relationship with my father, and I did not want to know. But she stood out in this parking lot ranting at me for visiting when she wouldn't.

The McTavishes were complicated, and I wanted nothing to do with it.

"That is neither here nor there. You need to do better. Be the son that you've never been and actually do something for once."

Anything I would say would just rile her up or make her believe she had won. So instead I pushed past her and got into my SUV. I nearly threatened to back into her, but she would probably like that too much.

She stepped to the side and toward her convertible, and I peeled out of the parking lot and headed toward my gym. As I did, she pulled out her phone, and I figured she was probably calling her lawyer again. It always made me roll my eyes when she did that. She had been trying to get me out of my trust and inheritance my entire life. But my grandfather's lawyers were better than hers. She was never going to be able to touch anything of mine. She had already done enough of that.

Feeling a little ill, the memories of my family once again taking root, I opened all the windows in the SUV and made my way down the highway toward the gym. I turned on a familiar rock song to full blast and screamed along with it.

I pulled into the gym parking lot, then turned off the engine. I did my best to calm down, because I needed to walk in there and look as if I knew what I was doing. After all, this was my gym. I knew my friends joked that they didn't know if I was the owner or not, because I let my managers run it, but I was the financer.

This wasn't one of those pretty gyms with perky instructors who did their best to sell memberships. No, this was one filled with boxing rings, different martial arts sections, bags to beat all to hell, and places just to get free. It was a safe place, and one that was just mine.

The staff knew I was the owner, because after a while it was harder to hide it, so now the secret was out of the bag. I didn't mind at this point, too many secrets meant for too many betrayals and hurt feelings. But between my dreams, not seeing Aria for a week now, and the shit show of my morning, I needed to hit something.

I walked inside the gym, that familiar feeling starting to release the tension in my shoulders, and bypassed my team. If they needed something, they would've texted me already. But since they hadn't, I was just going to get a workout in. I stretched, grabbed some water, and wrapped my hands in the familiar way I had done for all of my life.

Lex had known I had been hurt as a kid and had tried to help me heal the bruises. Aria had found out later. Because there was no hiding things from her. Even when I tried. And Lex and I had both started taking classes in order to try to fight back. Lex had invaded then. But he had done them so I had someone to spar against. And his parents had helped me along the way. Had tried to get me out of the situation that there was no getting out of. I knew without a doubt if I had let them, they would've taken me out of that home.

But the part of me that had been belittled into nothing had thought I deserved stay.

It'd taken a shit ton of fighting, and even more therapy, for me to realize that I shouldn't have stayed. That wasn't my fault. But that still didn't mean I didn't have those demons. And bringing Aria into any of this would have just made things worse.

Cursing, I once again pushed her out of my mind. There was no reason for me to even think about her. She wasn't mine. I wasn't even sure she was my friend anymore. Not with the way that she'd looked at me. She'd been so damned scared of me. I could have killed Travis that night, and she would've watched. Because I had been out of control.

And I couldn't protect her.

I started hitting the heavy bag, using my training so I could zone out, and just let my fists work. This was the only time I could breathe, the only time I could just let my mind flow without worrying about what I needed to hide, what others saw.

My breath came in pants as I continued to beat down the heavy bag, my fists aching. I moved to the speed bag, but that didn't help, so I went back to the other, the pain harder. I didn't know if I was bleeding at this point, but I had a feeling I was. Because my hands had already been bruised from losing control over Travis.

And I deserved that pain.

Out of the corner of my eye I realized I wasn't alone, and part of me felt the disappointment that it wasn't Aria.

But I didn't think she was going to come back here.

Not when she'd seen me lose control.

And not when I hadn't been fast enough to save her. To keep her from any pain.

Instead Lexington and Kingston stood by and watched me, but didn't say a thing. They didn't need to. They took up spaces beside me, not ending my workout, but doing one of their own, and let me be.

This was where I was best. Silent, lashing out at my demons, knowing that they would never go away. I might've woken up with Aria in my dreams, but that's where she needed to stay. I came from the worst, and that meant there was no going forward knowing the path behind me.

So I lashed out until I bled, and the Montgomerys once again were by my side.

Just not my Montgomery.

Chapter Four

Aria

I needed to call Crew.

It should have probably worried me that I had that thought on a constant loop in my head more often than not. And not just because I had put him in this difficult situation.

Difficult.

That seemed like such an odd word for this callous series of events. Yet perhaps it was the only word that made sense without me screaming into the abyss—something I did often these days.

My phone buzzed in my pocket, startling me out of my thoughts. I pulled it out, checking the screen once more. Noticing the familiar name, I immediately sent them to voicemail, knowing it was far past time that I blocked them completely.

Only doing that felt as if I was giving up on them, not just on who I thought they could be.

If I blocked Travis completely, and he did something to harm himself, I wasn't sure I would ever be able to forgive myself. And while I knew I couldn't put all of his actions on my shoulders, that didn't help the sleepless nights. I might be pressing charges on him for the assault, but he was out on bail, had his family name to keep him out, and there was nothing I could do in this moment.

I slid my phone into my pocket and rolled my shoulders back. I had plenty of things to do today, and focusing on a friendship long since broken wasn't going to help anyone. Instead I needed to get back to work.

While my father and his talent had made our family far past comfortable in terms of money, it wasn't as if I was going to touch my trust after using part of it to build the family business.

Alexander Montgomery was one of the most world-renowned photographers in the world. He had won countless prizes, and people knew his name. And it wasn't even the recognition that truly set his career apart from others. It was the depth that he brought to every single piece he showed the world. My father could bring out raw and unending emotions within his subject with the simple click of his finger. Though I knew there was nothing simple about what my father did.

My father was an alcoholic—something he told us whenever the situation arose. He had been married before he had fallen for my mother, and while I didn't know the details, I knew the situation had been horrific. And my father had turned to alcohol in order to ignore his pain and demons. It wasn't lost on me that Travis did the same thing. Though I knew Travis did so because he wanted to prove his art was something, and not because of the tragedy that had befallen my father.

My father hadn't had a drink in over thirty years. He didn't stress out about it around us, and it was just something that was part of who he was. He told us so we knew that he wasn't perfect. That all humans were fallible.

Though in my eyes, my father was the perfect man. He was my hero, the one who could literally hang the moon if he so desired. The way that he looked at my mother made me believe in true love, happiness, and the connection that came when you found your person.

Maybe that's why I had tried so hard to prove that I could be the person Travis needed. In the end, however, the connection we'd had paled in comparison to my parents' happiness. And perhaps it worried me that anything with Travis couldn't hold a candle to how I felt when Crew stood near me. But I couldn't think about that now. Not when I needed to find a way to make things right with him.

Before I could do that however, I needed to find the words. So I stood in my studio that happened to be in the back part of the Montgomery Gallery building. I knew one day we would outgrow the place and have to move into another building, but I loved what we had now. While the other three businesses in the building were one level, ours was two story. It used to be a bicycle shop before things went terribly wrong, but now everything was family.

The Gallery was our peace. There were separate sections for different mediums and needs. If we needed the community feel of working next to another person, we had sections for that as well. Though I knew most of my family tended to want to work alone. Sometimes, however, it was nice to work on the matting for my project while my cousin Nate painted in a corner, or Colin held a piece of clay.

Sometimes Oliver would have his sketchbook in hand, leaning against the wall as he talked me through my next project. And all the while, Riley would bounce between us, making sure that we were ready for the next show and forcing us to teach these small classes pro bono. Something we would do anyway, but it was nice watching Riley get forceful in keeping us on our toes.

We were a family business, and I loved every part of it. Only it wasn't just family. Crew worked right beside us. When he wasn't in his home studio, he'd have his paintbrush in hand, music blaring, and he would just *work*. Watching the way that he painted took my breath away. And I wasn't ashamed to say that many of my hidden photographs were of him—still photos of the intensity of his work. The way he would frown at his piece, his brows lowered, his teeth biting into his luscious lips.

Those photos would never see the light of day.

And not only because I wasn't a portrait photographer. Instead the world was my canvas and I tended to focus on the landscape. The way that the earth shifted from our doing, and its own. Part of me knew I had focused on that and not people because I didn't want to stay in my father's shadow, but I had leaned into this. And I enjoyed it.

Only, I felt as if I had nothing left in me.

No art, no desire to bring my camera with me.

And that worried me.

"Aria?"

I closed my computer and looked up as my father

walked toward me, a smile on his face. While it did reach his eyes, I saw the worry there. His gaze went to the bruise on my cheek, and his jaw tensed.

While Sebastian had done his best to keep the family away, there was only so much you could do to keep the Montgomerys out of your business. Especially when one of us was hurt. So the next day my parents had been over, both of them trying to act calm, and yet I knew all they wanted to do was take me home and tuck me into my childhood bed.

I didn't blame them, but I had needed to be alone.

My other two siblings had come over as well, the second set of twins my parents had somehow brought into the world. They had been louder, ready to kick some ass. And then they had left when Sebastian forced them out.

I knew Sebastian was only giving me so much of a reprieve because I had done the same for him. I wouldn't have much time left before the cavalry arrived. I had a feeling that some of it stood in front of me now.

Though part of me tensed, the rest of me couldn't help but set everything down and run to my father. His eyes widened only marginally, before he opened his arms and caught me just as he always had.

Alexander Montgomery twirled me around a few times, before setting me down and hugging me tight. He rested one hand on the back of my head, as I wrapped my arms around his waist and let out a deep breath against his chest—something I had done ever since I had been tall enough to do so.

We stood there for a moment, as my breath finally eased. I didn't cry, which surprised me, but hearing my father's heartbeat under my ear settled me.

"That was the welcome that I wanted," he murmured.

I smiled against him before finally taking a step back. "I always like to keep you on your toes."

"You never have to worry about that, Aria. You have always been that way." He winked and gestured toward my table. "Working on anything fun?"

I tried to hold back the cringe, but I wasn't successful. My dad studied my face, frowning again.

"What's wrong? Beyond the thing that I know you do not want to talk about right now."

Grateful he wasn't going to broach the Travis conversation, I let out a breath. "I'm not working on anything." I shook my head. "I should be working on something. We have a show coming up soon, and I'm not going to have anything for it."

"You don't need to show something every week. Or even every year. You want me to look at anything?" He held up his hands. "Which is pretentious as fuck for me to even say. But if you want to talk about it, I'm here. Hell, my camera is in the truck. We can head up I-70 and see what we can capture."

Tears pricked at my eyes, because I had the best father in the history of ever. I knew he had been surprised when I had followed in his footsteps. Mostly because I always hid my passion for photography. I had wanted it to be something of mine and hadn't wanted to be compared to my father. I knew the chip on my shoulder was probably large enough to have its own zip code by this point, but I couldn't help it.

In answer I shook my head. "Not today." I paused, freeing my hands in front of me. "I just feel off. Frankly I need to talk to Crew."

It was funny, because while I usually liked to keep my thoughts to myself, I also knew that I could tell my parents anything. I had never been forced to keep secrets from them. Never worried about what they would think. And yet, I wanted something just for myself. So I wasn't even sure why I had said Crew's name at all.

"I would offer to drive you there, but if Crew and I are in the same room, we're going to get in the car and go do something that will probably end badly for both of us."

My lips twitched at that, even though I knew it

wasn't a joke because my father was a boxer just like Crew and had been in fights before I was born. I was pretty sure he had been in a few afterward, but he had hidden those from us. Sebastian most likely had been to a few with him and by himself, because somebody had to train my brother before Crew had entered our lives. I had never really been interested in the whole boxing thing, except for when I watched Crew work out.

But those thoughts were for myself.

"You're probably right."

I looked at my desk again, my fingers itching. Maybe I should take my dad up on his offer. It would give me more time to think about what to say to Crew, and it would be nice to take photos again. Or just watch my dad do it. Maybe I'd find what I needed then.

But before I could say anything, someone I didn't recognize walked into the back room. A woman with ruby red hair, a nice linen suit, and a broad smile looked around the space and danced on her toes. "Hello there, I don't know if I'm supposed to be back here, but I was just looking around and couldn't help but take a peek."

"This is the work room, so no, it's off-limits to guests for privacy and safety reasons, but I can take you up front to see any art pieces you like," I said, using my most professional voice.

But the woman wasn't looking at me. Instead she

stared at my father, her eyes wide. She put her hand on her chest and staggered back. "You're Alexander Montgomery. I saw your work in Washington, as well as Paris. The life you bring to your studies is just amazing. And amazing isn't even a good word for it. I'm a fan clearly."

My dad, always uncomfortable in these situations, put his hands in his jeans pockets and smiled. "Thank you. It's always nice to meet someone who enjoys art."

I did not look at my dad's face because if I did, we would both burst out laughing.

Then the woman looked at me. "Oh, you must be his daughter. It's so nice that you followed in his footsteps. He must teach you so much. You're going to do so many amazing things one day. With those genes, you have to."

Every word was like tiny shards of glass sliding into my skin before rubbing a rough towel over the punctures and burying that glass deep within.

I knew I wasn't my father. I did not possess his talent. But sometimes I couldn't help the voice that told me I had zero talent at all. That I was just playing pretend with my father's old camera.

Then the voices would grow louder when people said things like that straight out as if they couldn't wait to toss me in the shadow of my father's presence.

And I couldn't even blame them.

My smile turned brittle, but I wasn't even sure the woman noticed. Thankfully I didn't have to say anything, because Riley was there, running in behind the woman, a scowl on her face one moment before she smiled it away.

"Hello, ma'am. I'm going to take you out front. I'm sorry, this is where the artists work, and we need to keep it private."

The woman sighed, but her smile stayed in place. "Um, I'm so sorry. It was lovely to meet you both."

Riley practically dragged the woman away, and I stood there, the echoes of her words bouncing around in my head, reminding me why I hadn't picked up my camera in recent memory.

"Aria—" my father began, but I couldn't let him finish.

Words lodged in my throat, and my hands fisted at my sides for one moment before I forced myself to relax, or at least fake it enough for my father, before turning to my desk and grabbing my purse. "I need to head out. But thank you for visiting. I love you."

I didn't even realize I was running until the sounds of my dad's footsteps followed.

"Aria!" he called out.

But I ignored him and jumped into my car, grateful that I had parked so close to the back door. I pulled out of the spot, my father staring at me, confusion and hurt in his gaze. I ignored it, because I couldn't stand to see that pity. I was Daddy's Little Girl, and I wasn't good enough.

Just ask anybody who looked at my work.

I hadn't even realized I was driving toward Crew's gym until the building came into view. While part of me tensed, knowing I needed to speak with him, the rest of me coiled in anticipation. I needed to block that feeling. No good could come from it. And yet I had been trying to do so for years.

Knowing I should turn this car right back around and go home, or even call my father and apologize, I got out of my car instead. It was as if my body had a mind of its own, and I couldn't help but walk toward where I hoped Crew would be.

The gym was closed since there were no classes that day, so I used my key to get in. Part of me should've wondered why I even had a key, but Crew had given it to me. I hadn't asked for it, nor asked why. But he had done so anyway.

He growled while he did it, and I had taken the key.

I walked down the empty hall, after locking the door behind me, and made my way to Crew's office. I didn't know why I knew he would be there, but as I turned down the hall, Crew leaned against the doorway, a scowl on his face and his phone to his ear.

"Yeah. She's here. I got her. Don't worry." Then he slid his phone into his pocket and moved to stand in front of me.

My breath caught, the nearness of him too much. He didn't touch me and yet I felt scalded, embraced. His. "I need to apologize to my father for running out like that."

Crew shook his head. "That's between the two of you, but I don't think you need to say you're sorry. He told me what that lady said. She's wrong. She was starstruck about one person, and she didn't think about her words. But fuck her anyway."

My lips twitched, and I let out a breath, somehow the world feeling calm for a mere moment. "Did you call him? Or did he call you?" I wasn't sure what answer I wanted.

"He called me. Thought maybe you'd come here." He gave me a look that I didn't have answers for.

"I'm sorry, Crew."

He shook his head. "For what?"

"For getting you sent to jail. For Travis. For continuing to try to help him when all it did was get you hurt. I'm sorry for being such a bitch every time I'm around you recently." He raised a brow at that. "Sorry to keep taking you for granted. I miss my friend, Crew. And I really hope you're still there. Even though I'm a mess."

He studied my face for so long that I was afraid I had once again said something wrong. Something cracked deep inside, a loss I couldn't quite grasp. And I knew it was my own fault.

He stood up and rolled his shoulders back. "Fine. Get in the ring."

I blinked. "What?"

"Get in the ring. You're going to need to protect yourself. If you're not going to let me do it, then I'll show you how to do it yourself. Get in the fucking ring, Aria."

"Crew—"

"No. I'll show you a few moves. That man is out on the streets even though he needs to be behind bars. I'm so damn angry, Aria. I need to get it out somehow. So, let's go."

He moved forward, pulled my purse from my shoulder, and gestured toward the ring.

I looked down at my leggings and T-shirt and realized I didn't have any reason not to do as he said.

So I followed him to the ring and climbed in.

"I've taken your classes before."

"I know. And I know you used your moves, but he was strong, and high as fuck. You and I are going to prepare a little more. Because every time I close my eyes, I see his hands on you. So you're going to do this for me. Got me?"

Once again, my emotions clogged my throat, and I nodded. "Okay."

And I did the one thing that felt right. *I let Crew lead.*

By the time we were done, I was sweaty and exhausted but felt a little more powerful. And Crew's shoulders finally loosened.

"You hungry?" he asked afterward, handing me a towel.

"I could eat."

His lips twitched. "Come on. I'm going to feed you."

I shook my head. "You don't need to feed me. We can get something."

"You like my cooking. I'm in the mood. Let's go eat, Aria."

I wasn't sure what to say because he was right, so I followed him to the parking lot, and then to his home. It felt almost as it once had. Before we had drank a little too much and leaned into each other a little too hard. I had finally given in to kissing my cousin's best friend.

And every time he touched me, I felt cherished, even when I also felt a little heated. Neither one of us ever talked about it—at least not before the end. It was just something we did when the world got to be too much, and I knew it wasn't fair to either one of us.

Crew made a quick homemade béchamel mac and cheese and grilled some chicken and zucchini, looking at home in his state of the art kitchen. He filled the space with his presence alone and I wasn't allowed to move from the barstool. Instead I watched him work in silence, letting myself finally breathe.

"I need to go to the grocery store, so you get this."

I rolled my eyes, because of course the man thought this wouldn't be enough. I slid my fork through the mac and cheese and pointed at his mouth. "Open."

He glared at me but opened his mouth. I fed him his delicious mac and cheese, and he smiled at me.

That smile always did things to me.

We ate in a calm silence, both of us sitting at his kitchen island. I loved his place, the warmness of it, even though it was daunting as well. He didn't let a lot of people in here, and I never knew why. Maybe it was time for me to find out.

"Whatever happens now, whatever we do next, I'm not hiding from the family anymore."

I blinked up at him, surprised and yet worried his thoughts might have been similar to mine. "What?"

He met my gaze, the tic in his jaw familiar. "You know there's something between us, Aria. There always has been. So something happens tonight, or next month, I'm not hiding it anymore. I'm not your secret, Aria. I am not the accident that you fell into."

Those were the most words Crew had ever said to me about what we were. And just like that, the real reason we fought stood between us.

There was no going back.

Chapter Five

Crew

I was not a man of words. That wasn't who I was and frankly, having to talk about my feelings and what I wanted made me want to walk right out of my own damn kitchen and never look back. There was a reason my friends ribbed me about my dark and stoic attitude. It was what I did and what made sense. If someone needed to know what I thought, I'd tell them.

Or they didn't need to know at all.

Stating my intentions sounded as if I were speaking from far away, wondering what the hell I was doing.

I'd been so good about pretending I knew what I was doing with Aria Montgomery, that I knew if I didn't stand my ground, I'd regret it for the rest of my life. Or I'd lost my mind, and I clearly needed her to be the one to walk away.

Aria was my addiction. My drug. And whatever she fed me coursed through my veins and it was all I could do not to beg for another hit.

I hated the fact that Aria looked at me as if I'd gone crazy. Or maybe I was projecting. I didn't want her forever. A full on romance with complications and responsibilities? I had way too much going on in my life to have someone lean on me like that.

And yet I knew even thinking those words was just denial.

Because the hidden part of me wanted to lean on her in return even though I knew it was a mistake.

Everything I did for my friends was a responsibility. And just the fact that Aria and I had been sleeping together off and on for months was a complication that neither one of us had faced for all this time.

But I was done hiding.

Yet that seemed like all talk and no action. So maybe it was time to actually do something.

"I thought you hated me."

The words were like a punch to the gut, but I didn't blame her for them. After all, I wasn't a nice man. And I hadn't been kind to her. We had used one another when we had needed to feel, or perhaps not feel at all, and now we needed to face the consequences of those choices.

I knew her body, knew what she needed, but sometimes I felt like I didn't know her—let alone myself.

So how was I standing here?

"I don't hate you, Aria. I hate how I am when I'm around you."

She blanched, and I cursed under my breath. She spoke before I had a chance to. "I don't want you to change who you are. You're one of my best friends, Crew. And I feel like I screwed everything up by kissing you. By leaning on you when I felt like you couldn't lean on me. Or maybe *you* felt like you couldn't. I wasn't strong enough for you."

I shook my head, then leaned forward, cupping her cheek. My hand was so big compared to her face, it just reminded me how gentle she was. Breakable. Oh, she could fight back, that was clear. She was so damn strong. But she used that as a veneer. A shield against the world. Her family loved her, and they understood her, but I didn't think she understood what they saw.

It wasn't my problem to fix. Wasn't my responsibility.

But I wanted to.

And that scared me more than anything.

"You're not weak. If I needed help, I would ask."

She raised a brow at the lie, so I leaned forward and brushed my lips against hers. She gasped into my mouth as I swiped my tongue along hers, deepening the kiss for an instant before taking a step back.

The heat between us had never been a problem. But that heat scorched, left scars. And I needed to figure out exactly what to do about that.

For Aria.

"Let's just get some sleep, I know you haven't been getting enough, and we'll talk in the morning."

"I feel like I'm three steps behind."

Same. "You'll be better after you sleep."

"Are you ordering me around?"

"Maybe you should let me for the moment. Because you've been trying to lift up everyone else around you for so long, you forget about yourself."

"That's not true. My family doesn't do that to me."

"They don't. But you also don't let them help you. Don't lie. You keep them at arm's length, just like you do everyone else. Just like you do me. But unlike your family, I'll call you out on your bullshit. So go put on one of my shirts, get into bed, and we will both sleep. I won't touch you unless you ask. But with those dark circles under your eyes, you need to catch a few Z's."

"Why are you so bossy?"

I leaned down and kissed her hard on the mouth. "Because you like it. Bed. Now."

She stared at me for a moment, before shaking her head and doing exactly like I had ordered.

I didn't know why that pleased me so much.

I cleaned up our mess in the kitchen and gave her a few moments to herself. It took everything within me not to go in there and help her. It wasn't that Aria couldn't do things on her own. It was that she had put so much into keeping Travis alive, that she had forgotten about herself. And she had punished herself for not being enough in Travis's eyes.

I didn't know if I was the punishment, and I didn't care if I was. Because I loved her. And that wasn't something I planned on saying aloud any time soon—if ever. Especially when I had no idea what the hell she was thinking. I might like to pretend, but she was still a mystery.

I finally made my way into my bedroom. She stood on her side of the bed, tugging at the bottom of my old T-shirt. She looked so damn sexy standing there in it that it was hard to breathe. I needed to know if she wore panties or if she was bare. When my cock pressed against my zipper at the thought, I willed myself to calm down. Tonight wasn't about that. Tonight was just about sleep. To remind myself that she was okay. That Travis couldn't touch her.

And that she could make her own decisions.

She looked up at me then with wide eyes. "I don't know why I keep going along with whatever you say. It should worry me."

In answer, I stripped my shirt up over my head. I watched as her gaze traveled over my body—the ink, the scars, the rigid planes that came from countless hours of working out. She knew some of the history behind those scars, but not all. Nobody did. Nobody needed to know.

Of course that just reminded me of the man who had screamed at me, and the woman who had done the same. But I wasn't going to think about them in that moment. Instead, I shoved off my pants, keeping my boxer briefs on, before walking into the bathroom to brush my teeth.

I splashed water on my face, hoping it would cool me down. But as I looked down at my waist, my cock stood on end, tenting my boxers. We were both just going to have to deal. It wasn't as if she hadn't seen all of me anyway.

I made my way back out to the bedroom, where she had gotten into the bed but hadn't lain down. Instead I watched as her nipples pebbled against the too thin T-shirt.

It was going to be a long night, but all I wanted to do

was hold her and remind myself that she was okay. Except I saw the bruise on her cheek, the ridge of her lip slightly swollen—same as my knuckles. And that reminded me that we weren't okay.

Without a word I turned off the light and got into bed beside her. It was still early, but I was just as exhausted as she looked. I hadn't had a full night's sleep since the night I had said it would be our last time. Since part of me had broken because I had known if we kept doing what we'd been doing to one another, we would shatter.

But everything had changed when I had seen Travis's arm against her neck. And I refused to let her go. So she was going to have to figure out what she wanted, and I was going to have to find a way to make sure that was me.

"Lie down, Aria."

"You're really bossy tonight."

"I'm always bossy. You like that about me."

Underneath the slight glow from the moonlight glancing through the blinds, I saw her lips lift into a smile. But she did indeed lie down, but instead of turning away from me, she faced me.

When she let out a deep breath and slid her fingers beneath mine, I licked my lips. It was hard for me not to lean forward and take more, but it wasn't the time.

"I've missed you."

Those words were like a balm to my soul, and I squeezed her hand. "I've missed you too. Just sleep. I'll be here when you wake up. I promise."

"I love the fact that I believe you."

And with that, she closed her eyes, our hands twined together, and I listened to her breathing even out. And thankfully, as she continued to sleep, I fell right beside her. The tightness in me easing, my breaths coming slowly, I finally slept.

THE NEXT MORNING SUNLIGHT SCATTERED through the blinds, waking me before the alarm I had forgotten to set. I cracked open one eye and realized that Aria was firmly against me, her backside pressing along my morning erection, and her hand gripped around my wrist. She lay pillowed on my arm, and my free hand was underneath her shirt. In my sleep I must've cupped her breast like a damn security blanket.

Aria Montgomery was just supposed to be my friend. Just like the rest of them. And though the others had joked that I wanted to be part of the family so damn much that I would marry in, none of them realized how close that taunt was to the truth.

I wasn't meant to fall first, only I had without thinking.

While I knew that this probably wouldn't lead to anything but heartache, considering where I came from, I wanted to be selfish enough to at least try it. I wanted to wake up like this every morning until we both realized we weren't better apart.

I was a self-centered asshole, and I didn't care in that moment when I had Aria's tit in my hand and that sweet ass pressed against my dick. Aria moaned and arched into me.

I held back a groan, my fingers slowly moving against her breast, plucking at her nipple gently. When she rocked into me again, my dick sliding between her legs, I licked my lips at the heat pressing against me.

"I need you awake, baby. Tell me you want this."

The little moan sliding through her lips nearly made me come. "Please. I always want you. Just make me feel good."

I smiled at that and pressed a kiss to her shoulder. "I can do that."

"As long as I can do the same for you."

My Aria. So giving even when she thought she was selfish.

I groaned, rocking my hips so the friction of that already wet pussy against my dick tempted me beyond reason. "You always make me feel good, Aria. Even when you're annoying the hell out of me."

That startled a laugh out of her, and a broad smile covered my face.

"You are such a jerk." Her voice turned breathy as I continued pinching her nipple between my thumb and forefinger.

"And?"

"Nothing really."

"Good. Because I know you like when I'm a jerk." I pinched a bit harder, and she gasped. "Do you want me this morning?"

"Yes."

Do you want me every morning?

I didn't ask. I wasn't even sure I wanted the answer to be yes.

"Does your pussy want me?"

"Crew. Stop teasing me."

"I bet your pussy is hungry for my cock. Why don't you use that free hand to slide beneath those drenched panties and tell me. Come on, Aria. Touch yourself for me."

With the moan, she slid her fingers underneath the seam of her panties, and I watched as her arm moved slightly, trying to get herself off. I removed my hand from her breast and reached down to grip her wrist.

"Don't. Your orgasm is mine. I'm the one who lets you come. Now tell me. Are you wet?"

"You know I am."

"Show me."

I let her slide her hand back out from under her panties, and she lifted her fingers up to me. I slid them into my mouth, tasting that tartness that nearly sent me over the edge. Controlling her arm by my hold on her wrist, I sucked every last drop off her fingers before moving my hand to where hers had been. I speared her with two fingers before she could even take a breath, and she gasped into me.

"You're such a fucking dirty girl. Already wet for me and I haven't even touched you. Do you want my cock? Tell me if you want my cock, Aria."

"I always want your cock."

"That's a good girl." Then I worked myself in and out of her, slowly at first, finding that bundle of nerves. I wrapped my other arm around her, cupping her breast as I finger fucked her. She let out little moans, little gasps, and I soaked in every single one.

And when she came, her body quaking in that way that told me she was all mine, I rocked into her, the friction of her thighs pressing around my dick nearly as tempting as her wet heat.

I pulled my fingers out of her, and then shoved them

into her mouth. She gagged, but I saw the excitement in her eyes as she lay back in my arms.

"Lick them. Taste yourself."

She nodded, gorging on my fingers before I pulled them out.

Then I shoved the comforter off us, and rolled us so I was on my back and her thighs were around my shoulders.

"Hold onto the headboard. I need my breakfast."

She shook her head, her eyes glassy. "Crew. I just want you. Please."

"And you'll have me. But if you aren't riding my face in the next thirty seconds, I won't fuck your ass later while you beg for it."

She blushed that pretty blush I knew spread all over her skin, and I winked at her.

"And take off my shirt. As much as I love you drenched in my scent, I want to see those pretty tits bouncing as you ride my face."

She blushed again but whipped off my shirt in an instant. Her breasts were large, full, her nipples tight. I loved sucking on them and bruising them with my mouth. They looked like a masterpiece when I came on them, painting them with my cum. It was territorial as fuck, and I didn't care.

I gripped her thighs, and then looked up at that

beautiful pink pussy above me. So sweet, and all mine. I licked and sucked as she moved against me, her hips doing that little rocking motion that told me she was once again close to the edge.

I wrapped my lips around her clit and twisted, and her thighs shuddered. When I dipped my tongue inside her, she gasped and continued rocking. I gorged on her, eating every ounce of her, before she finally came again, calling my name.

I ignored the squeeze of my heart at that sound, because I knew she was just in the moment and I had no idea what she felt. Nor did I want to know because that meant I would have to face my own feelings.

So I shoved those thoughts to the back of my mind before adjusting us once again on the bed. I slammed my feet on the floor and pulled Aria to her back so her head rested slightly over the edge.

"Open up. I told you I would feed you."

She smiled wide at me before chuckling. "I thought I was just having mac and cheese last night. But dick? I'll take that too."

"Yes, Aria. You're going to take it. Now open up so I can fuck that pretty face of yours."

She smiled up at me and opened. I slid the tip of my cock into her mouth as she teased the slit with the tip of her tongue. I squeezed the base of my dick, groaning.

"Hold on to my thighs so you don't fall. I've got you."

She nodded, my cock in her mouth, as I slowly worked my way in and out of her. I was too big to go balls deep inside her this way, but I didn't care. Her mouth was so warm, so inviting, that I slowly moved in and out of her, loving the way that her throat worked as I filled her. She gagged slightly, and then swallowed, the tip of my cock going deeper down her throat.

I used my free hand to cup her breasts, pinching each nipple, before trailing my thumb along her throat as I filled it with my cock.

"You're so fucking beautiful."

And then I continued to work my hips as I leaned over to rub two fingers over her clit.

I slid three fingers in her in one move, and her pussy clamped around me, swollen and pink. And when she came again, and I knew I was close to the edge, I pulled out of her.

Both of us sweaty, and Aria nearly spent, I moved us around once again before shoving her ass to the edge of the bed and wrapping her legs around my waist.

"Are you ready for me?" I asked.

She gave me a lazy look, that cat and cream smile the most beautiful thing I had ever seen as she cupped her breasts. "Always."

"Do we need a condom?" I asked, telling myself I needed to hold back.

She shook her head. "We're both clean. I'm on the pill. It's just us." She paused. "Always has been."

I swallowed the emotion in my throat, telling myself it was just the high of a near orgasm, before I nodded tightly, gripped her hips with bruising force, and thrust it into her so hard her breasts bounced and her pussy tightened around me. I let out a groan as she let out a scream of pleasure.

Balls deep, I sat there for a moment as I tried not to come right then and there. One stroke and I was already nearly ready to fill her.

"Look down at us," I ordered. "Do you see how your pussy is grabbing my cock? It wants me."

"*I want you*," she corrected as a small smile played on her face.

I grinned right back at her before pulling out and slamming back in fully.

"Crew! My God."

I froze, remembering exactly what had happened to bring us here. I looked down at the bruises on her neck and face, and at where my hands gripped her. Because I would leave similar bruises if I kept this up.

She must have seen the horror spilling onto my face at the mere thought of hurting her. "Don't stop. I'm not fragile. This is exactly what we both like. I love your marks on me. Because they're the ones I *want*. And because you give them to me with my consent. *You're not him*."

I nodded tightly, knowing she said that for both of us, not just me, before doing exactly as she asked and going as rough as she wanted.

As rough as I wanted.

I rocked in and out of her, hard and fast so she nearly fell off the bed, and I grinned. She sat up, gripping my shoulders, so I moved my hands under her ass and lifted her.

"You want like me this?" I asked, teasing.

"I just want you. Please. Come, already. You're going to need to catch up."

I shook my head, laughing. Because of course I could laugh with Aria while I was fucking her. Even when we hated each other, we could make each other laugh.

"I'm going to make you come two more times for that remark. You don't think I can last?"

"We both know what I think." And then she rolled her hips again, nearly making me come.

I lifted her over my cock and slammed her back down, over and over until we were both panting, sweaty. Nearly ready, I set her back down and continue to move my hips as I crawled over the bed. We laughed together, the movement slightly jerky, unpracticed, until we found a rhythm again. And then my hands were tangled with hers, our mouths pressed together as we kissed and licked and sucked. And when she came again, her cunt clamping down around my dick, I followed, meeting her.

I groaned into her mouth as we clung to one another, both of us still as the orgasm washed over each of us.

It had always been amazing with Aria. That was the problem. Because at first it had just been because we wanted it. It was a test to see exactly what we could do to each other.

When it became more, we had run. But not far enough.

Without another word, I kissed her temple, her nose, her forehead, and then the tears from her cheeks, before finally pulling out of her. I stood up on shaky legs, and then lifted her into my arms, cradling her as I walked us to the shower.

"Crew," she whispered, her voice breathy. "Why are you so sweet sometimes?"

"I'm not sweet. You just made me come so hard I was seeing double. It's just the endorphins."

She shook her head, and neither one of us believed

my words. But I turned on the water, and we each reached for the soap.

It was odd as she washed my body and I worked on her hair. It felt as if this was our routine, and perhaps it had been somewhat. Only I didn't shower with women. It wasn't my thing. But somehow it had become that way with Aria. Because we were friends, of course we were. And yet it had become more when I hadn't been watching.

When we were finished with the shower, I turned off the water and grabbed one of my fluffy towels that I knew she liked and wrapped it around her. Then I wrapped another around my waist and walked out into the bedroom so I could grab some clothes.

I tossed her a pair of jeans and a T-shirt she had left here once, and she pressed them to her nose, a small smile playing on her face.

"I love the smell of your detergent."

I snorted. "I'm pretty sure Lex bought that detergent. Sorry."

She licked her lips and nodded before we finish getting dressed, and awkwardness settled in. "So what is this?" she asked after a moment.

I shrugged, trying not to put too much into it. We were friends. I couldn't hurt that. Pushing her away as I had before because I had needed an ultimatum had hurt her. But watching the way that she had tried to save Travis repeatedly had been worse.

"Whatever you want it to be."

Aria reached out and gripped my forearm, her tongue darting out to wet her lips. "I was never with Travis."

I froze, my world shifting in an instant.

"I thought I needed to be. I thought he was my friend. And I could maybe save him. But he was just a man who took advantage. And I don't think he was ever my friend."

My heart thudded in my chest. "Aria. You're a good person. That's why you kept trying. Even if we hated that you did."

"Everybody hated that I did. But it wasn't because I loved him. I didn't. Even though the family thought I did." She met my eyes and swallowed hard. "You aren't a rebound, Crew. You never were."

That rocking motion hit again, and I pushed it down. I didn't know where this would lead, and I knew it probably couldn't lead to anything good. I was the product of my parents, so I knew exactly what happened when you wanted more than you deserved. But for now, I could have it all. I hope to hell I didn't fuck it up.

"Good," I finally said, before kissing her hard on the

mouth and tugging on her belt loop. "Now time to feed you again. This time food, my cock later."

She burst out laughing, her eyes finally full of such emotion, rather than the wariness that had been there for so long. And for once, I let myself relax.

Chapter Six

Crew

Before.

The taste of whiskey settled on my tongue, and I did my best just to sip. What I wanted to do was slam it back, and then have another. And then another. With the way my week was going, maybe if I buried myself in the bottle, I wouldn't have to think about anything else. However, that wasn't how I worked. I'd seen too many people rely on that bottle, and the so-called sweet elixir within.

So I set my half-empty glass on the bar and picked up the water next to it.

The bartender gave me a look, and I shrugged, not really caring what he thought.

If I didn't finish that two-hundred-dollar two fingers

of whiskey, I didn't really care. I had the money, and if I wasted it, it felt like maybe I was just wasting my parents' money. Even though I technically refused to touch it. The money I had on hand was all mine. And if I was thinking about my parents and their money, I was one sip too close to issues. Instead, I took my water and slid off the barstool.

What I really needed was to get laid. It had been far too long, and jerking off to images of one of my best friends wasn't helping anything.

"Why are you growling at me?" Lex asked, as he glared at me.

"I'm not growling," I growled.

Lex gave me a look, and then burst out laughing. "You're ridiculous. And now, I'm going to leave you alone because I'm pretty sure the woman at the end of the bar is giving me the eye."

"It could be dust. It's probably dust."

Lex flipped me off. "Fuck you."

I met his gaze, my lips twitching. "Didn't we already establish that I wasn't going to fuck you?" I muttered. I didn't care if anybody heard, but considering Lex was looking to get laid tonight, I thought I might be better off not shouting that last part.

His cheeks pinked even under the dim bar lights, and I just grinned. "You are the one who asked, not me."

I shrugged and didn't deny it. Lex and I were friends, nothing more. There could've been a little attraction between us, but it hadn't amounted to anything. We were better off as friends, and a kiss here or there just because we could. And to keep people on their toes.

But I didn't want Lexington Montgomery.

Sadly I wanted one of the Montgomerys currently on the dance floor.

Lex's gaze followed mine, and he clucked his tongue. "Playing with fire there, brother."

"Please don't call me brother after the conversation we literally just had," I said dryly.

"And on that note, I'm going over to the other side of the bar. The redhead wants me."

"Wasn't it just a blonde?"

"I said what I said." Lex snorted, and then headed off to go hit on the redheaded woman. Lex wasn't a creep. However, no one else in our friend group was looking for serious.

The fact that my ex had found her serious partner should've probably made me worry. But it hadn't. Daisy and I had just been good friends in the end. The sex had been great, but I liked the way she was with Hugh. And in one fell swoop, she gained a daughter. Instant family and all of that. It was perfect for Daisy.

And yet all I could do was look at Aria on the damn dance floor.

She had come with another one of her friends who wasn't related to the family, and was now dancing between the group, as well as five different guys who seem to be prowling like hyenas on the safari.

I wanted to rip one of the dudebro's arms off, but I figured that might be going a little too far. Especially since I hadn't even spoken to Aria tonight. There was just something about her, even though she annoyed the fuck out of me. Maybe that was why I wanted her.

Apparently, I was a masochist and hadn't known before this moment.

Dudebro number two slid his hand up her shirt and squeezed without even a hello, when Aria twisted, elbowing the man in the gut. I hadn't even realized I was moving until I was there.

Aria had taken care of it herself and the guy was already breathing heavily, but I still couldn't help myself. I had the man pinned to the wall, my forearm pressed against his throat in two steps.

"You think it's okay to touch a woman without consent?" I said, my voice so pointed, it was scarier than a growl.

"Who the fuck are you?" the guy rasped.

Considering the man could talk, I wasn't pressing hard enough. So I leaned in. "Different answer."

The guy's eyes bulged. "Shit." A choking rasp. "I didn't realize she was yours."

She wasn't. And never would be. She was off-limits for so many reasons.

"You're really not getting this. You touch a woman like that without asking? You deserve to get your nuts ripped off. So why don't you apologize."

The guy blinked and looked over my shoulder to where I knew Aria stood. "Sorry," he croaked.

"You know, it took you a little too long to get to why what you did was wrong. So maybe I'm the one who will take your nuts instead of him," Aria said the threat so sweetly, that my dick got hard just thinking about it. Damn, that woman was something.

"Sorry," he said again, looking a little scared. About time.

Before I could do anything though, there was a tap on my shoulder, and I raised brow at security. "Hi Jim."

The guy rolled his eyes. "Thank you for handling this for now. But I can take care of it from here."

I glared at the man. "You were a little late handling it *now*."

"I was right behind you, but I didn't realize you were a

sprinter, instead of just a boxer," he said with another roll of his eyes, and I let the little weasel go. Jim and the rest of security dragged the guy out, as well as his friends. Most of the women in the club cheered, and I shook my head.

Men. Disgusting creatures.

And as my cock pressed against my zipper by the mere presence of Aria, I included myself in that.

"Well, I'm going to get another drink," Aria said, and I watched as she walked back to the bar, my gaze glued to her ass. I cleared my throat as I caught Lex staring at me. I saw the worry in his gaze for his cousin and the fact he'd moved away from the redhead and toward us. I shook my head, letting him know I'd handled it, and he backed down.

Mistake.

I followed Aria to the bar, like she was the Pied Piper and I couldn't stay away.

"Tequila?" she asked.

The thought of it made me want to gag, but I nodded in answer anyway.

She held up two fingers, and the bartender immediately slid over to accommodate her. When the guy met my gaze, he moved his hand from the well to the top shelf, and I nodded.

As I owned the place, I only got the best. Not that anyone knew I owned the place. The fact that some guy had dared to touch Aria underneath *my* roof, he was lucky I hadn't killed him. And Jim would be faster next time.

I trained him for a reason.

"Why do you always get the fancy things without saying anything?" Aria asked as she tilted toward me.

I shook my head. "This stuff is good enough you don't need salt or lime. I get the fancy shit because I'm a gentleman."

She snorted, and I just grinned.

With my gaze on hers, both of us tapped the glass to the bar and took the shot with ease. The tequila was so good that there was no burn, and it was probably better as a sipping drink, but I didn't do swill. I'd been born with a silver spoon in my mouth, after all, and some things never went away.

We set our glasses down, and Aria shivered.

"Cold?"

"Maybe. The tequila was damn good though. Going to have to drink with you for always."

"Somebody sure is getting bougie," I teased.

"I can't help it. I like pretty things." She fluttered her eyelashes, and I chuckled, shaking my head. She checked her phone, for what I realized had to be the fifth or sixth time in a short amount of time, and I frowned.

"Waiting on a call?"

"Travis was supposed to meet me here."

Just the sound of that man's name set my teeth on edge, but I did my best to school my features. Aria hated when we questioned her about that man. He was useless, a user, and drained every ounce of spark from the woman in front of me. But if we said anything about it, she fought back. Because I knew she wanted to see the best in him. To try to keep him on the good path.

Only I knew it was a lost cause.

"Maybe he'll show later," I lied.

She met my gaze and sighed.

"Are you okay?"

She shrugged and looked down at her dress. That's when I realized that one of the double straps had torn, and my jaw tensed.

"Did he do that?" I asked, my voice so low I could practically see the ice crystals forming in the air.

"It's fine. It happened when I got out of his grip."

I was already moving toward the back door, hoping I could catch that little asshole, before she could even say a word. I made it all the way to the hallway where it was just the two of us, before she put her hand on my arm to stop me.

One touch and I was in her control.

How fucking weak was that?

"Don't. I don't care about him. I'm fine."

I let out a breath. "You shouldn't be so nonchalant about a man groping you."

"I'm not nonchalant. But security took care of it, and I don't want to think about it anymore. Okay?"

I turned then, caging her to the wall. Her eyes dilated, and I looked down at her, both hands pressed against the wall beside her head. "Fine. But if I see him again, he's a dead man."

Her chest rose and fell as she took a deep breath. "Just don't go looking for him. And you don't have to keep protecting me. You're not my brother."

I narrowed my gaze. "Thinking about you as my little sister is the furthest thing from my mind."

Aria's lips parted, and I cursed.

"You should go home, Aria."

"But what if I don't want to?"

In answer, I broke my cardinal role, and I slammed my mouth to hers.

Now

"What do you have on your docket today?" I asked as I leaned against my kitchen counter. We had eaten breakfast—after I had eaten her out again—and now I stood with my second cup of coffee, just watching thoughts pass over her face in quick succession. Sometimes I could read her. Sometimes she was an open book.

And other times, like now, I would do anything just to see what was going on in that mind of hers. A single note of the lyrics that was the melody of her soul. A single line of the verse that stroked against her heart.

"Family dinner was moved to Friday, so I don't really have anything."

I tilted my head, staring into those gorgeous blue eyes. *The Montgomery eyes.* "You want to go for a drive?"

A small smile played on her lips even as her eyes brightened ever so slightly. "You don't have to work today at one of your many mysterious businesses? Or paint?"

I took a sip of my coffee before shrugging. "I have a few projects in various stages but I don't have any commissions. Just doing what I feel like."

"That must be nice," she said wryly.

"What about you? Any projects or commissions?" I asked as if I didn't know what project she was working on. Hell, I knew that she knew every single one of my art pieces.

I loved her photography. She could capture an exact

moment in time in a way that few others could. It wasn't portrait work, but another type of art that was all beneath the surface.

"I just did a large spread for *Adventure*, and have three more coming up, but it's the wrong time of year for what I want. So now it's just what I can sell on the website and in-house. Thankfully my last payday was enough that I don't have to worry for a while. Which is always a relief."

I drained my coffee and set my empty cup in the dishwasher next to hers. I didn't know why that sight made me so damn happy, so I pushed those thoughts away. No need to get sentimental. It was just a damn coffee cup. Just like her damn toothbrush was next to mine in the bathroom.

"Well then, let's go get some air. We can take the convertible up I-70 into the mountains until it gets too winding for us."

Her eyes widened. "Just like that?"

"Just like that. Bring a hat if you want, or let the wind make your hair go in a thousand different directions. Anything you want, Aria."

"Anything?" She smiled then, before walking toward me and putting her hands on my chest. She was so damn short that she had to go to her tiptoes in order to kiss the bottom of my chin. I did not lean down to make it easier for her. I couldn't help but relish the warmth of her. I really needed to calm the fuck down.

"Go get your shoes and stop teasing me." I leaned down quickly and bit her bottom lip, before smacking her ass.

She yelped and glared at me, before she burst out laughing, and went to the bedroom.

I shook my head, wondering what the hell I was getting into.

By the time we were in the car, music blaring and wind in her hair, I could feel the stress and tension easing from her.

We couldn't talk that much with the top down, but it didn't matter. It was a perfect Colorado day. Not a single cloud in the sky, and not too hot or too cold. We'd souped up the engine of this beauty so I knew she could handle these roads as she had before. Maybe next time I would go up on my bike, with Aria on the back, legs spread around me. I shifted slightly in my seat, trying to adjust myself.

Out of the corner of my eye I saw Aria give me a look, that smirk on her face making me want to kiss it off.

"You keep looking at me like that, I'm going to give your mouth something to do," I shouted.

"Promises promises," she called out over the wind.

And then she leaned back into the seat, that relaxed smile on her face.

I hadn't realized how fake and forced her smiles had been recently. But right then and there, this was the real her.

We pulled up to a rest area where there were a few park benches and got out. I took the cooler with me, and Aria just stared at me.

"When did you have time to pack that? And why didn't I know you have it?"

"It took you thirty minutes to do your hair and makeup, even though you just let the wind have it."

"It took me like ten minutes. And I had to call my dad."

I froze in the act of unloading our lunch and tilted my head at her. "Everyone okay?"

That curious expression on her face did something to me I didn't want to name. "Yes. I just wanted him to know that I was sorry for running out like I had." She moved closer, and we unpacked the cooler together, acting as if we had done this countless times before.

After a moment, Aria finally let out another part of what had been bothering her. "I hate the fact I always feel weird about my dad and our work. I know that he loves me. And I know that he loves my work. And yet I can't help but feel like the little girl standing in her dad's too big shoes, wondering why she keeps tripping on her face."

When I set her camera bag next to her, she blinked down at it before running her fingers along its edge. She'd always had her camera on her for as long as I could remember. But recently, she'd stopped bringing it with her everywhere. It wasn't my place to push her, but if I could at least show her what she *could* have... Maybe it was for the best. Maybe I wasn't making a mistake.

She smiled up at me and I let out a relieved breath, grateful I'd gotten it right.

I pulled the tab on Aria's soda before handing it over to her, and she raised a brow.

"I'm well aware you can open it yourself, but you did just get your nails done with Daisy. So why ruin the manicure?"

She snorted and shook her head. "Why do you notice things like that?" She looked at her nails and grinned. "But I do like the steel color."

"I do not understand the need for fake nails like that, however I did like them digging into my back last night and on my shoulders this morning. So you do you so you can do me."

Her cheeks blushed again, and I had to adjust myself in my jeans once more.

We sat down with a cheese and meat concoction

that I had made up with some fruit, a couple of spreads, and crackers. It wasn't much, but if there was cheese, I knew Aria would be happy.

"You know, we should probably talk."

I drank the rest of my soda, before pulling out a water. "I hate those words."

"Of course you do. And not just because you're a man. But because you're you."

"I feel like I should be offended."

"No. I'm in the same boat as you. I hate talking about my feelings. But we might've said that whatever is happening between us is what it is." She gestured with her fingers at the two of us. "But it's a lot more complicated than that."

I shrugged. "Yeah? So?"

"So." She rolled her eyes. "When we slept together the first time, we didn't say anything. And then every other time we always said it was the last time. And we were mean to each other about it." Her teeth bit into her lower lip, and I reached out with my thumb to rub the sting.

"I was mean to you because I wanted to keep you. Is that real enough for you?" Tears filled her eyes, and I cursed. "Shit. Forget I said that."

"No. I'm not going to forget. Because it was the

same for me. When did you get so good about speaking about things?"

"I'm not. But I don't know." I sighed. "You had to deal with a liar for how many years? I don't want to be that guy. Even if we just end up friends that talk about things. I'm not going to be the guy that lies to you. Or uses you. Or pretends that I need you in my life. I'm just going to be me. Are you okay with that?"

A single tear fell down her cheek, and I moved to sit next to her on the bench, straddling it. I wiped away that tear, before licking it off my thumb. The salty taste brought me back to the present, and I wondered if I was moving too fast. Especially because I didn't know what I wanted. Or what she needed.

"You're not him." She let out a breath. "I'm going to tell you a story and know that I just need to get it out. So you understand. I'm not comparing you two. Okay?"

I nodded even though I didn't want to hear about the asshole. However, he was the ghost between us even if the man still breathed.

"The first time I met Travis, I was trying to keep up with Sebastian on my skateboard. And not completely failing."

I raised a brow. "How did I not know you used to skateboard?" I loved learning new things about her. I should have realized long before this how gone I was for this woman.

"Because I only did it for a little while. It was Sebastian's thing. And Raven's now that I think about it," she said, speaking of Sebastian's wife. "Marley would stand back with me, both of us pretending we were having fun and knowing what we were doing." Marley had been Sebastian's high school girlfriend and had died while giving birth to their daughter. I had no idea how Sebastian even moved day by day with what happened. But now he had Raven, and their family was a unit. The man was far stronger than I was.

"I can picture that clearly."

"Well one day, Marley couldn't make it because her parents were being assholes." She rolled her eyes at that, and I figured it was a common refrain from what I knew of the couple. "So Sebastian and Raven and a few of the cousins were out there, doing what they did best, and I was trying to keep up. It didn't matter that Sebastian was my twin, he always acted like the older brother. It's just who he is. But he was in a bad mood because of Marley's parents, so he left me behind."

"I'm not going to like this story, am I?"

She gave me a small smile that wasn't an answer. "Maybe. Anyway, I fell hard, and though I was wearing a helmet, I had foregone my elbow pads. Because I was a

Big Girl and had taken them off when my family wasn't watching." She rolled her eyes. "So stupid. My parents were watching, and running over, but this other kid came over and immediately helped me. He had an ice pack in hand, a bright smile, and made me laugh. Because Travis was accident prone."

"So he saved the day," I bit out.

"Yes, and then he continued to do so." She met my gaze, as if willing me to understand. And the sad part? I did. Because Travis hadn't always been the wraith he was now. "We clicked right away. He was my friend, and then someone I crushed on. Don't get that look," she warned, and I tried to fix my face. "He never crushed on me. When college came around, I got my business degree because I wanted to make sure I could handle my affairs with my art or if I stayed with Montgomery Security. And then I ended up working with my cousins in security, because I liked the idea of owning a business. In the end, that wasn't the right move for me, so I sold my shares in that, and put together the art house with my other cousins." She shrugged. "I had my plan, even though it went in a few different directions. But Travis threw himself into art. He's a brilliant sculptor, Crew."

I tensed, hating the truth. "He is. When he's sober enough to do something about it. I'm not going to lie,

Aria. He's fucking talented." I let out a breath. "Even though I hate him."

She squeezed my hand, and I ran my thumb over her skin, needing that connection. "He *is* talented. And, of course, then he realized he was talented and thought he was a goddess's gift to earth. And while it's good to have self-esteem, something that I do not have in large portions right now, he took it too far. He wanted to be that Tragic Artist. And leaned into it. I couldn't hold him back. The boy who eased my hurts and saved me, was out of my grasp. And I know it's ridiculous. I know that it is not my fault. But that doesn't help the little voices screaming that it is."

"I want to hit him all over again."

"I know you do. But you can't. He left town."

My eyes widened. "Oh?" I did my best to make my voice calm.

"Yes. He texted to say he was taking a break and leaving town. I don't know where. I don't want to know anymore. I'm honestly tired of everybody walking on eggshells around me. So worried about me because they think I'm deeply in love with that man."

I raised a brow. "Instead you were upset with yourself for not being able to save him."

"Pretty much. How self-righteous is that?"

I ran my hand over her hair. "You're a damn good

person, Aria. And we're going to go back to that self-esteem thing."

She gave me a wry smile, her fingers dancing over the denim on my thigh. "Of course you would pick up on that."

"I'm a jerk like that." I frowned. "If we're going to talk about past people we dated or didn't date, you know Daisy and I only hung out for a little while, right?"

She nodded, though I saw the tension sliding back into her. I hated being the one to do that.

"It was more of friends figuring out what we wanted, and it wasn't real."

"But you were having sex. And *good* sex according to Daisy. Because she went into detail." At my widened eyes, she continued. "Daisy is one of my best friends. Practically my sister versus my cousin. Of course we tell each other everything."

I winced. "I don't really want to know any more, do I?"

"She was very supportive." Her voice was its most prim and proper.

I threw my head back and laughed, thoughts of what exactly had been said filling my mind and honestly terrifying me. "Dear God. Women really do talk about everything, don't they?"

"Maybe." She held up her hands a little over ten inches apart, grinning far too widely for my taste.

I ran my hand over my face. "Aria Montgomery."

"What?"

"Please do not tell any more of your family members the size of my dick."

She burst out laughing. "I will do my best not to. Although Daisy knows."

"Daisy is married, and not going to talk about my dick anymore. At least I hope not."

"No, there's a code. She only talks about her husband's dick." At my look, she grinned. "No, she keeps that dick to herself. Don't worry."

"I think I should be worried." I cleared my throat. "Lex doesn't know what my dick looks like either." I paused. "No, wait, that's wrong."

Aria had just taken a sip of her soda and spewed it over the table. "What? I thought you said you and Lex were just friends."

"There are showers at the gym. And we have peed next to each other. At a urinal. Outside. Camping. And a group of us skinny dipped in the lake once. So I'm pretty sure I've seen a few Montgomery dicks. But not in a fun way." I did my best to keep a smile off my face, but at her wide eyes, I couldn't help but grin.

"We've said the word dick a lot."

My shoulders shook. "We can talk about cock if you want. Or penis. What innuendo would you like?"

She studied my face, her smile softening. "I like you like this. Laughing and smiling. You don't do it often enough."

"You haven't recently either." I reached for a chip even though I wasn't hungry anymore. "It feels weird to think about ever even being with Daisy. Or people thinking I'm with Lex. They are family."

"But I'm not," Aria said, even though it sounded like a question.

"Sleeping with you would be fucking weird then. Wouldn't it?"

She burst out laughing, and I tugged on her waist slightly so I could press my lips to hers.

"You're not like the others, Aria."

Her eyes widened, and I knew that was enough of baring my soul for the day. As it was, everything felt a little too rushed, a little too weird. And I wasn't sure I liked it. I didn't like this feeling. This happiness that seemed to be seeping through my pores.

We sat there a little longer and when Aria pulled out her camera, fiddling with the buttons, I leaned back and watched her work. I was decent with a point and shoot, but nowhere near her caliber. As she lifted the camera to her face, adjusting the lens, I held my breath. Then she turned toward me and snapped her first photo. Her shoulders relaxed, that tension she'd been holding for so damn long beginning to leave her.

Then she moved her focus to the trees behind me, taking another photo, then another. We didn't say anything, we didn't have to. She'd find her frame. Her center.

And I'd watch her work knowing this would always be one of the best parts of my day.

My phone buzzed in that instant. When I looked down at the readout, I realized that any feeling I had was only momentary.

"What is it?" Aria asked.

I tilted my phone to her, because she was one of the few who knew my mother was a bitch. They didn't know everything. I wasn't sure I would ever tell them. But this text I could show.

SATAN'S MISTRESS A.K.A. MOM:

I see you're finally showing your worth by getting arrested.

SATAN'S MISTRESS A.K.A. MOM:

I had to hear about it at the Club.

SATAN'S MISTRESS A.K.A. MOM:

If you're going to keep shaming me,
I'm going to ensure the world knows
how useless you are.

"I really hate that woman." The ice in Aria's tone matched the ice in my veins.

Chilled, I lifted my shoulder before putting my phone away. "It's nothing new."

"You were arrested because of me."

"If you say that one more time, I'm going to spank that ass." At her widened eyes, I shook my head. "No, that's not a good deterrent because you like it when my hand makes your ass all pink."

She narrowed those blue eyes of hers. "I should spank yours instead."

"If you can pin me down, you're welcome to try. Later," I promised. "The arrest was Travis's fault. We've already discussed this. Stop backtracking."

"Fine. As long as you realize that your mother is an evil person, and you don't need to listen to anything she says. I would say that you could use my mother as a good mother, but then we get into the weird family thing again." I knew she was trying to make me laugh, but I didn't have any words. Instead I lifted her onto my lap and held her close. She seemed to understand, and she wrapped her arms around me, pressing her cheek to mine.

I knew this wasn't forever. That we'd accidentally fallen into this moment, this connection. That would have to be okay with me.

But for now, I would take this.

Chapter Seven

Aria

It had been a week since something had shifted in my universe. If someone would've asked me even ten days before if I would be smiling at a text message from Crew, I'd have called them on their bullshit.

Not that he couldn't make me laugh. He'd always been able to do so and we'd texted daily until recently. Us being friends was never in question—at least before our last fight. But things had been strained as Travis had gone downhill. I'd spent so much of my time and guilt trying to help the man I thought was my best friend, that I'd nearly lost so many others in my life.

I'd pushed away so many people because I'd been trying my best to keep Travis safe.

Now as I looked at my phone, my lips couldn't help but lift.

CREW:

Your brother is hovering.

ME:

Which one?

CREW:

You know who. If it were Sebastian, I wouldn't be texting. Because he would just stick his daughter on me. You know I can't say no to anything Nora asks.

ME:

That is true. She has the entire Montgomery clan and their representatives wrapped around her little finger.

CREW:

Is that what you're going to call me? Your representative? I didn't realize representatives was another word for your seat. Considering where you sat this morning.

ME:

I am sitting on the other side of the studio from you blushing. I know you can't see me since I'm in the other room, but the others can see. I know everybody's going to want to know what I'm thinking.

CREW:

Because you're wet reading my texts? You think someone has had sex in that office yet? There's a lot of paint around here. I bet you we could have some fun with some art.

ME:

This is my family's place.

CREW:

And I am your representative.

ME:

I do not need one of my countless family members to walk into the office while I'm riding your face. Or with your cock in my mouth.

CREW:

Now I'm standing at my easel with my cock pressing against my sweats. It's not like I can hide that. Your brother is now glaring at me.

ME:

Why is Gus there? I thought he was at school.

CREW:

Graduate students don't need to be in class all day apparently. Come save me.

ME:

I'm afraid of my younger brother. So I'm going to need an incentive.

CREW:

If you don't come and save me from
your brother, I won't let you have my
dick. How about that?

"Aria Montgomery! You know I can read his texts over his shoulder!" Gus shouted through the building.

I put my phone in my pocket, my cheeks-stained red. "Mind your business, Gus Montgomery!"

"Do I want to know what you're texting Crew while you're in the same building?" Riley asked, her brows raised.

"Just the usual things," I lied as I scurried toward the other half of the building where Crew was set up. Because we wanted the right light for certain mediums, it wasn't an open floor space. I had been in the darkroom for most of the morning because sometimes I liked to work with film. That meant while Crew and I were in the same building, we had only seen each other for a few moments. I had spent the night at my own house, because I knew if I spent the night at his house every night, and if he did the same with mine, we would be moving way too fast.

As it was, it felt like we were in a whirlwind, and I was just trying to keep up.

"So when did this happen?" Gus asked as he stepped toward me, gesturing between Crew and me.

The rest of my family who happened to be in the building all stared at me, the silence thick.

I met Crew's gaze. The man looked unrepentant. He shrugged, then leaned against the doorway. I looked down at his tented sweats and raised a brow. He rolled his eyes, then adjusted himself, but I knew that wasn't going to help.

"I have no idea what you're talking about," I lied, knowing the others were staring at me and waiting for an answer.

"Finally!" Riley said as she threw up her hands. "I've been waiting for this day for years. It's a friends-to-lovers. Our time has come!"

"Do I want to know what that means?" Crew asked dryly.

"Wait, you and Aria? Why?" Nate asked. Only he wasn't looking at me, but Crew, as he said it.

I threw a couple of pieces of paper at my cousin. "Rude," I barked.

"She's so high maintenance," Colin joked, grinning at me. "I guess we're going to owe you a few drinks for taking her on, Crew."

Nate snorted. "From the way that Crew is glaring at you both right now, I'm pretty sure you should watch where you sleep."

Oliver just shook his head as he packed up his

sketchbooks. "As much as I love hearing about who my cousin is banging, I'm out. I promised Mom I would help at the store today. And I have a feeling traffic up to Boulder is going to be a bitch."

"Say hi to Holland for me." I leaned forward to kiss Oliver's cheek.

"Will do. And let my big brother, Kingston, know that he owes me."

"For working at your mother's shop? Or for something else?" I asked.

"Hell no," Oliver said mysteriously, before he walked out the building with a two-finger salute.

"Crap. I'm running late for lunch with James," Nate said, speaking of his twin. "He says he has something to tell me."

I clapped my hands, excited. "Is he going to propose to Sarah?" I asked. "Oh, I hope so. Those two have been adorable since they were like fourteen."

"You don't have to tell me. James can't stop talking about her, so hopefully he finally popped the question. And then that will keep Mom and Dad off my back. And Brooklyn's for that matter." And with that, he ran after Oliver.

Gus cleared his throat. "As much as I love all the family dynamics of everybody else in this room, I want to know when you and Crew became a *thing*. Because now I have to go bleach my eyes out after looking at those texts."

Crew shrugged. "You shouldn't have been reading over my shoulder. Do you want me to steal your phone and see what you've been texting?"

My younger brother blinked. "No. But I still want to know when this whole thing happened with Aria. I thought you two hated each other."

"That was just flirting," Riley said as she leaped onto the desk next to Colin and crossed her feet at the ankles.

"That's what I always said, but Leif didn't believe me." Colin shook his head at the mention of his older brother.

"You know I have been friends with your family for many years, and I still can't keep up with who is related to who." Crew took a few steps forward, and my heart finally eased because he was near. Or maybe I just needed a little more sleep. When he lifted my chin with just a brush of his knuckles and pressed his lips to mine, I sighed into him, wondering why I had been avoiding this for so long.

Riley squealed while Colin snapped a photo with his phone, and Gus let out a disgusted grunt.

"Stop doing that in front of me," my brother whined.

"You're the one who made me lie to Mom about

certain old school magazines you had in your room. So don't even," I warned.

Everybody burst out laughing as Gus flipped me off.

The man I was falling for—*or maybe had already fallen for*—held me tightly. "Seriously though, I'm going to need a family tree."

I leaned into Crew's hold, feeling right for some reason. "We'll get you a manual. Although you probably should've already had it."

"That's right. You dated Daisy. And Lex." Gus pointed at Crew as if he had made a huge discovery.

"You are going to want to lower that finger, son. Just saying."

"Shiver," Riley mock-whispered.

"Stop it," I teased.

"Why are you shivering, baby?" Patrick asked as he walked into the back room and immediately went to Riley's side. He pressed his lips to hers for long enough that I couldn't help but blush even as I winked over at Crew.

"It's an epidemic," I teased.

"I'm just enjoying seeing Gus squirm," Crew muttered.

"I heard that," my brother said.

"It's getting a little too touchy-feely for me," Colin

complained. "I'm headed over to the café to get some coffee. You want anything?" he asked.

Crew shook his head. "I'm about to take Aria out for lunch, so not us."

I raised a brow at Crew. "You weren't going to ask?

"You skipped breakfast and I know you don't snack while you're in the darkroom. So you're going to eat lunch," he said so matter-of-factly, that I just shook my head as Gus whistled.

"This is going to be fun," Riley teased.

"Good luck, man," Patrick said with a laugh. "Dating into this family has its perks, but it is a little overwhelming.

"Good thing I've been dealing with Montgomerys for a while," Crew said with a snort.

"You know Mom is going to want you to bring him for dinner," Gus warned.

I froze, and Crew rubbed his hand on the small of my back. "I'll be there Sunday."

I turned to him, wide-eyed. "What?" My heart raced, and I wondered why I suddenly felt so nervous.

Crew rolled his eyes. "We haven't been very subtle, so you know your mom already texted me and asked me to dinner. I've eaten at your place plenty of times. It will be fine."

The others laughed while I just stared at him, worry

sliding through. "You've gone as our friend. Because you know Sebastian and me. But this will be different."

"I know. It'll be okay, Aria. Stop worrying. For once. Just breathe." And then he leaned down and kissed me again, as Riley sighed happily, and the others chatted along.

Crew acted as if he had all the answers while I had none. But maybe that was okay. Maybe he actually had a plan. That would be one of us, and perhaps it would help the overwhelming sense of anxiety currently crawling up my spine.

At least I hoped so.

"I can't believe you texted him," I whispered.

My mom just grinned. "Of course I did. You weren't going to invite him over to meet the parents. Some things are simply needed."

I grimaced. "It's only been a week and a half. People usually get months before this moment." Or longer. Not that the Montgomerys were anything like normal.

"Most people don't have their daughter's significant other's phone number to make an evening meal happen." Tabitha Montgomery winked. "I love that something is happening between the two of you, and I won't ask for details. That's your business. Even if there wasn't, however, I would've wanted him here for a meal. With everything that happened in these recent months, he deserves a little comfort as well."

I relaxed completely, leaning into my mother's hold. "You're right. I'm glad that he has you and Lexington's parents. And frankly *all* of the aunts and uncles."

"I've never met his parents, but I know a few things and they are lucky I don't find them and run them down with one of the many cars we have and love. I am blessed with my parents and my in-laws. But I know a few of my sisters- and brothers-in-law had issues with their families. And knowing that they always had us to lean on helped them. Crew would've been invited here no matter what. That man needs to have a safe space—and we're it. And of course, he helped my baby. I'm going to make sure he gets cake."

I threw my head back and laughed before hugging her tight. My heart swelled at my mother's words because she was right. Crew needed us even if sometimes I felt as though he forgot that in his urge to take care of everyone else. "Cake solves everything."

"I thought that was cheese?" my younger sister Dara asked as she skipped into the room and threw her arms around me. She kissed me hard on the cheek and beamed. "Thank you for bringing that beautiful man for dinner."

I cringed. "Why did you make that sound like *he's* the dinner? Plus don't talk about Crew that way." *My* Crew.

My mom just pressed her lips together, holding back a laugh, thankfully not saying anything.

"He's edible. You know that."

Pushing at her arm, I tried not to laugh and let her win. "Is he out with Dad working the grill?" I asked, looking throughout the house for him.

"Yes, he's out there last I saw." Dara turned to Mom. "Oh, Mom. I forgot to mention that I needed that one paper you mentioned. Is it in the kitchen?"

"Yes, let me show you." Mom kissed my cheek. "Go rescue your man. Though your dad isn't as hard as my family was when it came to the third degree."

Laughing, I pulled away and headed to the back of the house. She was right since I knew my uncles had questioned my father for daring to touch their precious sister, but now they were all best friends. I visited Pennsylvania often to visit that set of cousins and my dad still playfully growled with his in-laws.

My parents' home was always so comforting. It wasn't our childhood home, as we had moved a couple of times when I was growing up as the family expanded.

The fact that my mother had birthed two sets of twins was a ridiculous feat. I still didn't know how the two of them made it all work even with the family helping.

And then after Sebastian had Nora, we had all moved into a larger house to accommodate the growing family. I had been in college, while Sebastian had been taking courses, raising his daughter, and preparing to buy into the tattoo shop. Gus and Dora had still been in school, and my parents had done everything to make sure that we were safe, loved, and had two feet on the ground.

My mother was an organizational queen. She kept Montgomery Inc., the family's first construction company going. Yes, Uncle Wes and the others were fantastic at what they did, but my mother was the planner extraordinaire. My father was a little messier, but not by much. I knew that part of his recovery had been taking control in what he had and that meant he didn't leave any messes. Even his dark room was pristine so he wouldn't accidentally harm one of his projects.

The walls were covered in art, some by family members, some by friends. And there were photographs everywhere. Of our childhood, of the family. Mostly ones my father had taken over time. And then a few of mine. That always made my stomach hurt, because I couldn't help but compare myself to my father. And I knew that was just in my head. Except maybe it wasn't. Especially because people like that woman couldn't help but give their opinion on my work.

I wanted to grow, I wanted to get better. And I would. But I still couldn't help but wonder if I would ever get to a point where I felt like I knew what I was doing.

A hand slid around my waist, and I looked at Crew. "Dad grilling you instead of dinner?" I asked, honestly a little worried.

Crew shook his head. "Nope. We were just out there grilling real food, waiting for Sebastian and his family to get here."

"Oh, are they here now?" I asked as I went to my tiptoes to look over his shoulder. Crew kissed the top of my head, and I blushed, knowing that my family was outright staring at me. We were all getting used to this new side of my relationship with Crew.

"They were just walking up."

I pulled on Crew's hand and tugged him to the side door. Before I could even open it though, Nora made her entrance, her dark hair in pigtails, and her smile wide.

"Aunt Aria? Mom and Dad said that you and uncle Crew were dating, and I had to not ask any questions. Can I ask a couple? Because I have a whole list."

I threw my head back and laughed, as Crew let go of my hand to bend down and meet Nora's gaze.

She was almost seven and had the Montgomery height. The height I hadn't gotten. I was more like my mother, but Nora got her genes from her father. Sebastian might be my twin, but sometimes I wasn't even sure we looked like we were from the same family. I knew his daughter was probably going to outgrow me quite quickly.

"What are your questions?" Crew asked, and I bit my lip, telling myself not to let my ovaries have control of this moment.

Nora ducked her head, blushing, and my eyes widened as I looked over her head at Sebastian and an adorably pregnant Raven. Nora never blushed. She was so confident, so this was a surprise. "I don't know where to start. But how about, if you and Aunt Aria don't work out, will you still wait for me?"

I pressed my lips together, trying not to squeal at the cuteness.

Crew reached out and tapped Nora's nose. "I promised you. When you're thirty-five, and if neither one of us is married, I will fight your father to see if I can have your hand in marriage. However, I'm pretty sure you're going to find someone your own age. I'll be old and gross by the time our deal works out."

Nora let out a relieved sigh. "You can never be gross, Crew." And when she fluttered her eyelashes, Raven and I both burst out laughing as Sebastian growled at the situation.

"Nora Montgomery," my twin snapped. "Are you serious right now?"

"You always said I had to be ambitious." She reached out and put her hand in Crew's, and the man I was slowly, okay, not so slowly, falling in love with, just winked at me.

Crew shook his head. "You have some competition."

"I see that." I put my hands on my hips before giving Nora a mock scowl. "You need to stop hitting on my man."

"So I'm your man?" Crew whispered.

I blushed as Sebastian growled once again.

"First, stop hitting on my sister. Second, Nora, Crew is way too old for you. And you're never going to date."

"I love this family," Raven said as she walked in and gave me a hug.

She took my hand and put it on her belly, because she knew I wouldn't do it myself. The baby kicked and I sucked in a breath, my eyes prickling with tears. And I couldn't help but smile at how happy she looked. I knew that Sebastian was worried about the pregnancy. After all he had lost his first wife in childbirth. And

Raven had PCOS, so she had her own worries but did her best not to show them—not that we let her hide them away. They had been surprised when she had gotten pregnant, but I knew they were so excited for this baby. Hell, I was excited for my next niece or nephew.

"How's Baby Coffee Bean doing?" I asked.

"Just fine. Although I really want coffee of my own. Considering I own and work at a coffee place," she said, her voice a little strained as she stared at her husband.

Sebastian scowled. "You know the rules. In fact, you've been standing for too long. Let's get you settled with your feet up."

Raven just rolled her eyes, gave me a look, and let her husband take care of her.

Nora skipped toward her grandparents, and I leaned into Crew, wondering exactly why this felt so right.

"You doing okay?" I asked, my voice low enough that the others couldn't hear.

"You don't have to worry about me, Aria. I like your family. I know them. Maybe it makes this part weird, but I don't really care. They make you happy, and they want what's best for you. So if they question me like I'm a suspect later, I'll take it. If I can handle your attitude, I can handle theirs."

I narrowed my gaze at him, shoving his shoulder.

"You were doing so well, so caring, and then you veered right off and were a jerk to me again."

"I can't be too sappy. You would think I was a pod person or something. I have to pick at you every once in a while to keep you on your toes."

"I don't know why but it makes me happy," I grumbled.

He pressed a kiss to my temple, ignoring the way that both of my brothers glared at him, and then pulled me toward the group. And once again, everything felt far too right.

Dinner went off without a hitch. Of course my family nudged at me and laughed, but they didn't poke or prod into my relationship. Even my brothers seemed to only be glaring out of habit rather than necessity. Things felt normal. Except for the fact that every once in a while, Crew would wrap his arm around the back of my chair or graze his knuckles along my knee. Then there was the fact we already had a routine without second thought. I wasn't a fan of cherry tomatoes on a salad, and Crew didn't like green olives and only liked black ones. So when we dug into the huge Italian salad my sister had made, I had picked off his olives, and he had done the same with my tomatoes.

While my father had just shaken his head, a small smile playing on his face, I realized that this wasn't the first time we had done this. Crew and I were friends. Yes, we had fallen into each other out of wanting to hide our feelings before, only now there was no hiding.

Except maybe from ourselves.

Us knowing each other's habits and food preferences wasn't new. Maybe that's why it felt like we were going full steam toward whatever came at us. And that worried me. So I wasn't going to focus on it too carefully.

My phone buzzed as we were cleaning off the table. I looked at the screen, my chest tightening.

TRAVIS:

I'm sorry, boo. You know what happens when I'm in the middle of a project. You just have to remember that sometimes I'm in my own head. But I'm sorry. Can you see me? I miss you.

I put my phone back in my pocket, not bothering to answer. Crew had been standing next to me, and his jaw clenched, but he didn't say anything.

"I'm not going to answer him."

He gave me a tight nod, and I hoped he believed me. Honestly, I hoped I believed myself. Because I didn't know which Travis was texting me. The one who felt remorseful, or the one who needed something. I was afraid it would always be the latter.

As Crew went off to help my mother with something in her office, my dad pulled me to the side. I tensed once again, thinking about that text and what this dinner meant.

"I'm not talking about Crew." I hadn't meant to blurt the words, but I was so afraid to say anything that would ruin what was just starting, that I needed these moments to myself.

My dad just smiled. "I love Crew. I trust you."

My eyes widened. "What?"

"We were going to ask Crew to dinner anyway because we wanted to check on him after the incident." My dad's eyes darkened and we both swallowed hard. "The fact that he now seems to be dating my daughter is a recent development. And I'm not going to get all alpha male and sit on the porch with a shotgun. Hell, if your mother's parents had done that to me, I don't think I ever would've made it past the front door. Especially as the man I used to be."

I reached out and squeezed my dad's wrist. "You're the best father. And Mom says you're the best husband. Just saying."

He shook his head. "I wasn't a good husband to my first wife. But then again, she wasn't a good wife. We said and did things we can't take back, but I'm not that man anymore." I didn't wince as he said it, they were very open about their past, but it still hurt to hear. "My opinion of Crew is that if he hurts my baby girl, I will hurt him. But I'm not going to get in the middle of the relationship."

"I love you, Dad."

"I love you too, baby girl. But while we talked on the phone about it, I want to talk about that day in your studio."

I tensed, and my dad pulled me to the porch swing, and we sat next to each other, my toes brushing the hard wood as my dad and his long legs pushed us back and forth.

"I never know how to approach you when it comes to photography. And that might be on me, or it just might be who the two of us are. But the first time you picked up a camera and wanted to learn was one of the best moments of my life." I smiled at him. He put an arm around my shoulder, and I leaned into his familiar hold.

"I'm always so nervous."

"Because of what it can mean? Or because of me?"

"I don't have an answer to that."

He nodded, and we were silent for little bit longer. "I don't know how to fix that for you. And maybe it's not my job to fix it. I'm always here if you need me."

"I know." I shook my head. "I just hate the fact that I

always feel like I'm searching for something. And that maybe I'll never find it."

"I don't know what I'm looking for when I work on a project. Sometimes it calls for me, sometimes I stumble into it. I don't have to work every day to breathe, but the feeling that comes from it? That keeps me steady. Just like your mom does."

"My camera's in the front foyer. I didn't want to leave it in the car. But I brought it with me."

"Good. *Good.*" And I heard the relief in that. He and Crew had both noticed I hadn't brought my camera with me everywhere like I used to. It hadn't felt like an extension of myself like it once had. Honestly, I hadn't even noticed the lack of it until Crew had set it down on that picnic table.

Now it went everywhere with me. Even if I wasn't always ready to take a photo.

"I'm going to say something, and I don't want you to hate me for it."

I tensed at my father's words but nodded.

"Watching you with Travis reminded me of what your mother saw before we were together, and I hated that for you. I don't like the man that I was, and I am grateful every day that you never had to meet him. And I hope to hell that one day Travis finds peace. That he figures out how to help himself. Because that will always be the first step. But I'm going to be a selfish bastard and say that I'm glad you are taking time for yourself too."

I wiped away a tear and leaned into my father more. "I love you, Daddy."

He let out a rough chuckle. "I love you too, baby girl. Now, let's go inside and interrogate your boyfriend."

I shook my head. "Let's not do labels. Labels are scary."

We stood up as my dad laughed. "I will never understand this generation."

"Okay, Grandpa."

"You say that, but your brother made me a grandpa when he was nineteen. Any gray hair you may see is all because of him."

Laughing, we walked into the house as my mother and Gus began to serve cake. Crew walked right up to me and took my hand, a curious expression on his face. In answer, I kissed him softly, and then walked to the foyer to get my camera.

My dad winked at me, and as my family ate cake and softly interrogated Crew, I snapped a photo, and then another, finally breathing.

Chapter Eight

Aria

I stripped off my jeans, tossed them across my bedroom, then reached for the lacy, flowy green skirt. I wiggled inside it, wondering if I needed to change my panties, but figured the thong was going to have to do. I was already running late enough.

I had on a cute cotton eyehole black crop top and a jean jacket over it. Since the skirt was pretty short in the front and yet longer in the back, I put on my knee-high brown boots and called it a win. It was a little southern, not quite matching, and I figured with some chunky silver jewelry, I could make it work.

And why was I so stressed about what I was going to wear to meet Crew?

"Maybe because this is a real date, dumbass." I

shook my head at my own inner reflections and told myself everything was fine. Crew and I ate meals together all the time. We went to games, movies, and events together routinely. Either with family and friends, or just the two of us.

Crew taking me to a new place without telling me exactly what it was, wasn't anything special.

I stared at myself in my reflection, finger combing the curls out of my dark hair.

I was lying to myself. Because today *was* something special.

I pinched my cheeks, annoying myself because I had gone pale just thinking about an actual date with Crew, and quickly finished my lip gloss right as the doorbell rang. My stomach tensed, and I tried not to run to the front door.

After all, I didn't want to seem too eager, and I didn't want to trip in these heeled boots. Crew had a key to my place and could walk in whenever he wanted to— just like I could at his place—but we set our own boundaries. Yet when I opened the door, my breath caught in my throat and all ideas of boundaries flew out the window.

I had always thought Crew was especially handsome. But with those high cheekbones, and strong jaw you could see even beneath that big beard of his, it was hard not to stare at him. His light eyes were piercing as he studied me, and my gaze raked over his body. He had on a dark Henley, worn jeans, and biker boots. I couldn't help but notice the way his jeans were tight around his thighs, and I remembered the last time I had been kneeling in front of him, my fingernails digging into the muscles of his thighs as he thrust in and out of my mouth. His cock was so huge that my lips had been stretched to the limit to accommodate him, my teeth scraping along his length.

I might've been the one sucking him down, with his hand wrapped in my hair, but he was in control as he fucked my face. Then I'd slid my hand down to between my thighs, fingering myself because he'd told me to—not coming until he'd let me.

I pressed my thighs together at that thought, and when Crew raised a single brow, that smirk on his face, I knew my blush was showcasing all of my emotions.

"If you don't stop looking at me like that, I'm going to bend you over in that skirt and see exactly how wet you are."

With the growl in his voice, I nearly turned around to bend over so he could slam into me. Except I was trying to act normal. Meaning, a normal date. And not wanting to fuck his brains out every time I saw him.

"I have no idea what you're talking about. However, I'm hungry. You promised me food." I leaned to the side to pick up my crossbody bag and loved the way that I could practically feel his gaze on me as I did so.

There had always been a combustible chemistry between us. But ever since we had stopped fighting the pull, it had increased exponentially. I wasn't quite sure what I was supposed to do with that information, so I set it to the side and brushed against Crew's body as I walked past him. Of course, the action backfired, because it just made me wetter as he let out that oh so dangerous growl of his.

"You are playing with fire, girl."

I ignored the warning in his tone and made my way to the passenger side of his lifted truck. "Again, no idea what you're talking about." Then I gestured toward his truck. "You usually drive the SUV, the convertible, or the bike. What is with the compensation mobile? Because I've seen what's between your legs, and you don't need to compensate for anything." I winked as I said it, and Crew threw his head back and laughed.

Then he leaned forward, gripped the back of my neck, and slammed his mouth to mine. It was rough, sensual, and everything I needed in a kiss. And when he pulled back, we were both panting. "I needed to get this one out of the garage for a bit. It's not good to let them sit idle for long."

"You know, you have way too many cars, rich boy."

He rolled his eyes at that, then opened the door for me and gripped me by the waist. Before I could say anything to the contrary, he lifted me with ease and set me in the passenger seat. I jokingly fanned my face at the action, and he snorted, closed the door, and walked to his side of the truck.

I looked around at the decked out interior and shook my head. I knew that Crew had money. He had always been pretty secretive about it, and I didn't blame him. The difference in incomes, money, and privilege always came with strings. And Crew was a pretty private person, even if he was always nosy as hell when it came to me. But he couldn't hide the fact that his house had to be worth a few million dollars, and he had way more vehicles than anyone I knew. A few of my family members had money and they liked to play with toys just like Crew did. And while my family's investments meant that we had been very comfortable growing up, technically, we had come from blue-collar roots with my parents' upbringing. My photography at the moment paid well enough that as long as I continued my investments and savings, I wouldn't have to worry about retirement, but it was nowhere near in the sphere of Crew. I had no idea how many businesses he owned, if he had more than that one house, or how many zeros he had to his name. But I knew that it wasn't any of my business. We might be dating—something that was still a novel idea to me—but some things were personal. And if he wanted to tell me all about his family money and every kind of toy he owned, I'd be there. But for now, I was still getting used to this new aspect of our relationship. Like how we actually had a relationship.

"Your mind is going in a million different directions over there. Care to let me know what you're thinking about?" Crew asked, and I realized when I had been lost in my thoughts, he had started the truck, and we were already on our way to wherever he had planned.

I shook myself out of my far too serious thoughts and smiled. "I was just thinking about how much I'm enjoying the fact that you're now my Sugar Daddy." I fluttered my eyelashes, hoping he understood the joke. Again, we didn't talk about money. However, me ignoring it completely would just make it awkward.

Crew's hands tightened on the steering wheel for an instant, and I was afraid I had said the wrong thing. Then he smirked over at me and clucked his tongue. "You know, that's right. That makes you my, what,

Sugar Baby? I should be taking out interest at this point. So what is it, an orgasm for a dinner out?"

Chuckling, I shook my head. "You really think your orgasm is worth a dinner? I don't know what you think more highly of. Your dick or my mouth?"

"I suppose we will have to see later. But first, you're going to want dinner."

I tried to hold back my laughter and failed. This was a ridiculous conversation, but I loved making him smile and act all possessive. "I wouldn't mind your cock. Just saying. It's a nice cock."

"You say the sweetest things, Aria." He paused, and I leaned back in the seat, enjoying the smooth leather. "You never ask about the money."

I stiffened and looked over at him. "I was just thinking about how it wasn't my place. You let me pay for dinner sometimes, and we've always been good about helping each other out. And I think you like the mysterious act when it comes to you owning the gym."

His lips twitched as he pulled into the parking lot of the place I had never seen before. "People get weird about the money. Especially my family."

My hands tightened into fists. "My family and I aren't typical people." I held up my hand. "Joking aside, you've always been just Crew to us. Even though it's taken me a while to realize what 'just Crew' means to me." I swallowed hard, ignoring that knot of emotion. "But your family also makes me want to throw something, so I tend not to think about them at all. If that makes me a terrible person, I'm sorry."

Crew looked at me for a moment, and once again I was afraid I'd said the wrong thing. Then he leaned forward and brushed his lips along mine. "You just do something to me, Aria Montgomery," he whispered before he shut off the engine. "Now, as much as I would like to talk more about this and figure out what is going on inside that big, beautiful brain of yours, you haven't noticed where we are. And I, for one, am shocked."

I frowned at him, my heart racing because it felt like we were having a moment here. A moment for what? I didn't know yet. But it was something. And then I turned to really look at the building in front of me.

"Oh my God. It's the Cheese Bar?" I turned to him, my stomach rumbling, my mouth watering. "You can't get reservations here. It takes months."

"You can when you know the owner because you happen to own the building next door."

"I love all of your Machiavellian connections. This place not only has a cheese bar, but on Wednesdays, it's all you can eat charcuterie, and they have a special menu depending on the week. I follow them on every social media, trying to get ideas for dinner with the family. It's so hard to get in here, I've never been able to come."

"Well then I'm glad that I brought you here." He paused, looking a little uncertain. "I've never brought any other Montgomerys here. Just thought you should know." And with that, he hopped out of the truck and made his way to my side.

Feeling oddly warm inside, I let him help me out of the truck, and then slid my hand in his as we went inside.

I froze as I looked at the gorgeous wood interior with comfortably warm booths and tables set up everywhere. It was one of the most inviting areas I had ever been to, and I nearly wept at the center of the room.

Because there, in all its glory, was a conveyor belt of cheese.

"Is this heaven?" I whispered, and the host laughed softly under his breath.

Crew wrapped his arm around my waist and led me toward the table. "I think the look on your face means I did a good thing."

"You did an amazing thing." Even in heeled boots, I went to my tiptoes, cupped his face, and kissed him softly on the mouth. It wasn't one of those hard and fast kisses that we used to gauge one another. One that would let the other know they were craving them. No, this was much softer, much kinder. And as our gazes met, I swallowed hard.

The host cleared his throat. "Here you go, you'll have this corner area of the belts, and if you'd like to sit at a table, for fondue or a full meal, let us know."

We took our seats, and I practically danced in my chair as I looked at the menu. The server came over and began explaining a few things, and I kept dancing.

"Are you going to be able to sit still for this?" I could hear the humor in his tone, but I didn't care.

"No. Not at all. I can't believe it's all you can eat on this belt right now."

Our server smiled. "And we can add extras. There's this Kirkham's Lancashire paired with a Yorkshire fruitcake that sounds awfully pleasing."

"I'll take fourteen of them," I teased, and I couldn't help but feel as if I had found my true home at this place.

Cheese and meat plates went around the conveyor belt, calling my name, and I laughed as Crew snapped a few photos of me, knowing I probably looked ridiculous. When he took a bite of a soft cheese and fig jam combination, I was the one to snap a photo.

"Are you going to show that anyone?" he asked, his voice low against my ear.

I wiggled in my seat and moved to whisper so only

he could hear. "No. Because I'm pretty sure you look like that when you're coming."

He barked out a laugh, kissed my cheek, and we moved on to the next phase of our dinner.

I wasn't sure when I had had a more fun meal in my life. And it didn't all have to do with the amount of cheese in front of me. Yes, we probably ate too much, but I didn't care. Everything was fresh, delectable, and the pairings made it feel like it wasn't too rich.

Full, but not overly so, I made sure my to go container of Yorkshire Parkin tiramisu and clotted cream panna cotta were safe in my hands as Crew drove me back to my place.

"Is it wrong that I could eat more?" I asked, rubbing my belly. "I probably shouldn't have worn a crop top."

"You look fucking sexy, and if you want to eat a second round of dinner later, I'm all for it. But first, let's get you home so I can have my dessert." He gave a pointed look between my legs, and I snorted before setting the to-go containers safely in the section between the seats. Then, meeting his gaze for an instant as he drove down the highway, I hiked up my skirt ever so slightly and spread my legs.

"Aria, do you really want me to wreck this truck right here?"

"I have no idea what you mean," I teased. And then

I slowly slid my hand under my skirt. I knew he couldn't see exactly what I was doing, but as my fingers slid over my clit, a moan escaped my mouth.

"Fuck. Don't you dare."

"I'm just imagining my fingers as your tongue."

"If it was my tongue, I'd be lapping up that sweet cunt of yours, teasing you. I'd spread you before me, making sure you were right at the edge, but not close enough. You'd beg me for my cock, but I wouldn't let you have it. You'd be squirming, your nipples hard little points, but still, I wouldn't let you come."

I hadn't realized I was panting until I arched my back, my middle finger slowly sliding in and out of my pussy. "Crew."

"Is that pussy of yours swollen for me?"

"Please. I need to come."

"You're really going to come right in my truck, are you? When we're only two streets away from your house?"

I nodded, nearly there, the edge so close. And then Crew slammed on the brakes at a stop sign, leaned over, and speared me with two fingers. Shocked, I arched my back, coming with the intrusion. My toes curled in my boots, and I rocked my hips against his hands. Somehow Crew was still driving, his fingers deep inside me, but I couldn't think.

When he pulled out of me, I whimpered, and realized we were at my place. Blushing, I nearly screamed as Crew ripped open the door and pulled me out of the truck after he undid my seatbelt.

"You are going to be punished for that," he growled.

"I'm pretty sure I was rewarded." I laughed. Thankfully he let me grab the desserts, then he carried me over his shoulder into my house and slammed the door behind him.

"Go put those in the fridge, while I try not to walk with a fucking limp."

He smacked me hard on the ass, then set me down on my feet. I looked between us, and because his cock was so hard his jeans were straining, I licked my lips.

"You're going to hate yourself for wasting a cheese dessert, Montgomery."

Blushing, I practically scampered into the kitchen to put everything in the fridge. I wasn't even sure what shelf I put them on, because as soon as I closed the door, Crew was on me.

He pressed himself to my back, pushing my hands over my head.

"Did you like nearly wrecking us? By touching that sweet pussy without my permission?"

"I don't need your permission to come," I snapped back.

Crew licked my neck before gently biting down. I shivered in his hold. "We'll see about that."

Then he shoved up my skirt and tore at the side of my panties.

"Hey! I liked those."

"Did you?" he asked, and I was afraid of what that meant. However I had my answer when he stuffed my panties in my mouth and gagged me.

Eyes wide, I arched my back for him, needing him. He pulled up my crop top, shoved down my bra, and fondled my breasts to the point that my knees went weak. He was rough, and yet I knew the moment that I needed him to, he would be gentle. Because that was Crew. Always knowing my needs before I did. That should've worried me, but it didn't.

Instead I moved into his touch, letting him take control. And at the sound of a zipper, my inner walls clenched, and I rubbed myself on him.

"Stay still," he snarled. And then, with one tease at my entrance, he shoved into me in one stroke.

I gasped, my body stretching at his length and girth, knowing that I would be sore tomorrow. But I didn't care.

Instead, Crew kissed at my neck, then tilted my head to take my mouth before he took me.

He pounded me into the fridge, and I held on for

dear life, meeting him thrust for thrust. "That's it. Take my cock."

"Crew," I panted through my panties.

He pulled out of me, and I whimpered. But before I could feel the loss, he turned me around and lifted me up by my thighs. I wrapped my legs around him, rubbing my pussy against his cock as he walked me to the bedroom.

"I want to see those eyes when I come. I want to see your face as I feel you. Can you do that? Can you come on my cock when the only thing that matters is us?"

Tears pricked my eyes, but I nodded, taking his mouth. He kissed me hard, and then tossed me on the bed. He shoved my skirt up fully, my boots still on, and I reached for him, my gag falling out.

"Take off your shirt. I need to see."

He nodded, his eyes so dark I couldn't even tell where his irises were. Then he took off his boots and stripped off his pants as well. He stood there naked, glorious.

And all mine.

I quickly pulled off my shirt and bra, and tried to do the same with my skirt, but he didn't let me finish. Instead he lifted me up by the waist and licked up my slit. I moaned his name as he continued to feast on me, licking and sucking his fill.

"Play with your tits. I need you to come on my face when you're making those nipples even harder."

Somehow, I knew if I let him, I could come from his words alone. This man just did things to me. But I listened to him, cupping my breasts and rolling my nipples between my thumb and forefinger.

He continued to eat me out, licking and sucking before finally my inner walls clenched, and I came right on his face. Before I could do anything, still orgasming, Crew had his mouth on mine, and I could taste myself on him.

Tears slid down my cheeks, and I couldn't help them. So he kissed them away and teased me with the tip of his cock.

"Are you ready for me?" he whispered, the question so fragile that I couldn't speak. Instead I just nodded, and then he sank into me, inch by inch.

This time was different. It had started hard and fast, and yet there was so much more in this moment. He rocked in and out of me, one hand lazily playing with my breasts, the other wiping away tears.

I cupped his face with one hand, the other arm wrapped around him, and smiled.

"Mine," I whispered.

"As long as I can claim you too."

And as I nodded, he picked up the pace, and I came

once again, my body growing lax. And he filled me, one thrust after another, whispering my name into my mouth as he took me. When he came, I threw my head back, my body shaking.

I realized I was shaking as he pulled out of me, leaving gentle kisses on my cheeks. Then he slid his fingers over my mouth, and I realized he'd covered them with his cum and I couldn't help but lick them clean.

"Those fucking boots just do something to me," he said with a laugh.

I grinned up at him and then down at my boots and haphazardly put together skirt. "I would joke and say that it was the cheese, but we both know that would be a lie."

He came back from the restroom with a wet towel and chuckled. "It's okay if it was both. This time."

I blushed as he cleaned me up, wondering when this would start to feel real. Because it still didn't. It didn't matter that we had slept together long before we had allowed ourselves to think about that. Everything still felt new. I was so afraid somehow we would mess it up.

But I pushed those thoughts away for now, because I didn't want to fulfill my own prophecy.

"Come on, I'm sure you want dessert now," he said roughly.

I could have called him out on it, but he wasn't wrong. "It's shouting my name."

"Pretty sure that was me," he mumbled.

I finally took off my boots and skirt, and reached for a tank top and tiny shorts to sleep in. Crew and I usually slept naked, but I really didn't want to walk around my kitchen that way.

"Crap." I paused.

"What?" Crew asked as he pulled on a pair of gray sweatpants he had left here a few nights ago.

"I'm going to have to scrub my kitchen. My family eats in there sometimes."

He rolled his eyes and left me alone in the bedroom. "I'll go get the bleach," he called out.

"You know we had to scrub your living room last time," I replied.

"True. I have a cleaning team that comes in but I'm not about to have them clean up after orgasms."

I shivered. "No, thank you."

Crew pulled out two forks, and then gestured for me to sit at the breakfast bar. I hopped on the barstool, and he took a seat beside me as the two of us opened the cartons and began eating.

"This feels so domestic," I teased.

"It's food. And talking. So sure." He rolled his eyes, but I saw the blush on his cheeks. This was different for

Crew as well—whatever this was. So who knew what we'd do with this.

I licked the whipped cream off my fork, before setting it down and hopping off the chair.

"Where you are going?" he asked, a frown on his face.

"I forgot I got you something."

"It's not my birthday. Is it because I made you come? Because I think you owe me a few more gifts."

I rolled my eyes and pulled out the box I had put together earlier that day, and feeling suddenly self-conscious, I handed it over without looking at him. Then I hopped back on the barstool and took a huge bite of dessert.

Crew gave me a weird look, and then pulled the top of the box open, his eyes widening.

"I forgot you took this," he whispered.

He set the fork down and looked over at the photo I had given him. I didn't do portraits often, because it wasn't my specialty—it was my dad's. But I couldn't help doing this one.

It was from our picnic in the mountains, when Crew had been laughing, and then glaring at me. I had somehow caught the in-between moments, when he was just himself. With the mountains and green trees behind him, and just that look in his eyes that said it was the two of us.

I put it in a dark frame and adjusted the color a bit so his eyes stood out, so it wasn't fully black and white.

"You do damn good work, Montgomery."

"It helps that the subject is pretty."

He snorted. "Pretty, my ass."

"Well, your ass is also pretty." I paused, self-conscious. "I don't know...I just wanted you have it. It's just a gift. A token."

He met my gaze, but he didn't smirk like he usually would have in the past. Instead he leaned forward and brushed his lips against mine. "Thank you. I have some of your artwork in my place, but I always want more. I'm greedy like that."

I bit my lip and leaned back into my seat. "You always make me believe I can do more. Without making me feel as if I'm doing less."

He stared at me for a moment, before finally setting down the photo and pulling me into his lap. "You have always been spectacular, Aria Montgomery. Even when I pretended to hate you. So you are going to have to get used to the fact that I believe in you. Got it?"

For some reason tears pricked my eyes again, and I leaned into his hold, letting him cradle me. "This means

I get to have one of your paintings in my place though, right?" I teased, needing to lighten the moment.

"I'm expensive."

Laughing, I snuggled into him more. "I'm sure I could get a few orgasms out of you. As payment."

He threw his head back and laughed. I settled into his hold, finally feeling happy for the first time in a long while.

And hoping to hell I didn't fuck things up.

Chapter Nine

Crew

Music blared from the speakers, a pounding beat that I could feel against my heart. I rolled my shoulders back, letting the so-called "dad rock" get me in the mood to finish this painting. I wasn't on a commission, this was just for myself, but I needed to get it out of me. Frankly, I rarely worked on commissions. I didn't like the idea of paint by numbers or paint on demand. And I didn't need the money.

Many of my contemporaries did however, but they were all of the same mindset. If somebody wanted a commission, they would get what they got, given a slight direction, rather than a firm checklist.

One of my sculptor friends said it was easier for

them to make a bowl or a vase for some clients, and still have their own inspiration in it.

The eight foot by ten foot painting currently filling my studio, however, wasn't something I could whip up in a breeze. I frowned, wondering why I was harping on that. It didn't matter what anyone else did with their art. Just because I had the privilege of doing whatever the fuck I wanted, didn't make anyone else less of an artist. I was in a damn mood since the memory care center had called twice in the past week. My dad was declining rapidly, and there would have to be some decisions made soon about what facility would be best for him.

God forbid my mother actually did something. Instead it was on my shoulders. Because apparently the son who hadn't been worth anything while the father could remember, was the one who was supposed to decide quality of life.

I dipped my paintbrush in a deep and vibrant red I had blended together earlier and went to war with the canvas. Sometimes I went abstract, sometimes I went portrait or realistic. Today I was in the mood to work with oils, meaning everything was a mess, and I'd have to deal with the clean up later. The art called me in this instant and I wanted to see what I could do with this, and that wouldn't go away.

Hence why I wanted to get this painting out of my

studio. Either in the trash, out on some tour, or in some-body's house who could get something from it.

I kept going, adding a slightly different red, then changing techniques with black and grays. The layering itself felt as if it were jagged edges of whatever the hell feelings wouldn't get out of my brain. I just kept going, knowing that if I didn't finish this soon, I'd be unpleasant to deal with later.

I added a touch of purple, and then went into shad-ing, when my phone alarm finally went off.

Startled, I pulled myself out of the zone and set down my paintbrushes.

I was in my home studio, tarps and drop cloths draped everywhere, and I looked like I had rolled in my paint right along with it. I wasn't always this messy, but it had been a hell of a day.

Using my nose to turn off the alarm because it was the only thing not covered in paint I could use, I began cleanup. I didn't like working on a timer, but I had some-where to be.

A smile finally covered my face after the day from hell, and I couldn't help but wonder when exactly I had fallen into this.

Aria had an art show later today, as well as some students from the Montgomery Gallery, and a few of the other Montgomerys themselves. I was excited to see what she was going to show since she had been secretive about it. That was the way she was sometimes though. Art was personal, even when you told yourself it wasn't.

Hell, I didn't like the art in front of me, and I didn't know if I would ever, but if I looked too deep, I would realize it was because I didn't like the person I became after dealing with my parents. I didn't need additional therapy hours to come to that conclusion. I'd already been through enough therapy to get to this point.

I snorted as I finished cleaning up, shaking my head. Considering my therapist was the one who told me to finally shit or get off the pot when it came to Aria, I couldn't really complain.

Of course, the old man who listened to my troubles and usually had a good word to say, wouldn't be that vulgar. He would have some elegant way to say that I should focus on what I had and speak about my feelings.

Only I wasn't quite sure how to tell the woman who I was just now seeing that I had been in love with her for years.

That wouldn't go well for anyone.

Aria was like a deer in headlights. And she had just blinked, slowly moving to the other side of the road. But if I revved the engine, or made any sudden movement like turning off my lights, or saying something as idiotic as I loved her, she would either freeze once again or run.

And I'd seriously taken everything out of that metaphor apparently.

She was just getting out of whatever hellscape relationship she had with Travis. And while I knew it wasn't a romantic relationship, it was still a tethered emotional one. Because her past with that man wrapped around the history I shared with her. Every single pivotal moment between us until recently had been due to Travis and his addiction, or our reaction to the space he had made.

I wasn't quite sure I liked putting it that way. But then again, Travis would always be there.

No, she was no longer helping him. No longer actively trying to make him a better person than he was, but the man was still out there. And that, combined with dealing with both of my parents today, meant that I needed to get in a better mood before I saw Aria.

She needed me to be the strong one. Because she always got so stressed-out during art shows. And one where people would actually be seeing her pieces, my worry over a man who had nothing to do with this, would just make things worse.

I had no idea where we were going, what the hell she felt, or what I even wanted out of this, but considering I was the one who brought us this far, I wasn't going to back down. I shook my head, wondering why I was being so introspective, considering whenever I finished a painting, that's when I could purge everything. Except Aria always did something to me.

I quickly showered, grateful for paint remover, and changed into dark gray pants, nicer biker boots that fit the suit that Aria had bought me one day since I hated dress shoes most days, and a dove gray button up shirt. Honestly, I could've worn anything I wanted to this. It wasn't going to be formal, but Aria had mentioned she was going to wear a dress, so I might as well not look like a heathen next to her.

I winced, knowing that at some point the two of us needed to talk about what the hell we were to each other. But that wasn't right now. Instead, I grabbed my phone, wallet, keys, and headed to my car.

I called Aria on the way, knowing that I was meeting her there, rather than picking her up like I wanted. We had been sleeping at each other's homes nearly every night, and I was getting used to waking up next to her.

Before, when we just used each other to get whatever we were feeling out of the other, we hadn't slept over. I hadn't let myself think we would even want that. But now, waking up with her in my arms, with that sweet little ass pressed up against my cock every morning, I wasn't sure I wanted it any other way. I probably should be listening to the warning sirens at that, but I wasn't. That was a warning in its own right.

I pulled into the main parking lot, happy to see it was nearly full. A few people were already parked on the street, and I was grateful there was a small employee area. I noticed Aria's SUV in the corner, and I quickly made my way inside.

When she had said she would wear a dress, I should've asked her what kind of dress.

Because my tongue stuck to the roof of my mouth, and my eyes nearly rolled out of my head.

She had on this asymmetrical flowing piece of fabric that made my mouth water and my cock standing at attention. The slit on the right side was high enough that I could see long swaths of tan thigh. She had on stiletto shoes to match the dress, and while the front of it was pretty demure with the neckline being right at her collarbone, the back was nonexistent.

You could see all of the ink that her family had given her over time because she had pulled that dark hair back into an elegant bun thing. The dress left her arms bare and the rest of the dress showcased those luscious curves I had licked every inch of. And the deep, vibrant ruby color of it made her stand out in a sea of mostly black and white. Of course, there were a few other colors among some of the patrons who had strolled in as well, with one guy wearing this peach suit thing that reminded me of an older movie. But I only had eyes for Aria. Then again, that was usually the case when it came to her.

With a smile on her face, she spoke to Lex. My best friend had a worried look, but it was gone in a blink. I knew I'd have to get the information out of him soon. Her cousin wore a dark purple shirt with black pants, the two of them laughing at something Lex said. And while Lexington looked like he meant it, I saw the tension hiding in his smile.

Ignoring others calling for me, because I had forgotten that I had a piece in this as well, I made a beeline toward Aria.

Lexington's eyes widened as he saw me, before a clever smile covered that face of his. "I think you're about to be stolen from me."

Aria turned, a frown on her face, before her shoulders relaxed marginally. "You're late."

"I was working."

"Taking over the world or painting?"

I leaned forward and kissed her jaw. She smelled of roses, and I had to swallow hard. She kept changing that scent on me. It was like a surprise every time I was near her.

"Painting."

"That's good considering your piece over there already sold," Lexington said, gesturing with his champagne flute.

I looked over my shoulder and frowned at the dark landscape painting I had set aside a few months ago. I could see the errors in it, but I still liked that piece. I had captured that moment in the mountains after an event with the Montgomerys. When Travis had shown up drunk, and Aria had done her best to try to save her friend. And in the end, the first fracture in my friendship with her had begun. We had sealed it now, because we had done the one thing we were never good at before: communicate. But I could still remember that night, when another one of us had nearly died, and Aria had lost part of herself along the way.

Her hand slid into mine and squeezed. "Are you okay?"

I nodded, swiping a champagne flute from a passing server. "Just thinking about that painting. I forgot Riley was using it."

"It was okay, right? You signed for everything but I'm sure we can change it if we need to."

"Oh it's fine. I was just thinking about your work, and my current project." *And my parents.*

"You artists always surprise me with what you can do," Lexington said with a shake of his head. "But whoever bought that is lucky. I was looking at it, but it's too rich for my blood."

"You know I would paint anything for you," I told one of my best friends. "For a price."

"And there it is," Lex said with a laugh, gesturing with his drink.

Aria leaned into me, her eyes filled with nerves. "Will you walk with me to the other side of the room, so I don't have to see people looking at my art? I'd rather hang out in the student area. They've done such fantastic work."

I leaned forward and brushed my lips against her ruby red ones. "Of course. But you have nothing to be worried about."

"I didn't say I was worried," she bit out.

I winced, knowing I'd read her wrong. Maybe we *weren't* communicating the way we should. "That's not what I meant."

"I will leave you two to it." Lex practically ran down the hall and toward another group of our friends.

Aria wrung her hands together but didn't look at me. "I know it's good work, and I know it'll sell. If that's what I really want. I'm fine."

I tilted my head to study her face. "Then what's wrong?" I asked.

"Nothing. Just always feel awkward at these things."

"Then let's go see how the student section is doing and keep your mind off it."

"Why are you being so reasonable when I'm being a bitch?" she muttered as we went to the front of the gallery where a few student pieces were being showcased.

"I can be an asshole if you want. I'm pretty good at it. But you're not being a bitch."

"If I agree with you, then I'm once again that bitch," she said, but her lips twitched.

My girl had layers and we both knew this. Aria made sure everyone around her knew they were at their best but was harder on herself than anyone else. "These things don't make me nervous. I don't know why. Other shit with this job makes me nervous, but not this. So I just take it in stride. If you want to lash out at me, I can take it out on your ass later," I teased.

Her cheeks flushed, and I just grinned. She opened her mouth to say something, but then her face lost all color, her jaw tightening. Worried, I set down my glass and turned, only to come face to face with the person I had hoped moved on into oblivion.

"For a woman who declared her love for me, you moved on pretty quick," Travis slurred, his eyes glassy. He had lost weight since I had last seen him, the dark circles under his eyes growing. He reeked of booze, and from the way he twitched, he had to have something else in his system.

The showing hadn't been invite only, so anybody could walk in from the streets. However, we did have security considering the Montgomerys owned the company. Travis was a usual so perhaps the others hadn't gotten the memo he was no longer wanted. Or worse, maybe Aria had invited him. I ignored the ache in my gut at that thought.

Daisy and Noah were already walking toward us, ready to deal with the situation, and as people turned, the spectacle growing, Aria tensed beside me.

"Travis. Please. Not here. Not now." Aria's voice was calm, but I heard the strain beneath it.

"Oh? You're going to dictate what I can do now? You've always done that." He turned to me. "Is she a better lay than I've heard? Because she's always been a frigid bitch. I assume she's like that bed too. I'd have fucked her since I knew she wanted it. But she was too easy. Always was."

Without thinking, my fist collided with Travis's jaw. The man crumpled, and people started shouting. Noah pulled me off him, and I held out both hands.

"I did my part."

"I think you did enough," Aria murmured before she

looked at Travis on the floor, as some of Noah's team began to drag him out.

Then she looked up at me and I staggered. The disappointment I saw there enraged me even more. "What?" I barked. "Are you really mad at me?"

She just shook her head and walked off, the sound of her stilettos on tile echoing throughout the gallery.

"Go after her," Daisy snapped.

I looked at my ex-girlfriend and frowned. "Where the hell do you think I'm going? I don't know why she's angry though."

Daisy studied my face before shaking her head. "Maybe because you used your fists? And once again took care of it so she couldn't."

I glared. "And I'm supposed to let her handle everything when he talks like that?"

"Maybe stop arguing with me and continuing to make a scene, and go after her," Daisy whispered, before turning her back on me and following to where the others had taken Travis.

Anger coursing through my veins, I moved through the crowds who continued to ask questions, murmuring with one another while some recorded everything with their phones. Because of course I wanted this on the internet.

"Where is she?" I asked Lex, who narrowed his gaze.

"In the office. She's pacing in there because she wanted to leave, and I told her that it was better if she stayed. Then she yelled at me. You go handle this. And thank you for hitting him because I wanted to cut off his balls."

That made me feel marginally better. "At least someone agrees with me."

"I'm not going to touch that. But tread lightly, Crew."

I snarled, ready to go find Travis and kick his ass once again. "I didn't do anything wrong."

"Then you should be fine." And with that, he shook his head, leaving me alone as I walked down the hall to the main office.

Riley, the Montgomery who ran the gallery, had another office down the corridor, but this was the main one that people used when they needed to get paperwork done when not at their studio.

Aria stood at one of the message boards, chin lowered as she stared at her hands. I closed the door behind me, finally letting out a sigh. She turned toward me, her eyes dark. "Did you really have to hit him?"

Staggered, I took step back. "You're really worried about him?" Of all the things she could have said, I never thought it would be this. That I'd done it wrong. That I'd failed her. Again.

Then she surprised me.

"I don't care about him. Which makes me feel like a horrible person because he was one of my best friends. But no, that man out there isn't the Travis I knew. And I've spent five years trying to be there for him. And he's consistently hurt me and pushed me away. So I had done my best to cut him off. He can come to us, *to me*, when he needs help. But I'm not going to be his punching bag. But, Crew? You don't have to continue to use your fists to solve my problems. You think I'm that weak?"

I threw my hands into the air. "I don't think you're weak. But you're allowed to let people help you."

"Then show him out the door. I don't care what he says about me. Yes, it's cruel. It's embarrassing. It's probably all over the internet since people were recording. But he doesn't matter. *You* do."

"Aria—"

"You matter, you dumbass." She shook her head. "I'm sorry. But you matter, Crew. More than anyone I let myself get close to. But Travis? He'll press charges. And once again, you're going to end up behind bars because the person that I trusted is breaking both of us. You keep getting hurt because of me. Look at your hand.

And it's the hand that you use to paint. It's already swelling, Crew, and you're not putting ice on it. Meaning you're not taking care of yourself. You are too busy worrying about me, but you never think about yourself."

Her chest heaved as she spoke, but I saw the worry there. I didn't know what to do with it. Others didn't have to worry about me. I was the one who was there for them. It's what I'd been good at since it wasn't like I'd grown up learning how any other way.

"I'm fine, Aria."

If possible, her eyes went molten. "You're not. You keep preparing yourself to stand in front of a bullet for me, but you won't even let me pull you out of the way."

The thought of Aria in front of a bullet nearly made me pass out, bile coating my tongue. "That doesn't make any sense."

"Let me get you some damn ice." She stepped toward the mini fridge, then pulled out a tiny ice packet.

"How did you know that was in there?" I asked.

"Because Riley uses it for migraines sometimes so I'm going to borrow it and use it for your knuckles. I just don't want you to be hurt. Especially for me. Not again."

"You know I would do anything for you." My heartrate was finally starting to slow down, but I was still confused at why she seemed so damn angry at *me*.

She met my gaze, her eyes steady. "Maybe stop hitting him for me. Maybe think about yourself."

"I wasn't going to let him just walk out of there after saying those things to you."

Finally she looked away, her shoulders sagging. "Crew. What am I going to do with you?"

"He's lucky I didn't kill him. After the day I've had, he's damn lucky."

"What happened today?" she asked, her gaze pleading when she looked back up at me.

"Just stuff," I lied.

"And there it is again. You keep everything to yourself because you're afraid it'll be too much for me. But it's not. Travis wasn't the be –all, end-all of my life. I can be there for my family, my friends. And I sure as hell can be there for you. What happened today, Crew?"

I frowned, realizing I *didn't* tell her things. I kept them to myself because that's what I always did. It's where my issues belonged. It's what my parents had taught me, even though the Montgomerys and their boisterous nature might be different, it didn't change who I was.

"I'm not good at this," I whispered.

She traced her finger along my jaw, and I shivered. "Just one thing. Tell me one thing, Crew."

I swallowed hard, that crevice in my heart pulsating

even though I did my best to ignore it. "My dad forgot me again. Then he threw his book at my face. I didn't duck completely." I pointed to the bruise forming right beneath my hairline, and Aria's eyes widened.

"Crew! You're hurt and I couldn't see it with your hair brushed that way. Oh, baby." She moved forward and cupped my face. I turned to kiss her palm, and she scowled.

"Stop being so sweet. I'm mad at you for getting hurt and not telling any of us. Because I know you didn't tell Lex. He'd have told me."

"I can handle myself, Aria."

Her hands dropped away. "Then why can't you let me do the same?"

I leaned forward and brushed my lips against hers. "Stop."

"Stop what? Stop caring about you? Stop getting angry when you punch Travis? Stop wanting to yell at the world right along with you because of your dad?"

"Stop trying to be rational when there's nothing rational about this."

A tear slid down her cheek, and I set down the ice pack before leaning forward to kiss that tear away. And then the next. And then the next.

"I'm okay, Crew. Travis didn't wound me. I don't want you to be injured for him. He's dangerous. And I don't want him to be part of this." She pointed between the two of us. "I barely know what *this* is. I'm so afraid that once again he's going to break down something important to me."

"He can't do that," I lied once again. Because I didn't know what *this* was to begin with. And Travis would always be there.

The ghost and shade that would never leave.

"I need you to be okay too," she whispered, and then went to her tiptoes to press her lips against mine.

I deepened the kiss, caging her with my arms against the desk. It started gentle and then grew harder as she parted her lips for me and moaned. She tilted her head back, and I used one hand to tug on her hair. It fell from its bun, and whatever was holding it up clattered to the desk.

I nudged my way between her legs, and then used one hand to lift her up by her thigh. She let out a gasp as she balanced on the edge of the desk, and I slid my hand up the slit in her dress.

"Did you wear this red for me?"

"Crew."

"Aria. Tell me. Is this for me?"

Her lips trembled, her gaze dark. "You know I did. But we shouldn't be doing this."

"Doing what?" I asked as I used one hand to cup her

chin, slowly sliding my thumb into her mouth. "Suck." When she did, my cock pressed against the zipper of my pants. Then I moved my hand beneath her dress and froze.

"Are you not wearing panties?" I asked before moving my thumb over her cunt.

"They got in the way."

I growled before moving my hand to tug on her hair once more. She gasped, and then I speared her with two fingers. No preparation, no warning. But she was so wet the sound echoed through the quiet office.

"You're so fucking sexy. You're wet for me and I'm barely touching you. When you walk in those sexy heels for me, is your bare pussy out there for anyone to see if you bent over a certain way? Do your thighs rub together, humming along your clit? How close are you?"

"Crew, I was supposed to take care of you."

"You're doing it." All she had to do was give in and she bathed me in care and hope.

"I can't."

"You're going to." I worked my fingers in and out of her, a fast motion that drenched my palm as I rolled my thumb over her clit. As her moaning grew louder, I crushed my mouth to hers, keeping her silent. And when she came, she clamped down around my fingers, the sensation nearly making me come in my pants.

I pulled my fingers out of her, and then shoved them in her mouth. She gagged, then smiled as she licked herself off me.

"Do you want my cock, Aria? Can I give that to you? After everything that happened, do you want my cock inside you?"

She studied my face, a small smile playing on her face. "We shouldn't. They're going to know. But I always want you, Crew. And that's the problem."

"Then you're going to have to be quiet, but I'll let you come around my cock. You're going to have to take all of me. For punishment for not wearing panties. And for thinking I can't take care of you."

She frowned, her hand frozen in the action of rubbing over my linen covered cock. "For once, are you going to let me take care of you? Because we both know I can take care of myself."

We weren't just talking about sex just then, and I knew if we kept going down this path, we wouldn't end up with me deep inside her. Instead we'd fight once again. But I was so fucking angry that Travis was always *there*. That no matter what I did, he would be on the periphery, ready to break everything that we could make.

I wanted to claim her in front of everybody, no matter how caveman that made me feel. But I wouldn't do that. Instead I would just claim her between the two of us. And hoped to hell that Travis didn't ruin it all.

And that I didn't let him.

"Take my cock out," I ordered.

She met my gaze, as if still searching for the answers, before she reached for the button of my slacks and undid them. She slowly tugged down the zipper and pulled me out of my boxer briefs. She squeezed around the base of my shaft, and I groaned, running my thumb along her jawline.

"Your lips are already swollen from my mouth. I love looking at them when they are wrapped around my cock."

"Do you want my pussy? Or my mouth?" She fluttered her eyelashes so innocently, that I had to hold back a laugh. Anyone could walk into this room since I hadn't locked it. And we weren't exactly being quiet.

"The answer is always both." But before she could say anything, I crushed my mouth to hers, lifted her up slightly, and plunged into her. She gasped into my mouth, and I had to hold back a growl of my own.

I held her close, pumping in and out of her as she rolled her hips thrust for thrust.

I wanted to strip off that dress, watch her tits bounce as I fucked her hard, but that would have to come later. This needed to be hard and fast, and when she began to flutter around my dick, I pumped once, twice, and came, knowing that everybody would be hearing me nearly shouting her name. It didn't matter that we tried to quiet ourselves. There was no way I could ever be truly silent when it came to Aria Montgomery.

We stood there in the aftermath, with me still balls deep inside her, and I looked between us, at the way that we were connected, and let out a shuddering breath.

"I don't want him to ruin us," I muttered. "That means no matter what I do, I have a chance of ruining this."

A soft brush against my temple, and then fingers fluttering against my lips. "We won't let him. But you have to talk to me."

I leaned forward and kissed her softly, far gentler than before. "And you have to do the same."

I just had to hope we were telling the truth.

Chapter Ten

Aria

TRAVIS:

I'm sorry about last night. I just wanted to see you glow.

TRAVIS:

You are such a talent.

TRAVIS:

I miss you.

TRAVIS:

It's been so long.

TRAVIS:

I think about you.

TRAVIS:

Do you even think about me?

TRAVIS:

I went on a drive today. I saw the stars. They made me think of you.

TRAVIS:

Why are you ignoring me?

TRAVIS:

I thought you loved me.

TRAVIS:

You moved on quickly, didn't you?

TRAVIS:

So you are with Crew?

TRAVIS:

I knew you were fucking him all along.

TRAVIS:

I hear he has money. Is that why you spread your legs for him?

TRAVIS:

I bet nobody bought your art.

TRAVIS:

Do you know how long it takes me to create paradise with my hands? I'm a god with my art.

TRAVIS:

You point and shoot and sometimes get it right. I could do what you do with a cellphone.

TRAVIS:

I'm sorry. I know you hate my drinking. I'll do better for you.

TRAVIS:

You whore. Answer me.

TRAVIS:

Answer me.

TRAVIS:

Answer me.

I scrolled through the seventy-four text messages I had received in the past day and a half before I exited out of the app. I knew I needed to block him even though I'd turned off his notifications. It would be better for everybody if I did. But there was that small part of me that knew once I did, he would reach out to me in truth. And I would never forgive myself if I missed that text.

But he was escalating. There was nothing I could do about it right now, except be there when he hit rock bottom. That might make me sound like a horrible person, but he was no longer hurting just himself. I wasn't going to let Crew continue to be harmed because of me. Nor was I going to let myself fall down that rabbit hole.

Part of me knew I shouldn't show Crew the texts at all. He got so angry every time he even heard Travis's name—let alone heard about any of the other man's actions. And I didn't want to ruin his day. There was nothing he could do at the moment, so I ignored the texts and kept Crew safe.

"Everything okay over there?"

I slid my phone into my back pocket and grinned over at Daisy. "Everything is wonderful." Not quite a lie. "Although I'm still confused as to why we are bowling. I mean, you know what happened the last time I bowled."

My cousin held back a grin, but her eyes still danced with laughter. "Because you lost the coin toss. And don't worry. We'll get you bumpers."

"That is just mean." I shook my head, smiling for real this time.

Claire, Phoebe, and Phoebe's sister Isabella walked toward us at that moment, a tray of nachos, hot dogs, burgers, wings, and assorted snacks between them.

My eyes widened. "Oh. *This* is why we come here."

After they set down the tray on the tabletop, Phoebe tossed a tater tot into her mouth and moaned. "I know these are terrible for me, but I'm going to eat all of them."

"As long as you don't touch my onion rings," Isabella warned. She turned to me and grinned. "And the chicken sandwich. There's just something about a bowling alley chicken sandwich."

Phoebe shuddered. "That is all yours. The last time I ate a chicken sandwich like that I was fourteen, and it was right before a soccer game. *Big mistake.* I was on defense, and not only did I get a yellow card for so-called tripping a kid named Karl, a ball hit me square in the stomach and I nearly threw up on everyone."

I had just taken a bite of hot dog and paused.

Phoebe shook her head. "Sorry for the visual. But every time I look at a chicken sandwich, that's what I think. Actually, what I mostly think about is the fourteen-year-old kid who hadn't hit his growth spurt yet and went flying as he tripped over my foot. I got in trouble because he couldn't handle me and hadn't hit puberty."

Isabella looked dubiously at her sandwich. "Are there any more childhood horror stories that are going to try to ruin some of my favorite foods?"

It took me a moment to remember that although Phoebe and Isabella were sisters, they hadn't grown up together, nor had they even known of each other's existence until recently. Two of my cousins had ended up married or dating into that family, and nobody had realized the connection until everything had blown up. And for once, it hadn't been a Montgomery issue. I counted that as a win for the whole family. We tended to make messes, though we cleaned them up—usually growing stronger in the process.

"Okay, do we have these two lanes?" my other cousin Brooklyn asked.

Daisy beamed. "Yes. We can divide teams however we want, but Aria can't be in my lane."

"Why?" I asked, a little put out. Though not surprised since bowling wasn't my thing.

"Probably because you need the bumpers," Dara said as she ran toward us.

I held open my arms for my baby sister and hugged her tightly before shoving playfully at her shoulder. "Hey. You're supposed to be on my side. We are actually siblings."

"And I'm the one who not only had her toe broken, but almost got a concussion from the last time you bowled. I am not on your team," Dara said as everybody burst out laughing, and I felt the blush that covered my cheeks.

"Oh. Right." I cleared my throat. "Though I *have* been bowling since then."

Everybody gave me a look, and I threw my hands in the air.

"Is there evidence of this bowling?" Daisy asked, lifting her chin even though I knew she was laughing.

"You can ask Crew. He's the one who took me out." I paused. "Because he was afraid for my family's safety if we ever went bowling again without him," I muttered.

Everyone once again burst out laughing before we

broke into teams. Daisy, Isabella, and Brooklyn all decided to brave being in my lane.

"That does sound like a Crew thing to do. Sacrificing himself for the greater good." Daisy rolled her eyes as a little bit of uneasiness swept over me.

"Is this weird?" I blurted.

"Is what weird?" Daisy asked as we put on our ugly yet amazing bowling shoes.

"The fact that I'm dating your ex-boyfriend."

"Wait, you used to date Crew?" Isabella asked as she leaned toward us. Only interest covered her face, not any judgement.

"Yep," Brooklyn answered for us. "And I thought that Lexington did too, but he keeps telling us the two of them didn't date. I just thought that third time was the charm with finding his Montgomery Princess or Prince."

"You are thinking entirely too much about this," I told her.

"I find all of this fascinating." Isabella looked between us before she and Brooklyn went to start the game. "I thought we had the family drama in the Cages, but I am loving learning more and more about the Montgomerys."

"It's not weird at all for me," Daisy answered after a moment.

I bit my lip and tried to believe her. "Okay."

A wry smile covered her face. "Crew and I are just friends. And we have been for a while. In fact, I'm pretty sure we were nearly just friends when we were dating."

"It's the *nearly just* part that gets weird. Considering well...you know."

Daisy shrugged. "We are of an age, live in the same area, and have similar and decent taste in men. I'm surprised overlap hasn't happened more often in this family."

"I'm just going to say that Crew is hot, and if things don't work out between you two, I'll be there," Brooklyn said. "Three for three and all that."

I glared at her, and she held up both hands.

"Kidding. I mean, Crew kind of scares me. While that could be exciting, I like the two of you together. I'm going to go bowl now and try not to break any toes." She scampered off, Isabella beside her.

I let out a breath, confused and yet entertained. "See? Weird."

"Not weird. The two of you have had a connection for years. And in case you've forgotten, I'm married. I have a child. I am very much over Crew. Not that he isn't a lovely man. But he's not mine. He's all yours. But if *you're* worried about it, then you should talk to him." She paused. "Are you worried what *he* thinks?"

"I don't. He's always been who he is. He's good enough. Better than that. He's...he's Crew. He is who he is. I can't say this right." I felt like I was putting down the man I was falling for down, and that was not the case. He was just...everything. And always had been. I felt like I was learning who this new person in my life was even though he'd always been there. He hadn't changed. But maybe I had. Or how I perceived him.

She shook her head. "No, I understand. Because he doesn't need to improve. Other than how all of us as humans need to improve. The two of you just click. He talks more with you around. And it's not a growl or a grunt. I'm not going to ask what your intentions are or where you think it's going, because that's not my business. And frankly, it's weird when people asked about me and Hugh. But I'm here to talk. Or if I'm the last person you want to talk to, you know every single person in this group here, and those who couldn't come with us tonight, are here for you. We love you, Aria. In case you have forgotten."

I glared at her as I wiped away tears. "Why are you making me cry at girls' night?"

"Because it's my purpose in life. Now, I see my order has arrived."

I turned to see a waiter arrive with two trays of shots, and I rolled my eyes. "Really?"

"We have a car service to get us to the next place and a ride home. We are going to have fun."

I took the first shot with a thank you to the waiter, stared at my family, to blood and connections, and held up the glass.

"To girls' night."

"And not breaking any toes," Brooklyn added.

I glared at her, then each of us tapped the table with the bottom of the glass and tossed the shot back. Some reached for salt and lime, but sadly, I could shoot tequila without any of that. I couldn't touch dark liquor, and just the scent of rum got me buzzed, but tequila and I were friends.

We bowled, and I did not break anyone's toes. Though I did toss the ball over the bumper and into the next lane. The drunk frat guys next to us cheered me on and bought all of us a round shots.

So really, my bowling was the best. It got us free drinks.

Once we were done, we cleaned up our mess, made our way into the SUVs that Daisy had acquired for us, and the drivers took us to the next place.

"What on earth is a cupcake bar?" I asked, chugging water in the backseat.

"We get to decorate our own cupcakes and eat as many as we want," Daisy answered before she chugged her own bottle.

"This sounds like a bad idea in my case," Isabella said. "All that sugar after tequila?" She shuddered.

"There are also vegetable cupcakes, like carrot cake, and other things that aren't sweet. And cheese."

Every one of the Montgomerys in our SUV sat straighter, like prairie dogs sensing movement.

"Cheese?" I asked.

"Oh my God. It's real," Isabella burst out, and we all laughed.

"We lean into it, but don't worry, we also eat things other than cheese," I reassured her.

She looked dubious but nodded anyway. We all piled out of the SUVs, and then into the cupcake bar.

"One of Lucy's friends had a birthday party here, and they think they also had adult nights with wine, so I think it's going to be fun," Daisy explained.

"Now everything makes sense," I teased.

We each took a chair at one of the small tables, and the owner Margie walked out, exuberant and excited to talk about cupcakes. I might have eaten my weight in junk food already, but I was in the mood for all the sugar.

I didn't mix tequila and wine, so I stuck with water, that is, until Margie showed up with the margaritas.

"I heard you had tequila earlier, so don't worry, I have you covered."

"This is a mistake," I told Daisy, but we clinked glasses and took a sip.

"I'm just having the one," Daisy warned.

"Honestly, same." Because as much as we all were joking, none of us were getting truly drunk that night. Especially after everything that had happened the night before.

I had five cupcakes in front of me, buttercream frosting in one piping bag and cream cheese frosting in the other, and I had found my new heaven.

"I just want to eat this entire bag," Claire said.

"I feel there's a joke there but I'm on too much of a sugar high to figure out what," I replied.

We all burst out laughing and went on to decorate some amazingly beautiful and amazingly horrid cupcakes.

I stared down my lopsided creation and sighed. "This is why I am a photographer. And Crew does the painting."

"Has he ever painted *you*?" Claire asked as she set down her drink. "And that is enough tequila for me."

"My answer is no, but I'm not sure Aria wanted to

hear that," Daisy said, looked at her drink, then put it on the table. "And that means I will stick to water now as well."

Blushing, I drank some water and didn't answer. Which I suppose was answer in itself. Isabella toasted me with her glass, but the others didn't seem to notice.

By the time we boxed up the creations we hadn't eaten, I was full, slightly nauseous, and yet so happy we had gone out.

"I almost canceled," I told Daisy.

"I figured. You would've had every right to. But I'm glad you came out. And I see your ride is here."

"I thought the cars were taking us home."

Daisy just grinned. "For some. But with others, I have my ways."

I looked up to see some of the Montgomery men, Hugh, and Crew walking toward us.

"I guess the single ladies take the car service home," Brooklyn said with a sigh, before the rest piled into the remaining SUV.

I only had eyes for Crew. "Hey there," I said, my smile wide.

"I can't tell if you had too much to drink or too much sugar. But I don't mind." He leaned forward and brushed his lips against mine. When I parted my lips for him and groaned, he deepened the kiss.

"I love frosting," he whispered.

"I have extra for later." From the way that Kingston grimaced as he directed Claire to his car, I realized I hadn't whispered that.

"Let's get you home. And that frosting."

I narrowed my gaze at him as I tapped his shoulder with my finger. "Sweet things only stay above the waist. You know the rules."

He buckled me into the passenger side of his SUV and chuckled. "I do. I'll just eat your pussy for dessert if I want to go beneath the waist." He pressed a hard kiss to my lips before closing the door and walking around to the driver's side.

I must've dozed off, because soon I was in his arms, and he was carrying me to his bed.

"I fell asleep?"

"You were snoring."

"I do not snore."

"You do. But it's okay."

I looked around his place and frowned, confused but still happy. "I thought you said we were going home." I didn't mind being here. I liked Crew's house better than mine anyway.

Something odd crossed over his face, but he sat me down on his bed. "My home. Now let's get you naked."

"Then you're going to eat my pussy?" I asked.

"Not with you this drunk. You know the rules."

"I had tons of water though," I put in, disappointed.

"Future you will be happy with that decision."

He pulled off my clothes, and I wiggled into his bed naked, comfy, and feeling safe. "I always feel safe with you."

He swallowed hard as he brushed my hair from my face. "That's damn good to hear, Aria. I know you need to brush your teeth and everything. But I just want to hold you for a while. Okay?"

"Will you get naked?"

He rolled his eyes and pulled off his shirt. But he didn't take off his pants as he got into bed, holding me close. I couldn't be disappointed though, not with his scent wrapping around me.

"Did you have a good day?" I asked, knowing I needed to stay awake for a little longer.

"It was okay."

"What's wrong?" I asked, hearing the annoyance in his tone.

"Nothing."

"Is it your parents?"

He didn't say anything, and I let the disappointment go. If Crew wanted to talk about it, he would. I would just have to ignore the hurt that he didn't want to share. After all, it wasn't any of my business.

But sometimes it just reminded me that we were playing house. That at any moment this—whatever we had—could crumble.

So I leaned into his hold and told myself I was happy. That I didn't need anything else.

But part of me knew it was a lie.

Chapter Eleven

Crew

The scent of coffee woke me up. That bold flavor from one of my favorite beans that I had recently bought hit my nostrils, and my eyelids popped open. I reached toward the other side of the bed and frowned when I realized it was empty. It was still warm, so Aria must have been there recently, but I didn't like waking up without her next to me.

I rolled to my back, ignoring my morning wood, and the fact that it was currently tenting the sheets, and thought back to that idea.

Since when had it become normal? Routine that Aria would be by my side?

It hadn't been like this before. Not when we'd hate fucked and I'd hidden my feelings from the both of us. When we'd been sneaking around from the rest of our friends, acting as if we weren't on a precipice of inevitable failure. Only now it felt as if we slept at each other's house every evening. Not having Aria cradled in my arms, that rounded backside of hers pressed against my cock in the morning, felt wrong.

I liked waking her up by slowly sliding my cock between her legs, waking her up with pressure at her entrance, and letting her take charge by sinking down onto me. Letting her be the one to say yes. I loved that moment when I would slowly open my eyes and realize that I had palmed her breasts, her nipple pressing against my hand. I knew I played with it in my sleep, and sometimes she would wrap her hand around the base of my cock, rubbing me as she dreamed.

In other words, we always had our hands on each other. It was starting to scare me how much I wanted this.

I didn't have a reference for whatever the two of us were. Despite having so many friends who fell into serious relationships, I'd never had one. Daisy had been the closest, and it really wasn't even close to anything like what I had with Aria. I tried dating after Daisy and I had broken up, perhaps feeling like I *was* that character from *Frozen*, feeling not enough. Or maybe that was just what the Montgomerys had placed on me with their constant jokes about me kissing my way through the family to find my way in. I knew they were only joking, but sometimes I didn't truly believe it. However, there might be some truth to it.

The Montgomerys were the family I didn't have. That steadfast connection that I hadn't been allowed to even contemplate before leaving the family that had tried to destroy me and becoming friends with the people who truly cared.

They had that foundation that held rock-steady even in the face of terror and loss.

And I didn't have that. Hell, I was still having to deal with my father—a man who hated me even when his disease forced him to never remember me or his own reality. All because of a displaced sense of loyalty to the blood running in my veins. I didn't want to be in debt to the McTavish name but the person in me who had begged for their acceptance still held on even in denial.

My mother wouldn't even look at her husband but took out all her fear on me. It made no damn sense. Though I suppose it made perfect sense when I thought about the way my family operated.

And yet in this moment, I was disappointed that Aria wasn't tucked into my side when I woke up. And not just because I wanted to slide inside her and feel her around every inch of me. I just wanted to be by her. And that terrified me more than anything.

Because what would happen next? When would she realize that we weren't endgame?

I didn't even know if I had endgame in me.

And how utterly pointless and demoralizing was that idea?

I finally pulled myself out of bed since the scent of coffee had grown stronger. I shoved on the jeans I had tossed off the night before, not bothering to button them. I went into the adjoining bathroom, brushed my teeth, took care of business, and headed down to the kitchen.

The sight of Aria in my kitchen wearing my T-shirt and nothing else as she danced to whatever music was playing on her ear buds nearly took my breath away. She had piled her hair on the top of her head with a clip, and she rolled her ass back and forth as she cooked breakfast on my chef's grade stove.

Every time she would move however, the shirt would ride up slightly, and I could see a peek of the globes of her ass. I wanted to bend her over right there and slide my cock in between those cheeks, taking my fill of her and making sure she came around me.

I was a freaking monster.

A horny monster.

I padded my way into the kitchen, the idea of coffee and the draw of Aria herself too strong. I went to turn off the music on her phone, so she would be able to hear me coming up to her since she was near an open flame, and frowned as I looked down at the screen.

> TRAVIS:
>
> Why aren't you answering?
>
> TRAVIS:
>
> Fucking whore.
>
> TRAVIS:
>
> I'm going to end you.
>
> TRAVIS:
>
> I'm sorry.
>
> TRAVIS:
>
> I just need a little bit to get by. You know it's about the art.

There had to be a couple dozen texts from him. All left unread, all within the last two hours.

I just stared down at the screen, feeling as if a snake would slither out and strike me if I dared even touched the damn thing.

"Oh, you startled me," Aria whispered from my side as she plucked her ear buds out and put them in the case next to her phone. "Did the coffee wake you?" She went to her tiptoes and kissed my cheek, but I only saw that out of the periphery of my vision as I stared down at her phone.

"How long has this been going on?" I bit out.

I hadn't meant to sound so angry, but the fury riding my veins was far too much to deal with.

Her eyebrows lifted before she looked down at the screen. Then the blood left her face, leaving her gray. "I didn't realize he was texting again."

"*Again.*" It was as if I were spitting out the word through gritted teeth. "He's been harassing you this whole time? Why the fuck did you not tell me?"

"Why are you getting angry at me? I'm not replying back. But I'm letting him spew what he needs to in case he really does reach out for help one day."

"Don't be stupid. He's not going to reach out for anything other than to hurt you. Or money like he clearly wants. Do the cops know about these texts? Because he's out on fucking bail, Aria, and this is harassment. And why the fuck does he need money? He has his parents."

She stepped back as if I'd slapped her, and I cursed under my breath. Only she held out a hand to stop me when I moved forward. "Don't call me stupid. Yes, the cops know. Yes, they talked to him. I don't know what else they can do other than continue to talk to him until the courts figure things out. And you know that he has community service coming up to get out of the charges. It's not the same for him like it is for normal people. His parents got him out of it and there's nothing we can do about that. However, I realize that letting him say horrible things through a text message isn't good for me, but one day he might reach out. He might need help. I'm not going to beg him to get clean anymore. I'm not going to get him out of terrible situations, so he doesn't have to face his own consequences. But I will always be the person that he, or *any of my friends*, can truthfully hold on to during a time of crisis. He's not hurting me right now. I know you don't believe me, but his words in this state mean nothing. His words can't hurt me because I'm past them. I have to be."

"Aria."

She shook her head. "No. Don't give me that tone. That 'disappointed, you know better than me' tone. In the past his words would slice. But I can handle him by *not* handling him."

This woman.

I had no words.

She was way too fucking strong. And it broke me thinking about the power Travis could hold over her if she let him. "I just don't want him to hurt you."

Aria met my gaze, the determination within them astonishing. "He already hurt me. But everybody is standing around me trying to protect me and I am so grateful for who you are. Who my family and friends are. I just need you to know I'm not listening to his tirades. I'm trying to be the good friend that will be there if needed, but not take what he says now to heart. Because that is what I would want if I was facing my own demons. Or running from them in his case. That might not be what you want. But it is what I would hope my friends would do."

I licked my lips, emotions warring inside me. "You should've told me."

"So you could get angry again? So you could handle it like you did before?"

I blinked at her. "He was hurting you."

She shook her head before reaching forward to cup my face with her hands. "Not then. You walking into my home that night is something I will remember for the end of my days. I hated the fact that you got hurt because of what happened and that he could put you behind bars for even a few hours. And I will never forgive him for that. But I don't need you to always stand in front of me. And frankly the only reason I didn't tell you is that we are dealing with so many other things. I just want whatever it is between us in this moment to be nice. I don't want this to always be about the drama that I always bring."

I wanted to hate her words, to refute them. But I understood them and it annoyed me. "I bring plenty of drama too." I moved my head to kiss her palm before bringing her to my chest. "I don't want him to hurt you anymore."

"I don't want him to hurt me either. I'm going to do my best not to let him do that. I'm not sure I can block him, Crew. I have this nightmare that I do that, and he reaches out just like my dad did once to someone, and I'm not there. It might make me selfish, but I don't want to be the reason he doesn't find a foothold in this world."

So many emotions warred within me, and I wasn't sure what to think. Because I knew she had the best intentions, but I did not trust that man. She might be ignoring him the way that she could, but Travis would find a way to get inside and hurt her. And I wasn't about to let that happen.

I was so damn scared because I was falling for her. I fucking loved her. There was no falling. I had fallen long before. I had fallen in love with Aria Montgomery even when I told myself it would be easier to hate her.

"I'm sorry. For reading your texts. For overreacting. But, baby, you're way too damn good for me."

"That's a lie and you know it. Though maybe it means we're finally good for each other rather than the toxicity that could have infected whatever this is long ago. By the way, my phone was out on the island, face up, and not tucked away in secret. I don't want to hide anything from you. Okay?"

I pulled back so I could study her face and looked into those bright blue eyes that I loved. "I can do that," I said. I just hoped it wasn't a lie.

"I'm not a glutton for punishment. I promise. I'm not going to roll over anytime he begs me to. But one day he might find his way out and need that hand. And then I'm going to have to figure out what to do then."

"I'll kill him if he hurts you," I vowed.

Alarm raced over her features. "Don't say that. Because sometimes I feel like it's the truth." She went to her toes and kissed the bottom of my jaw before moving away to put our breakfast back on the burner.

I watched as she used my kitchen with such ease, as if she had done this countless times before.

I wanted her in my kitchen. I wanted her in my home. In my bed. And it terrified me. Because I wanted this so much. This domesticity. This idea that we could just talk to each other even when we were scared.

But it felt like something was coming.

Either Travis. Or hell, even my parents.

At the core of it, we were figuring out who we were to each other. Or maybe, I was figuring out what I was to her. Because I always knew what she was to me even when I was ignoring it. But the powers that be were circling. And someday they were going to hit home.

However, as I watched her bend over to reach for

another pan, teasing a glance of that sweet pussy, I held back a groan before pushing out all thoughts of the dangers to come.

And instead I managed to be in the moment.

Though I knew it wouldn't last forever.

"You know, I still don't know why I'm here," I grumbled at my best friend.

Lex just beamed. "What, you want to be at home with your girlfriend?"

"Oooh, girlfriend," Kingston teased. "That's a big word."

"I'm sorry that your reading comprehension is so low that 'girlfriend' seems like a big word," Lex drawled. "But it is appropriate, is it not, Crew?"

I sipped my beer and glared at the lot of them. Tonight was guys' night, a night that I usually enjoyed. But after the fight Aria and I had that morning, and our subsequent making up when I ate her out on the counter, I couldn't help but want to be home. Not hanging out with a bunch of dudes who were like my family and way too inquisitive.

"Not quite sure my relationship title with your cousin has anything to do with you."

"You see, that is where you're wrong," Dash put in. "Because she's family. And *you* are too. However, not in the way that would make this weird."

"Please, just stop talking," Lexington said with a start. "And, Crew? Is girlfriend an appropriate title? Because if you just say a friend with benefits, or chick you are banging, I'm going to have to use the baseball bat we are about to pick up for the batting cage and hit you with it. And then it will be a whole thing, and I'm just not in the mood to deal with the ramifications of kicking your ass. So much paperwork."

"Especially because we would have to clean up the blood, and whatever other liquids end up around," Kingston said with a mock shudder.

I grimaced as the others broke out into laughter. "That is such a visual. Thank you for that. Now, let's not ever talk about it again."

"Seriously though, girlfriend?" Lex asked, fluttering his eyelashes.

"Are you asking me out?" I joked.

"Not when Aria claimed you first."

"You know, this is why people thought the two of you were dating for so long," Dash stated as he pointed between the two of us.

I shrugged and drained the rest of my beer before picking up a water bottle and heading toward the batting cage. "My girlfriend, Aria, and I are doing just fine. Don't worry about us."

Although that was not quite the truth because I was worried. Waiting for the other shoe to drop, for there to be an issue, or for anything that kept circling us to finally break whatever fragile hold we had in this sense of peace. Because times like this didn't just stay as they were. They didn't just happen for people like me. Sure, my friends could go out and find the loves of their lives and keep them, but I knew the statistics. It wasn't always going to work.

One day soon Aria would wake up and realize she was so much fucking more than I was. That she deserved more.

She'd realize exactly what lay within her veins and leave. She'd go around the world and take photos that could rival anyone's. She'd continue to win the awards she always blushed at and thought she wasn't good enough for. She'd move on.

And leave me behind.

I didn't have to work. I didn't have to paint—no, that was a lie. I *did* have to paint. But it had nothing to do with income and everything to do with who I was. I might have money thanks to my family. I might like to keep businesses going and working with investments just to see what I could do with it.

But whatever screamed inside me needed to get out, and painting was that way for me.

It wasn't a job.

It was art.

And that made me sound like a damn idiot who couldn't make sense of what was truth and what was the artist's ideal. I wasn't the starving artist, but I fucking loved what I did.

Yet if I had to put down my paintbrush tomorrow, I wasn't sure if I could do it. Not because of what I needed, but what pounded within me. And I knew it was the same for Aria when it came to her photography. She might have a chip on her shoulder when it came to her father, but she was getting past that. I saw it with the way she spoke with her dad. With the way she always had her camera on her now. She was changing, seeing the light.

And maybe that had to do with leaving Travis.

Even thinking of his name made me want to growl, but it was the truth. Travis had always been a shit when it came to Aria's work. He'd always degraded her without most people even realizing he was doing it. He was so damn good at making sure the world knew *he* was the talented one and Aria "did her best." Aria put her own work and life to the side for him and there was no way I'd ever let that happen again. Even if me standing in front of her over whatever happened meant she'd hate me and try to push me away.

Hell, maybe I was the idiot here. The one who needed to learn more. To realize that maybe she didn't want me for the long haul.

And this was why I didn't do relationships.

I couldn't get out of my own damn head.

"Crew? You good?"

I blinked out of my own thoughts at the sound of Lex's voice and let out a breath. I clearly needed more sleep if I was going to spiral like that. Aria and I weren't that serious. Yes, I loved her, but I had no idea what she felt about me. So venturing down that path felt as if it would be better classified as a minefield.

Nothing good could come from facing Aria Montgomery and her feelings.

The best way to deal with the future was to ignore it and be there until she woke up out of whatever this was and walked away.

It would be better for everyone once she did.

I'd hate it.

Hate her.

Hate myself.

But it would be for the best.

"Yeah. I'm good. And ready to hit some balls."

Lex merely raised a brow, knowing I was lying

through my teeth before handing me my helmet. "By all means. Have fun with your balls."

"Always do," I snapped back turning toward the cage.

Having a projectile coming at my face at seventy miles per hour or more sounded a whole hell of a lot better than dealing with the idea that Aria only loved me for the now and not the forever.

A forever I didn't know if I even wanted considering my parents' idea of forever.

The crack of the bat against the first ball pushed all thoughts of my version of hell out of my mind and then I swung again. And again.

Until there was nothing left but the shell that I'd become.

SINCE LEX HAD DRIVEN ME TO THE BATTING CAGES as I'd wanted a few beers, he also drove me home. "You know, I only asked about Aria earlier because I think the two of you are good for each other."

I turned to him as he pulled into my neighborhood. "Yeah?"

Lex's mouth turned up into a small smile. "Yes.

You're both good for each other even when you're yelling at one another."

"I don't know if that's healthy, Lex."

"You only yell because you know you can trust each other completely. And you only yell because it's for the other person. Not for your own issues. It's weird that it took me so long to realize it."

I blinked. "I have no idea what you're talking about."

Lex parked in my driveway but didn't shut off the engine. "You both fight *so* hard for other people that you forget what you want for yourself. Aria went into business with the cousins at Montgomery Security because she was afraid of wanting to use her art for something other than fun. So she used her business degree to make sure Noah didn't have to do the initial set up paperwork on his own. And in the end, every other person involved had the same idea, so Aria ended up feeling like the odd man out."

I nodded. "I remember. We got into such a fight when I told her that."

Lex snorted. "Yeah. You *told* her what she was doing rather than talking it out."

I shrugged. "And she did the same to me when I was figuring out the gym."

"Exactly. It took you both too long to figure out how

to talk things out with each other, rather than pointing it out with sarcasm."

"I hate when she doesn't put herself first," I put in simply.

"And she hates the same for you."

"I don't do that." I scowled.

"The fuck you don't," Lex snapped. "You spend your whole day making sure your friends have what they need, that Aria is safe and putting herself out there but not risking her soul or sanity. Then when you're not doing that, you're dealing with the fucking problems that are your parents. And at some point, you find time for yourself and your art. I hate that you don't try to put yourself first in that but it's not your nature. I don't mind that Aria is your number one goal and *should* be. But don't forget yourself along the way, Crew."

I frowned at my friend, wondering where the hell this was coming from. "Why are you saying this, Lex? You're not usually the one who blurts out shit like this. Yet I don't think my priorities are so cut and dry."

Lex shrugged. "Maybe not. But I don't want you two to fuck up what could be the best thing in your life because you're scared."

"I'm not scared," I lied.

My best friend laughed. "Liar. I'm scared to death that I'm going to end up alone and be the one who has the most unsurpassed and fucking elite best man speeches in the world because that's what I'm good at but you're the only person I'd ever tell that to. So don't fucking lie to me that you're secure around Aria. You never have been, and I don't think you are now."

"I...Lex." I didn't know what to say about that revelation and I felt like such a shit friend. "You want to talk about that?" I finally croaked.

"Not in the slightest. I needed that self-pity party and now I'm done. But I better be your best man."

I shook my head. "I'm not getting married."

"Says the man who is going to get married next. That's the rules of a proclamation like that. Now, let's get inside because I have to pee since I had like eight glasses of water and I'm not in the mood to get into my feels anymore. Just don't fuck things up with Aria and hurt her or yourself and we'll be great."

And with that, he got out of the car, and I joined him, wondering if maybe I'd had too much to drink since my mind couldn't help but whirl. We walked up the path toward my front door, but I paused before I made it fully to the porch.

"What's wrong?" Lex asked.

"I don't know. Something feels off." The hairs on the back of my neck stood on end as I moved toward my garage. Then I cursed, pulling out my phone. "Fuck."

"What is it?" Lex bumped into me, then cursed as well when he got a look at my view. "You calling the cops?"

"Yep. Call your cousins. Someone had a hell of a time tonight. Let's hope we caught whoever it was on camera."

Because someone had broken into my garage, left the door open, and slashed every single tire of my most recent rides they could get their hands on. My bike, my truck, the SUV, the convertible.

Everything that Aria had ever touched.

And with that chilling thought, I dialed the cops.

And had to wonder if Travis had really gone this far...or if I had another enemy out there I didn't know about.

Chapter Twelve

Crew

"I think you're making a mistake."

Paintbrush in hand, I did my best not to reach up and pinch the bridge of my nose. I had enough paint in my hair at this point. "I will tell her, but when I see her in person later today. Calling her last night or interrupting her work would just worry her. And we're finally getting to a place where we can actually relax. I don't want to stress her out."

After the police had come to take their photos and do whatever they did for collecting evidence, Noah, Ford, Daisy, and Hugh had shown up, hands on hips, worry on their faces, and had gone through every inch of security I had put in. Considering they had been the team who had installed it in the first place, they were just as pissed as I was that someone had come to destroy my property.

The cameras hadn't caught who'd broken in since the person had worn all black and a ski mask like they'd watched too many movies. Though considering the damn routine had worked, I couldn't comment much on that.

The Montgomery crew would be coming back tomorrow to add more security throughout the property. They were hell-bent on helping me figure out exactly who it was, since the cops could only do so much when I pointed out who it had to be.

They had reminded me that my family was well known in some circles. That my father and mother were both assholes. Though they hadn't used those words. They had been a little kinder but not much. So maybe it had been an enemy of my family. Somebody who wanted access to our bank accounts.

Except they hadn't taken a damn thing. Instead, they had merely destroyed. Although it didn't truly feel like the word *merely* worked like that.

The intruder had taken out their hate, and whatever other rage they might've been feeling, on my cars. Thankfully it seemed to be just focused on the tires themselves. After all, those were easier to stab with a knife than the metal body of the vehicles. But it was still a mess. I had appointments to deal with the damage with our friends who owned a body shop. Lex and the rest of the Montgomery Construction crew would help with the damage to the building as well. Once Aria walked into that garage, she would know something was different. Not to mention she would notice the increased security.

"Are you listening to me? She's going to find out. And I don't want my cousin to get hurt because some asshole has his sights set on you or her or even just your tires."

I set the paintbrush down, knowing if I held onto it any longer, I would crack it in my hands. "Nothing is going to happen to Aria. I will kill the son of bitch before that happens."

Lex met my gaze. "You still think it's Travis."

"Who else could it be? While my parents are narcissistic, terrible people, they don't have violent enemies."

No, they kept their violence behind closed doors, and only for their son. But it had been a long while since they had laid a hand on me. Even in my father's misguided anger, hatred, and confusion, he didn't leave bruises like my mother had.

So no, I didn't think it was them. Or anything having to do with them.

"You're right. It feels petty. Targeted. Not something randomly to do with the business that you don't touch. He's high most of the time though, so I wouldn't have figured he'd have the energy to do this. I just can't believe how far that guy has fallen."

"And Aria still lets him text because she wants to be there just in case he reaches out. In case he finally sees the light and stops being so selfish. And there's nothing I can do. Because the angrier I get, the closer I feel I'm becoming my parents or even Travis. So I just have to let it happen."

Lex snarled. "I want to take her phone and throw it in the lake, but apparently that would be controlling."

I rolled my eyes at his dry tone. "So I hear. The problem is, I'd tell you the same thing in her shoes. If one of you guys needed me, I'd be there."

"If one of us tried to hurt someone though, we would have other people holding us back. And at this point I can't feel much sympathy for a man who tried to kill my cousin."

I let out a breath, knowing this conversation wasn't going to get anywhere. The words cut and reminded me that I would truly end Travis if I had to. "We both agree. He's a danger. The cops are looking for him to question him about the vandalism at least. Maybe this time he won't be able to weasel out of charges. His parents won't be able to game the system for him." His parents ran in the same circles as mine but I knew for a fact my parents would let me rot behind bars before they helped me unless it shined a black light on the McTavish name. "But until then, if I see that man, I'm going to kill him. He doesn't get to come into my house, hurt Aria, or threaten me. Because that's all he's doing right now, threatening *me*. The one time we're not in the house he just happens to break in and destroy my shit? No thank you. I'm done with him."

"You've been done with him for a long while," Lex put in. "You need to tell her, Crew."

"Stop fucking badgering me. I will. Today. You're right. If she doesn't know he's even more of a danger, it's just going to put her in the middle of it. And that could lead to her getting hurt. So, I'm not going to let that happen."

"You know, it is little ironic you've kept the secret for as many hours as you have, when you were just pissed at her for keeping the texts secret."

I flipped him off as I went through my notes for the next phase of my project. "Don't throw that back in my face. I have my reasons."

"And so did she."

"I thought you were on my side here."

"Of course I am on your side. And hers. I love you both." Lex held up his hands. "I don't love you like that.

I swear, this family loves to put me into weird situations when it comes to you."

"You're the one who started it." I raised a brow. "Other than wanting to talk about what happened, is there a reason you're here? Not that I don't love you. As my best friend. But shouldn't you be working?"

Lex ran his hand through his hair, looking far more lost than I had ever seen him. I had been so focused on my own life, things moving with Aria, my parents, that I was messing up when it came to my best friend.

"I'm just tired. And we finished our major project last week. I've been dealing with permits and contracts all day, so I took the afternoon off."

I blinked. "You don't take time off. You are worse than your uncle Wes like that."

"Uncle Wes takes time off because Aunt Jillian makes him. But you're right, I don't take time off. Maybe I should go on vacation. See the sights. Put down the hammer. Do something for myself."

"Now you're starting to worry me."

"It's nothing."

"It's something."

"Gia is getting married."

It took me a moment to realize who Gia was, and I blinked. "Your ex? That didn't take long."

"Tell me about it. She found the love of her life, and

apparently breaking up with me to do so was the perfect catalyst."

"You don't still love her, do you?" I asked carefully.

"I don't. Which is probably an issue all on its own. I just had a bad morning, and might've yelled at somebody, so I'm taking the afternoon off."

"Do you want to get out to do something?"

He shook his head. "No. I'm here because I want to make sure that you're okay. That my cousin is safe. Whatever is going on with Travis scares the hell out of me."

"You're not alone there." I paused. "You matter, you know. And we both know I hate talking about my feelings. So stop making me talk about my feelings."

His lips twitched. "You are so enlightened it's hard for me to even breathe. However, since we are talking about feelings, do you want to talk about what the hell is going on with my cousin? As in, what are your intentions? Because I'm in the mood to be nosy."

I gave him a look, barely resisting the growl escaping my lips. "Not sure how that's your business."

"Again, I'm a Montgomery. I don't know why you're so surprised about this fact. But stop being an idiot and talk to me. Or maybe, this is going to be a surprise, maybe you should talk to her about, oh I don't know, your feelings for fuck's sake."

I blinked at the raised tone and shook my head. "Why are you suddenly worried that I'm not?"

"Because you've been in love with her for years and you never did a thing about it. You watched her circle the drain while trying to help Travis, and you were always there to pick up the pieces. I was wrong. I thought that she loved him. But that wasn't the case. She wasn't in love with Travis. She wanted to help him because apparently, she has a savior complex. Much like we all do in this damn family. But every single time she fell right along with Travis, picking him up, you were there too. Picking up her pieces. So, for the love of the gods, just tell her you love her and stop worrying that she's going to run away. She loves you. We can all see it."

"You thought she loved Travis. So why the hell do you think she loves me?" I snapped. I hadn't even realized the words were there until they were already out of my lips. But it was the truth.

I had thought she had loved Travis in some way this whole time, and I had been wrong. So who was to say that she loved me? Maybe this was all in my damn head.

"It's different. And don't tell me how I know, I just do. But I hate the two of you dancing around each other for so long. And I know you, Crew. You're going to put her first, and in doing so, you might let her walk away to protect you both."

"What the hell are you talking about? We've barely started even dating."

"You're not telling her about this. I can see the way your mind works. You're thinking that if you worked with her, maybe Travis will stay away. Maybe she won't feel so insecure about you. But if you push her away to protect her, she's never going to forgive you. We both know that."

"You have no idea what you're saying."

Although, I knew that was a lie. I hadn't even realized that's where my thoughts had been going until he put it out there.

I rubbed my hand over my chest and set down my notes. "How did you know I loved her?"

"It's written all over your face, man. I'm surprised she hasn't figured it out. Or frankly, I'm surprised you haven't."

"We both know I figured it out a long time ago," I muttered, looking at the canvas, wondering if I was ever going to finish this.

It wasn't that it was a bad piece. I was just holding back. Each stroke felt as if I were ripping it from my soul, and the shades weren't aligning, the focus not quite there. Because if I put what I wanted to on the canvas, she was going to see everything.

And what if she didn't want that?

What if I was the person she hadn't been expecting, and yet was the one who held her back?

"Just talk to her. About everything. There's so much going on that if you don't, it's going to be thrown back in your face. Don't miss out on what could be because you're scared about what happened before."

"When did you get so introspective?" I asked, deflecting his words.

"Maybe when I realized everybody was growing up and I was still figuring out what I wanted to do with my life."

I studied Lex's face, wondering why he couldn't see the great man he was. No amount of me telling him though, would change the way he saw himself. Though I didn't have much to say on that. Pot and kettle and all that. "Lex. You are the most stable person I know."

"And isn't that a sad statement about the state of today's affairs? And on that note, I'm going to head out. I know you have to leave the studio soon and head back to see Aria. Where I don't know, but maybe you can have a conversation. That might be good for the both of you." My best friend leaned forward, cuffed the back of my head, and kissed my forehead. "Don't be an idiot."

And with that, he walked out, leaving me confused, tired, and yet, in the right direction.

Because I needed to talk with Aria. About so many

things. She was going to be upset about the break-in, then maybe I should actually talk about what I was feeling rather than pretending it didn't matter. And didn't that sound like pulling teeth?

Frowning, I went back to work, adding a few more colors and realizing maybe I could figure out where this was going.

At least I hoped so.

I stayed an extra hour before heading back to my place.

ARIA:

The hike with Dad went amazing. I am on my way to your house. See you soon?

ME:

That's good to hear.

ME:

See you soon.

ME:

Miss you, babe.

ARIA:

I miss you too.

I nearly texted that I loved her. And I wanted to yell at Lex for that. Just because I loved her, didn't mean she had to know.

Yes, I knew how stupid that sounded. But it wasn't time yet. What if she wasn't ready?

What if she was?

I shook my head. It took me a bit to get through traffic and I knew Aria had probably beaten me home. I pulled into my garage, grateful that they hadn't gotten to this particular car. It had been parked on the other side of the house, so it had been spared. But I was going to have to tell Aria everything.

I walked inside, the scent of garlic hitting me first, and I couldn't help but smile as Aria danced in my kitchen once again. She looked like she fit there. As if maybe she had always been there.

I didn't know if I was projecting, or if this was just what I wanted, but damn it, I didn't want her to leave. I wanted her to stay here. To be mine. And for there not to be any more questions.

Maybe Lex was right. Maybe I just should just shout the damn words.

Aria turned then, a smile on her face. "I am making linner. I hope you're hungry."

I blinked. "Lunch and dinner?" I leaned forward and brushed my lips against hers. She set down her mixing bowl, slid her fingers into my belt loops, and pulled me closer. So I put my hand around the back of her head, tangled my fingers in her hair, and deepened the kiss. She moaned, walking into me, and my dick pressed against my zipper.

"If you're not careful, I'm going to eat *you* in this kitchen. Not whatever you're making."

"You're welcome to eat me later. But first, I need actual sustenance." She winked, looking far lighter and happier than I had seen her in ages. Then again, this had been a gradual thing. She was digging more into her arts, spending more time with her family. Hell, spending more time with me.

No Travis.

No doubters at galleries telling her she wasn't good enough.

This was the Aria that I loved.

And I needed to tell her.

I opened my mouth to just say the words. Whether it was about what happened in the garage, or what I felt, I didn't know, but my phone rang. I frowned, knowing it was usually on silent, but that was the ring of the memory care center. Just in case of emergencies.

"Crap." I met Aria's worried gaze as I answered the phone. "This is Crew."

"Hello, Mr. McTavish. We had an incident at the center, and we really need you to come down here. We cannot get a hold of your mother."

I cursed under my breath. Of course they couldn't

get a hold of my mother. She was only there to throw shit then moaned and tried to forget that any of this was happening. Though, part of me wanted to do the same, the little kid inside couldn't.

And I really hated that.

"I'll be there soon." I paused. "Is he okay?" I bit out, hating myself for even asking. It wasn't like the man had ever loved me. He didn't even remember me now.

"Yes. He will be. But I think he could use a friendly face."

I hung up, snorting since I knew I wasn't the friendly face that he would want to see. But the old man didn't have anyone else.

How messed up was that?

"How can I help?" Aria asked. She'd turned off the burners and shoved everything into the fridge. She had done it so quickly and quietly that I hadn't even noticed until I looked up. I was grateful she seemed to be on top of things because I clearly wasn't.

"I don't know. The memory care center needs me down there. Something with Dad. I have no idea. I'm sorry."

She gave me a soft smile. "Don't be sorry. I know you have a complicated relationship with your parents. Believe me. I understand complicated. Can I come with you?"

I opened my mouth to say no, but she put her fingers across my lips.

"You know what. No. I'm going with you. You get to deal with me. You've spent so much time dealing with my problems, I'm not going to let you do this alone."

My shoulders fell, and I leaned down to press my forehead against hers. "It might be bad."

"All the more reason for me to be there. You don't have to do this alone. I think I remember a very sexy, bearded man telling me that once."

My lips twitched. "I hear he has a huge dick as well."

"I will have to do more research on that tonight. I'll let you know."

I smiled, not even realizing I could in that moment, before brushing my lips against hers. "It's not going to be pretty."

"I don't mind. I promise."

I let out a breath and took her hand, hoping to hell this didn't ruin everything.

Chapter Thirteen

Crew

"You don't have to come inside with me if you do not want to." I threaded my fingers with Aria's, dread settling in my gut.

I didn't want to walk inside that building. I wanted to walk away and leave all family obligations behind. And while I could do that with most things, I wasn't sure I could do that with the man whose blood ran in my veins.

"If you don't want me to go inside, I won't. But you're the one who repeatedly tells me that I don't have to do everything on my own. That I have an entire support system. And you were always not so quietly by my side even when I didn't realize I needed help. So let me be that pillar you lean on when it's too much."

We stood in the parking lot of the memory care

center, and I turned, our hands still clasped, and I used my free one to push aside a strand of her hair. "You were always too busy saving everybody else to worry about yourself. Somebody had to do it."

"Next time just talk directly into a mirror when you say that."

I let out a sigh before I began pacing in front of the entrance. I let go of Aria's hand, only because she stood back watching me. "I want to get my car and take you away from here. I don't want to go in there."

"Then we don't." She said it so simply but we both knew it was anything but. Yet she'd risk the world for me. Just like I'd do for her.

I had no idea how I'd been able to pretend to hate her for so long when all along it was this fiery passion and love I had for her.

This woman.

And that meant I didn't want her to have to face my demons—ones I didn't want in my life to begin with.

"Doesn't that make me a terrible person? That's my dad in there." I pointed toward the glass doors. Nobody was outside, and with the angle we were at, the only people who could see us were those in the security booth. What would they think of my hesitancy? They probably had tons to say, then again, if they knew who that man was, maybe they would be on my side.

Aria moved closer then, her hand outstretched to cup my cheek. I paused in my pacing at her touch. "That man is your genetic donor. You know that. I've only met him a few times, and you always got me out of there since it was too much for everyone involved. You protected all of us before he showed his true colors. But I know so many of your stories. Of the way he would belittle you. Of the way he wouldn't stand up for you but would shower your mother in affection after she did such terrible things to you."

"Why can't we just quit them?" I ground out. I ran my hands through her hair, knowing she was my anchor even though it might be too much for either of us.

Aria slid her hands over my chest, her fingertips playing with a small thread on my shirt. "In your case it's because there is a sad man in there who doesn't remember the terrible things he did. You're not here for your mother, as she feels it's easy to walk away when it's too much. And it's hard for me to even hear her name without wanting to claw her eyes out for what she did to you. She deserves to be in a jail cell. Not able to walk around this community with her head held high as people pity her for what her husband is going through. They don't know the truth of the viper beneath her skin. But we do. Our family does. We're not going to let her hurt you."

It was such a role reversal, her trying to protect me. It didn't feel right. I wanted to be the one to protect her, and here I was, ready to drag her into the lion's den that was this center with the man who had hurt me just as much as my mother even though it was rarely with his fists.

"Sometimes I feel like my dad is in his own prison. He can't remember the terrible things he did, but he can't remember himself. As he faces his own mortality and can't remember the path of hate and fear he paved. Because that's what this disease robs you of. It's taking away a man who hated me and leaving behind a shell that doesn't understand the complexity of how I feel. Hell, I don't even understand."

I'd never bared myself like this to anyone. Of course it would be Aria. There was only one person it could have ever been.

"We can walk away right now. You don't owe him anything. But you do owe yourself. If you need closure, we will help you get it. I just want to keep you safe. Just like you always tried to do for me."

I pushed her hair back from her face once more, wanting to kiss her, to hold her. I loved her so much in that moment, it was hard for me to focus.

I didn't even know when I had first felt that pull

toward her. That feeling had always been there, something I had hidden, pushed down. But it had always floated under the surface, waiting for me to acknowledge its insistence. And in the end, I couldn't ignore it. Because here she was, the woman who had wrapped herself around every ounce of my being. And I never wanted to let her go.

Only I knew once we walked through those doors, she could get hurt.

So what kind of love was that?

I let out a gruff breath. "The nurse sounded scared. Or worried. Let's just see what happens, and I'll take it day by day."

"Okay then. But you're not doing it alone."

I leaned down and brushed my lips against hers, just a soft caress to remind me I had someone to come home to. Though she didn't technically live with me. She might stay at my place more than I stayed at hers, but we were still separate. Still trying to navigate this new facet of our relationship.

I wanted so much, even though I was afraid to grasp it. That hope.

I once again tangled my fingers with hers and we walked inside the memory care center.

"Hi, Linda," I said to the familiar desk nurse.

She gave me a small smile before turning her attention to Aria. "Hello, you two. Crew, we have you all set up, I just need you to sign in. And who is this?"

"I'm Aria Montgomery. A friend of Crew's."

"Aria is my girlfriend, Linda." I squeezed Aria's hand, and she gave me a soft smile. "I already have her and a few of her family members on the list."

Aria widened her eyes as Linda smiled. "No problem. Let's get you set up with a visitor pass, and the doctor should be out soon to talk to you."

I ran my thumb along Aria's hand, once again needing that anchor. "Anything I should know?"

"It's just been a hard day."

At that solemn response, we finished signing in and put on our visitor badges. Everything was laminated on nice chains versus a sticky note or anything like that. Only the best for this care center.

Once the doctor and two nurses came out to speak with us, I nodded along, knowing that they were only doing what they thought was best. Because my father was never going to get better. They had to have an inkling of the difficult relationship I had with that man, but they still told me the inevitable. Only I wasn't sure what I was supposed to do with the information. Soon he'd have to be moved to another center with specialized care, but I didn't want that decision in my hands. It should have been in my mother's. I couldn't help but think this was another way for my mother to hurt me. It had taken me far too long to realize that. It was as if there was nothing left for me. The trainwreck of my childhood hadn't fostered the adult sense of self that could carry this burden—but the ones I met outside my house of terror had been there nonetheless.

We made our way into the formal living room where my dad sat in his favorite chair staring out of the bay window. I did not know what he looked at, but he loved that angle.

He had thrown books, his food, and any item he could get his hands on earlier and had broken another window in the building. He had screamed and shouted, before finally calming down, and was only now allowed to sit here with two burly orderlies watching.

I nearly tripped over my feet when I realized that he wasn't the only one in the room.

"It took you far too long to get here."

As I hadn't been expecting her, I flinched at the venom in my mother's tone. She stood off to the side, staring out another window. She had on her pantsuit and high heels, her twenty-thousand-dollar bag on her elbow. I knew she had jewelry that was probably worth more than a small house covering her. As well as the two-thousand-dollar perfume she drenched herself in.

I liked nice things. I knew how to spend money.

Hell, the jeans I wore were a couple hundred dollars because the cheaper ones I used to wear would wear out too quickly, and I decided to find a nice pair that would last. I knew my privilege.

But my mother lorded it.

I think what she wore bothered me because she was only skin deep. With poison beneath.

"I didn't realize you could walk through those doors," I volleyed back.

Aria squeezed my hand.

"Don't get snippy with me. Your father needs you."

"I do not." I turned as my father stood up, vitriol on his face. Pure hatred. "You are no son of mine. For all I know, your mother spread her legs for some lowlife. My true son would have more meat to them. More dignity. Instead you're covered with ink, paint, and have a whore by your side."

I was moving forward before I even realized it, and Aria pulled me back.

"He's not worth it," she reminded me, and I froze.

Because beating up an old and feeble man when all I wanted to do was drown the memories themselves truly wouldn't help anything. "If this is all tonight is going to be about, I am done."

My father narrowed his gaze toward Aria. "I remember this girl. They tell me I don't. But I do. She was always lapping at your heels. She probably wants your inheritance. Make sure she's good in bed before you give her anything though. Just because they can suck your cock doesn't make them worth a ring. She's pretty enough, but not from good stock. She's good for the side, but you need to marry well to keep the family name going."

My dad continued on rambling, and I finally realized that I didn't care. He could lash out at me constantly, but the moment he said anything about Aria, I was done. Completely done.

"Don't call again." I turned to head out, a quiet Aria at my side. I swallowed the bile rising in my throat and it was only Aria's presence keeping me steady in this moment.

My mother's voice brought me back to the nightmare that was my bloodline. "He might be sick, but he's telling the truth. You have responsibilities to this family."

I turned to her, chest tight. "You had a responsibility to raise me. Not to treat me like shit. Not to beat me." She looked around since we weren't alone in the room, but I didn't care who saw her for who she truly was. "You hit me, slapped me. Pushed me down the stairs. You used Dad's belt. You made me put my face over the steam coming off a boiling pot of water. You and Dad did all you could to belittle me and torture me to the point that I had zero self-esteem. If it wasn't for *her* family, I would be dead right now." I gestured toward Aria, knowing she had her chin lifted by my side. "We both know that. Maybe that's what you wanted, but from what I'm seeing, you want some kind of legacy? No. I'm not going to be your legacy. Fuck you. Fuck him. I don't care what happens anymore. I don't care what you want. Everything you have ever done to me, the lashes, the words, they took their toll. Fine, you went there. But I am done now. I don't care what you try to take from me, because I have already made myself without you. I have who I need. So fuck you."

"You are such a vulgar human being. Did you teach him that?" my mother asked as she turned to the woman I loved by my side.

"I'm pretty sure the words that constantly flow out of your mouth did that." Aria raised her chin before I could defend her. "You are a sorry excuse for a mother. You are supposed to love your children. Protect them. But you couldn't even protect him from yourself. And you're still doing it. I get that you might be scared about what's happening in your life right now, but hurting your son repeatedly isn't the answer. So if you want to come at him again, you are going to have to come through me. And everyone in my family. You do not get to hurt him anymore."

I moved forward and gripped her shoulder. "That's enough, baby. We can go. She's not worth it."

Aria glared at me as my mother stared at us both, such anger in her expression I couldn't process who the hell this woman was. But Aria wasn't done. "You don't have to defend me anymore because she doesn't matter."

My mother finally broke in. "If I don't matter, then why did you send the police to my home? Why did you have them question me like I'm common trash, like this little girl. I had nothing to do with harming your precious cars. Cars that my family's money paid for."

The woman who occasionally claimed to be my mother was lucky I refused to lay a hand on her. I wasn't that person, and I wouldn't become who'd she'd tried to mold me into. "First, I paid for everything in that garage with my money. With money I made from my art. That silly little hobby you hated. I guess I should thank you for not letting me starve and putting me out of the house when I was a little kid like you kept threatening. Because that roof you gave me over my head until I was sixteen allowed me to get through most of school and learn how to paint. Thank you for not killing me." The sarcasm dripping through my tone was so thick I could practically feel it in the air. "But there's a reason the cops talked to you. Because I don't trust you. You might not have stuck a knife in my tires, but you have done so many other things. We're done. I'm done with all of this."

I swallowed the emotion in my throat as I turned to my dad. Only I knew he couldn't recognize me again. That odd look he got in his eyes when he thought I was a stranger came back, and part of me wanted to cry. Because he wouldn't remember me. His own son. Yet wasn't that a good thing in some aspects? If he couldn't remember me, he couldn't hate me.

And that was the family I came from.

Not the family that tried to protect

"Goodbye, Dad. Goodbye." My voice nearly broke at the last word, and I turned, taking Aria with me. I tossed the visitor's badges in the bin next to the desk, ignoring the pitying looks on everyone's faces. Honestly, I was surprised they had let it go on for as long as they had. But perhaps they knew if it didn't happen now, it would happen again. It was inevitable after all.

I slammed my way out of the building, Aria on my heels.

When I got to my SUV, I stood there, chest heaving.

"Crew, baby. I'm sorry for what they said. They had no right to hurt you."

"Don't be sorry. You had nothing to do with it. You

didn't even have to defend me." I turned to her, throat tight. "I'm sorry my parents are such horrible people that they can't see who you are."

"They could never see who you were."

"I should take you home." My chest ached, hollow. I couldn't have Aria near me and taint her anymore. Couldn't she see where I'd come from? She didn't deserve that.

Her brows furrowed. "And what, leave me there? No. I'm not going anywhere. We're going to stand here and talk and you're going to lean on me for once. I am not some weak little girl that you have to constantly protect. Let me be the one there for you."

"Don't you see that I'm nothing but a stain on you and your family? That is where I came from. A woman who was going to gaslight every single fucking person in there to the point that I'm the bad guy. She wouldn't even walk through those doors before now, and suddenly she will have them wrapped around her finger. But that's what she does. Money talks, and she is fluent."

Aria tilted her head as she studied me. "She doesn't have any of us wrapped around her finger. You know that."

"Only because she thinks all of you are beneath her anyway. That is who my mother is. And that glimpse you saw of my father? That's who he always was beneath the surface and behind closed doors. Before this disease started to rip him from his own psyche. That is who I am. Who I came from. People who are so cruel it's comical."

"No, that's who *they* are. We are not the summation of our parents. Maybe we can take some of the good things, some of the tics. But in the end, we are who we make ourselves. And don't forget, you have been friends of the Montgomerys for long enough to take some of their traits. We wouldn't be with you—*I* wouldn't be with you if you didn't come out of that horrible home as a good person."

Why wasn't she getting this? "I'm not a good person, Aria. I treated you like shit because it was easier than having you. Easier than telling you I wanted you. I wanted you when you were with other people. How is that a good person?"

"I didn't say we were perfect. I am not perfect. I don't want perfect. I want you." Her lips twitched even as her eyes narrowed.

I snorted. "Well I'm far from perfect."

"I don't care. I'm far from perfect. But I want you to know that you are not your parents. I hate them. I want to go in and shank them. But that would only somehow make them feel better because then they can put me into jail. Just like Travis did with you. They don't matter. Your mother is never going to change. And I don't have any words for your father. Because I know it's a devastating thing to see. But you cannot come out of there and think that I'm just going to let you walk away from me because of some stupid words your parents said. I don't care what they think of me. I care what you think."

"I want to hurt them for saying those things about you." I cupped her face again, rage going through my body. "And I'm the reason you had to deal with it anyway. They could have hurt you because of me."

"What they said means nothing. All that matters is what you and I say to each other. I'm sorry that might be the last time you ever see them. And yet, I'm not. Because every time you come here a little part of you dies inside and I don't want that for you anymore. You deserve more."

She saw so damn much it terrified me. "I don't know what to say. I never want to go back."

"Then you won't. But I have one more thing to ask." She met my gaze, and I swallowed hard. "What is she talking about with your cars?"

I flinched, realizing that I hadn't told her yet. Things had happened too quickly, and now I had messed up. "The night Lex dropped me off somebody had broken into the garage and destroyed every single tire they could get to." I explained everything that happened, including setting up more security.

Each word seemed to cement the anger on Aria's face. "Why didn't you tell me?"

"I was going to tell you today. And then we came here instead."

"Let me get this straight. Everybody in my family that works for the security company knows. The cops know. Lex knows. I'm sure other people have details. But you didn't tell me. Why? Because you didn't think I could handle it?"

"Of course not." I paused. "I was just tired of so much shit coming at us. I just wanted one night where we could just be."

"I get the concept of that. I really do. But you yelled at me because I didn't know how to tell you about the texts from Travis. And I was wrong. I should've told you. He hasn't texted again thankfully, but I would tell you. So I need you to tell me when bad things happen. We can't make this work if we're afraid of hurting the other person with our own burdens."

"I just want you safe," I whispered.

"I'm safer with information. You were with me when I made the wrong decision. And I'm with you."

"Good. Because I love you," I blurted.

"Well I love you too," she shouted.

And then we stood there, staring at one another, a smile slowly covering my face. "You love me?"

"You love me too. And it feels kind of apropos yelling it at each other for the first time."

And just like that, all thoughts of anger, denial, and pain backed away for the moment. And I cupped her face. "I love you. So much so that it's hard for me to remember when it started. And I have no idea how to love someone, Aria. You're going to have to help me out, okay?"

Tears slid down her cheeks as she nodded. Then she slid her fingers in my belt loops and pulled me closer. "I can do that. Because I've never loved someone either. Not like this. And it's really scary. Terrifying even. But I'm not going anywhere, Crew. Even when we are scared that something in our lives could hurt the other. I'm in. All in."

And with that, I crushed my lips to hers, ignoring the rest of the world.

And just this once, the world let me.

Chapter Fourteen

Aria

Shoulders back, focus ready, I snapped the photo. The shutter clicked, a scene frozen in time. I repeated the action, sucking in a breath as the fawn moved slightly to the left, and its twin took center stage.

Another shot. Another.

The doe lifted her head, as if allowing the breeze to slide over her face. She had to be exhausted. Dealing with newborn twins in the wild while protecting them from predators and humans, while also nursing and trying to find food, had to take every ounce of her energy. But her babies looked healthy and moved around on near wobbly legs as they danced through the meadow as if they hadn't a care in the world.

I did my best to capture that magic. The moment where the doe could finally feel relaxed enough in order to check on her babies. Thanks to where I had situated myself, the deer couldn't scent me, and I hoped there were no predators around for all of our sakes.

I loved walking through the forest in the mountains, taking photos of what lay beneath. It wasn't a sunset, not just mountainous peaks that looked purple after a deep rain. Instead, I tried to take snapshots of life that crawled through. Of the fallen log that had rotted from the inside out, with life persevering.

Another tree that had been split in half by lightning, the dark brand of fire creating a scar.

The rocks themselves created their own beauty, with the wildlife that belonged in these lands making the mark.

I hadn't gone too deep into the forest, and was still on the trail, but part of me wanted to go deeper. To spend weeks within the Rocky Mountain National Forest. I was on my way to working in every single national and state park I could find my way to. I wanted to travel the world and see what struck.

Because while I didn't take photos of people often, my goal was to capture what humanity was slowly taking away.

The litter that dusted the canyon. The stream dry from a change in climate. The broken tree limbs and craters left behind from a mudslide thanks to the erosion our deforestation and building had created. Countless marks upon the earth from humanity. Because we all left scars and carried some of our own. In this moment, however, I snapped a photo of life. And then I turned to the side and took one more shot.

Crew didn't look up, but I saw his brow raised. He sat on a rock, booted foot over his knee as he sketched whatever was on his mind. I knew he wanted to get a few ideas for a showcase, and so we decided to take our date on a hike. He had packed a lunch because he was better at sandwich making. I hadn't known that was a thing until he had mentioned it offhand. The ensuing fight reminded me of the good old days where we spent more time fighting with each other only to make up, than we did laughing.

I pressed my thighs together at the memory, though that didn't help much.

"What is on your mind?" he asked, that deep voice of his sending shivers down my spine.

"Just thinking about lunch."

"I did have a damn good breakfast before we headed out." He smirked and I rolled my eyes considering what his breakfast had been. He had laid me out on his kitchen counter, my hands on my breasts, and had his fill. My thighs had been around his face, legs wrapped around his head.

He had licked, sucked, and speared me with two fingers so quickly that I had come once, and then another time when he continued his motions. I loved the way that his beard scraped the inner silk of my thighs. There was just something about Crew that always kept me on edge. Whether it was the tension, or just Crew.

"I suppose I had my breakfast as well," I said dryly.

He merely grinned, closing his notebook. Because I had ended up on my knees, his hand in my hair, as he slid that thick cock down my throat. He had been the one in control, fucking my face as he moved his length between my lips. I had flattened my tongue and swallowed the tip of him as deep down as possible without gagging. Then I'd made myself come by holding the dildo he'd bought me, rotating my hips up and down to fuck myself, as I had my other hand on his thigh to keep steady. Then I had swallowed every drop of him as he had come down my throat.

Seriously, the best way to wake up.

In the three weeks since I had finally realized I loved him and told him, it had been like this. The two of us doing our best to find our pattern in life. Staying at each other's houses, going into the studio together. Doing things like *this*. Me trying to capture what I wanted for my next large project. And Crew coming with me so he could find new inspiration.

And throughout it all, it felt like we were back to a new normal. Still arguing, still making love, and just being.

No more mention of his family because in the end, they weren't what was important. But plenty of mention of mine because they were always in our hair. In fact, a couple of my cousins had wanted to come out with us today, but I had nipped that in the bud. Frankly, I just wanted time with Crew. Everything felt so new and fresh. And it felt like if I didn't latch on to it now, it could fall at any moment. I hated that feeling.

"What's with that face?" Crew asked as he reached out to cup my cheek. I leaned into his hold and sighed.

"I'm just worried that I am too happy."

He gave me a look. "I swear you overthink more than anyone I know."

"I'm good at it."

He raised a brow. "It isn't the only thing you're good at," he whispered. At that deep rasp of his voice, the deer cantered off, and I moved back so I could put my camera away.

"I am not having sex outdoors with you. Last time

we did that, we nearly got caught by that couple who were trying to do the same thing."

"It's not my fault we were better at it than they were."

"And how do you know that?" I asked, laughing.

"Because the guy couldn't find a trail on a clearly marked map. How the hell is he supposed to find her clit?"

I burst out laughing, before pulling my camera bag over my shoulder. "I so happy that you were the perfect Boy Scout and can read a map."

"I'm always prepared. Don't worry. I'll never get lost when I'm down there."

I rolled my eyes, holding out my hand. He took it, lifted that curious brow of his, and we made our way back down the trail.

"When we get back, I have a few things to do before my meeting. Dinner tonight?"

The domesticity of the question made me smile. Was this what it was supposed to be like? People just figuring things out together. Making plans, whether they were huge or smaller ones. I had never had this before. I thought maybe at one point I could with Travis, until I realized it wasn't love I was feeling, but friendship and the desire to try to find peace. But any other relationship I had been in hadn't been close.

I scared myself. Because the more I had, the happier I felt, the harder it would hurt if it was ever taken away.

"Dinner sounds great," I said, wondering why I was so introspective and worried.

"I don't really want to go to this meeting, but I have to sign off on everything for the lawyer."

I gave his hand a reassuring squeeze. "But then you're done, right? Powers of attorney, other legal jargon that is beyond even my degree, but no more issues. You only have to deal with your own businesses."

He nodded tightly. "I'll have to deal with it later if they keep me in the will. And frankly, that's not a sure thing. She might keep me in it only to fuck with me, or she's finally cutting me off forever. She can't touch the trust or what I've made since, but she can do something with her personal will. However, I'm done. It might make me a terrible person, a horrific son, but I'm done."

"You are not either one of those. You are just protecting your peace. And you're allowed to do that."

"I yelled at you enough to do the same, I suppose I should eat my own words."

"Damn straight."

We made our way to his SUV, and I was grateful that his tires were new, and the added security at his place meant it wouldn't happen again. Still, an unsettled feeling slid through me as we got inside and made our way out of the state park. "They haven't found anything else since they spoke to Travis, right?" I asked, blurting the thought before I could even formulate it fully.

The hand that wasn't on my thigh tightened on the steering wheel. "After they questioned him, they didn't have much else. No evidence, just a feeling. So unless something else happens, they are out of luck. And he's been a good boy since, according to the authorities. His parents are keeping his nose clean."

"So let's just go with nothing happening."

"That sounds like a damn fine plan for me."

After the authorities had spoken to Travis, I received a few more threatening texts. We'd sent them to the authorities as well though there was nothing inherently dangerous about them according to the people in charge. Crew wasn't sure he believed that. And frankly, I wasn't sure either. Travis wasn't in his right mind. I didn't know what he was capable of anymore. But after those initial texts, he hadn't contacted me again. Nor had he spoken to anyone in my family from what I could tell.

It was as if he had vanished in these past weeks. And while part of me was relieved because I didn't have to deal with him, the rest of me was worried. And no matter how many times I told myself it wasn't my problem, I wasn't going to stop worrying. He had been my friend for years. And he was in trouble.

"If you want, I can have the private detective I hired see if he could help Travis."

I blinked, looking over at the man I loved. "Your detective is just trying to figure out who did that to your cars, right?"

"You could've been at the house. You could have been hurt. And I don't like thinking about that. So of course I'm going to try to figure it out on my own. I know the guy looked Travis up, but it isn't like he is following him around or anything."

I moved my hand, so it was over his on my thigh and squeezed. "Sometimes I feel like you can read my mind."

"I've been wanting you for so long, sometimes it feels as if I can."

I smiled at him as we pulled into the parking lot of the gallery. "That sounds creepily sexy. And I don't know what that says about me."

He barked out a laugh as he turned off the engine. "Well, your creepily sexy boyfriend will do anything you want him to."

"I love you."

Crew leaned forward and brushed his lips against mine. "I love you too."

"But back to your offer. I think following Travis is just going to make things worse. Which hurts to say."

"Anything you want."

"Well that's a loaded statement."

He snorted, and we got out of the SUV and headed toward the main building. Someone shifted out of the shadows, and Crew immediately put me behind him, his shoulders tense.

"You ruined everything," Travis spat as he jumped at Crew.

I staggered back as the ghost of my friend swung his arm wildly, trying to punch Crew. "Travis! Stop."

"You don't get to be happy. You left me alone. How could you do this?" Travis asked, his voice high-pitched. He punched out at Crew again, and Crew just moved out of the way, before shifting quickly to the other side. He had Travis's arms pinned behind him, the man I had thought was my friend kicking wildly.

"If you don't stop, I'm going to break your fucking arm."

My eyes widened at Crew, but I didn't blame him for the threat. Not right now. I heard people running in the distance, and I figured my cousins who worked at the security side of the building were on their way. After all, this place was covered in cameras.

"Don't you threaten me. I should have thrown you

in jail. There are so many things I could've done to you. Look what he's doing to me, Aria! All you care about is spreading your legs for him."

"Travis. Let us help you." He had to be high on something, his eyes wide, his body so thin. It looked as if he'd lost another twenty pounds. He had already had a small frame. Now he just looked like a shadow of who he had been.

Ford and Noah were there, arms outstretched because I knew they wanted to help the situation. But Crew seem to have it in hand.

"I don't need your help. If you had wanted to help me, you wouldn't have sent your pet cops at me. Wouldn't have left me alone. But you're nothing. I never want to talk to you again."

"But you *are* here. Let us help you. Travis. I know you're angry. I know nothing makes sense. But if you are hurting, let us help."

He spat at my feet before kicking Crew in the knee.

My boyfriend didn't move, instead he just growled under his breath. "There's nothing you can do right now. You need to stop, Travis."

"Come on, Travis, let's get you a cup of coffee," Ford said calmly.

"I'm *fine*. I don't need your help. I will come back. I don't need you anymore, Aria. You never came when I needed you in the first place. So why do I need you now?" Travis just tugged himself away, and for some reason Crew let him go.

I didn't stagger back, didn't feel as if he would hit me. Because I did not know the person in front of me. I didn't know what drugs and alcohol had done to him. And even if I stuffed him in my trunk and forced him into rehab, he wouldn't do anything. He would still hate me.

Just like he always had.

"Okay. If we can't help you, then you need to go. Staying here isn't going to work out for you, Travis. You're just going to end up behind bars because you're going to hurt someone. And I don't want that for you."

"I hate you," he snarled.

I ignored the barb because this wasn't my Travis. I wasn't sure I'd ever see that Travis again. It broke something inside, but I'd be here if that man I'd once known came back. "That's fine. Because I don't hate you. I don't know who you are right now, but I don't hate you."

Travis opened his mouth to say something, but instead he just took a few steps back before turning and running the other direction.

Crew moved slightly, as if to follow him, but I reached out and touched his arm. He immediately stopped moving forward.

"Stay. He'll find a way to hurt you and I...I just want the people I love safe. I don't know how to help him right now."

"I don't think you can," Ford said softly. "Kingston is on the other side of the property, and he and Daisy can head Travis off. Maybe get him some coffee. Or have him talk to someone. See what they can do. The cops are going to need to be called since I'm sure this is against the agreement he made. But his parents seem to get him out of everything. I don't trust him around you, Aria."

I nodded tightly, my chest squeezing. Crew was there then, pulling me into his arms. "Did he hurt you?" I asked.

"No. I was afraid I was leaving bruises on his arms though. He has like no weight left to him."

I closed my eyes, hating what had become of the boy I had once known. "Hopefully the others can do more for him. I don't like him out here on the streets."

"Nobody does. We will try what we can, okay?" Ford whispered.

I nodded, and my family did what they did best, and tried to help those around them. And I stood in Crew's arms, feeling helpless. "I'm sorry that he tried to hurt you."

"He didn't even get close. But damn it, if he

would've touched you, I would've ended him." I saw the rage in his gaze then and reached out to his cheek.

"Then let's not let that happen. Let's drop off what we need to and head back to the house."

He moved to kiss my palm, nodding tightly. "Fine. But I don't like leaving you alone."

"You're leaving me at my house under a full security system. And the only time I will be leaving my house is going into my attached garage to get into my car and drive toward you. I'll be fine."

"I'd rather take you with me."

"And I need to shower and do a few work things for the business, while you do your lawyerly things. You said we had to start living our lives? Let's try to do so. I want to be normal. Just for once, I want normal."

"You need to stop throwing my words back in my face."

"I love you. I can't help it."

He leaned down and brushed his lips to mine, but I still couldn't relax. Because Travis was out there, and he was in pain, and nothing I could do could help. But maybe someone else could.

Crew dropped me off at my place, made sure I was behind my security system, and went to deal with his paperwork. I put on music, showered, and spent the rest of my time at my computer with a hair mask and under eye patches doing their work. I was going to go on a date with my boyfriend tonight, and while I couldn't pretend that everything was perfect, I could at least try to move on.

My phone rang then, and I smiled at my father's face on the screen.

"Hey there."

"Hello, daughter of mine. I heard you had a run-in today."

I winced, grateful he hadn't video called. "Who told you?"

"Three of your cousins. And then Sebastian called because he heard it from another cousin and wanted to know if you had told me."

"I'm sorry. Crew dropped me off at home, and we talked it out. I should have told you but...I just needed a moment."

"I can understand that but your family loves you. Okay?"

"I know. I love you too." I paused, my throat tight. "Now I'm getting ready for my date."

My dad was silent for long enough, I was afraid I'd done something wrong. "You sound happy, Aria."

Tears pricked my eyes. "I am happy. I feel selfish that I am sometimes, but I am. I love him so much, Daddy."

"That's good to hear. My kids are all starting to settle, and I'm feeling like an old man."

"Whatever you say, Grandpa."

"Rude." He paused again. "I know the situation isn't easy with Travis. And there's not an answer that I can give. Your grandparents, aunts, and uncles all did their best to try to help me before I was ready for it. But as soon as I reached out, they were there. Just like I know you will be. Even though it pains me because I want you out of harm's reach. I don't know what's going on in Travis's head, because sometimes I don't know what had gone through mine. But you're trying. And you're living your life. I'm proud of you, Aria."

My throat tightened even as a weight lifted from my shoulders. Because of all people, my dad understood where I was coming from. He'd been on the other side of it, after all. Though he'd never hurt anyone—not like Travis was doing. "I love you."

"I love you too. Now, make sure you bring Crew over for dinner this weekend. Your mom is making noises about surprising you at his house since you haven't brought him over recently."

"Mom is? Because that sounds like a *you* thing. Mom makes intricate plans."

I could practically hear him rolling his eyes at me

through the phone. "Fine. It's my idea. Let me do what I want. You're my baby girl."

"We will put it in the books, that way Mom's planner is happy."

"Honestly, that is what I strive for in life. Making sure your mother's planner is happy."

I burst out laughing, knowing he was actually telling the truth. My dad loved making my mother and her planners happy. We said our goodbyes, and I went to finish getting ready.

CREW:

Are you sure you don't want me to pick you up? I'm almost done here.

ME:

I am spending the night at your house, and I want a car for tomorrow. I'll meet you there. Then I'll let you finger bang me in your truck later.

CREW:

Now I'm talking to my lawyer with a hard on.

ME:

You're welcome.

I snapped a photo of me in just a towel, my breasts nearly falling out of the fabric, and laughed when he sent back a middle finger emoji.

I dressed, added lip gloss to my look, and went to pack a bag, only to realize that everything I needed was at Crew's house. Hell. When had that happened? I shook my head, wondering exactly what that meant, and grabbed my purse. I went through my garage and walked to my car.

A small sound echoed behind me, and I turned. Only to meet with darkness as something slammed into the side of my head.

Chapter Fifteen

Crew

I pulled into the restaurant parking lot feeling lighter than I had. I was no longer connected to my family. Perhaps in a few weeks I would feel differently about the decision. Right now, it was as if the albatross around my neck was no longer there.

The people who had done the piss poor job of raising me were not my parents. They hadn't truly raised me. They had done their best to try to form me into what they thought would be possible. I never knew their endgame. They wanted me to be perfect, so they would break me to get there. Honestly, they didn't make sense. Perhaps it was because they never tried to. They wanted power, and I wasn't going to give it to them. Not when I had finally grown old enough to protect myself.

And find the family that I should've had along the way.

Tonight however, wasn't about them. It was about new steps.

I was finally going to ask Aria to move in with me. She practically had already, and I hadn't liked leaving her at her place. Not that I didn't love the cottage style house that the Montgomerys built twenty years ago. The construction company continued to keep it up to date with everything, and it was a beautiful home.

But I wanted her in my bed every night.

I wanted to wake up with her nestled in my arms, or dancing without panties on in my kitchen. I didn't like her having to meet me at the restaurant because she wanted her car at my place. I wanted it to be our place.

Hopefully she wouldn't fight me on it. Though, I never knew with Aria. Then again, fighting was what we did best. Because the making up had its perks.

I looked at my phone to see if she had responded to my latest text, but she hadn't. When I looked around the parking lot, I frowned. Her car wasn't there. I looked around the large truck beside me and realized it wasn't parked on the street either. Weird. Maybe she'd hit traffic.

I pressed her name on my phone, and it rang a few times before being put through to voicemail. But it hadn't rang enough to do that naturally, meaning she had pushed me to voicemail.

"What the hell?" I continued to pace and called again. Same thing. I texted, no answer. I quickly called Daisy, worry starting to sink in.

"Hey there. I thought you were going to be on your date."

"Have you heard from Aria?"

She must have heard the tension in my tone, because she didn't crack a joke. "No. We texted a few times when she was getting ready, but I thought she would be on her way to you by now. Is she not there?"

"She's not answering her phone, nor has she texted me back. I have a bad feeling."

"Was her phone ringing at all?" Daisy asked, and I heard the clicking of keys, telling me she was probably at her desk, her laptop at hand.

"Yes. So I don't think it's off."

"Okay, that's good. It's probably nothing. She's probably just in traffic. Let me check."

"You can track all of us?"

"Of course we can. With the normal apps and our own apps. We've all become hyper aware of things with recent events."

I nodded, not wanting to think about exactly what had happened to Aria's family members and my friends over the past years. There were too many hospital visits, too many stress factors.

"Her phone is on Huntington Bridge. That's weird as it's not in between the house and the restaurant you were going to. Were you still going to Parmigiano?"

I was already running back to my car as she spoke. "Call the cops. Do something. Anything. I'm on my way to the bridge now."

"I'll do that, and I'm calling the team. It's probably nothing, Crew." I heard the doubt in her voice, even as she was trying to reassure me. It wasn't working.

"Travis attacked us today. And somebody broke into my house already. If it wasn't Travis, it was someone else. Somebody that wanted to hurt us. I don't have a good feeling."

"You're not trained for this, Crew. We are on our way. Don't do anything stupid."

"Then get there before me," I snapped before ending the call and trying to call Aria again. No answer. Another chink in my heart and nerves.

I knew I was probably breaking a few traffic laws as I drove the few miles to the Huntington Bridge. But I didn't care. I needed to get to her. I knew Daisy would handle everything else, that's what she was good at, what she trained for. I just needed to get Aria.

Maybe it was just her phone, maybe it was a bad connection. Maybe it was nothing. But I didn't think so.

I shouldn't have left her alone.

Huntington Bridge was a small metal bridge over the river that bisected the edge of the suburb. It wasn't too tall, so during high precipitation times, people did jump off it for recreation. But there were signs plastered everywhere that you weren't supposed to. People had no idea what was beneath the surface. There could be logs, sharp rocks, or the river could be shallower there than in some other places.

However, the bridge was one of Aria's favorite places to sit and take photos when she needed to clear her head. There were countless angles, backdrops, and people that could create stories for her so she could focus on what she needed to for her next project. We'd been there recently so I had an idea of how high the water was, but it still made me fucking nervous.

Hell, I drew Huntington Bridge countless times because I sat next to Aria as she worked. We had almost gone there today instead of our hike.

Some part of me hoped she had gone there to snap a few photos, and got lost in her art. But that wasn't who Aria was. We were all worried about what happened today, so she would answer if she could.

The fact that she couldn't sent chills up my spine.

I ran a stop sign, ignoring the honking car beside me, and slammed on my brakes as I made it to the side of the road where I could see the edge of the bridge. There was nobody else there, since it was not a high traffic time and there was a slight chill in the air.

The scream echoing through the air made my heart stop.

I jumped out of my SUV and ran toward the bridge.

I knew the moment I saw the tableau in front of me, I'd break if I let myself. The picture in front of me would forever haunt my dreams. I would never paint it, never see it on canvas or in any media.

But I would know every shade, every angle, and every moment until the end of my days.

Aria stood in the middle of the bridge, on the other side of the railing, holding on for dear life, as Travis stood behind her, a knife to her throat. There was blood matted in her hair, and some of it on her cheek, and I knew she had to be hurting because she was unsteady.

One slip and she would fall into the river below.

From what I could tell, the river was moving fast enough that it was probably at the right depth that she wouldn't immediately break her neck if she fell. But there was no way I could know that. My blood grew icy, digging into my spine as I moved forward, not knowing what the hell I was going to do. It wasn't as if I could come up from behind Travis at this angle and stop him. Even if I did, one wrong move and he could slice her neck, or pull her down off the bridge.

"Travis. You don't have to do this. Put down the knife. We can just talk." Aria's voice sounded so calm, but I heard the fear beneath it. I didn't know if I wanted Travis to hear that fear.

"You never want to talk. You always tried to lecture me. *'Travis, you're drinking too much. Travis, you need to focus on your art. Travis, why don't you love me?'*"

"I'm sorry. I'm sorry I hurt you. But please, you're scaring me."

"Good. Do you know how hard it was to wait for the perfect time to get into your garage? How long it took for you to finally leave your precious house? And then I had to drag you here until you finally woke up. The only reason you're even standing beside me where you said you would always be is because I have a knife. You're a liar. If you really loved me, if you really cared about me, if you really followed through on any promises, you would've stood by me, doing everything you said you would."

Fear coated my tongue as I moved forward, hoping to hell this was the right decision.

"Let's just talk, Travis. You don't want to do this."

"Stop telling me what to do!" Travis yelled.

"I'm sorry. Just put down the knife. We can stand here. But you need your other hand on the railing, and not on the knife," Aria said calmly.

"Fine. But don't try to pull yourself over the railing. I'll pull you with me. You understand? You go with me just like you always promised you would."

I could see Aria's face pale from here, but she nodded slightly against the knife at her throat. "Okay. I understand."

Travis swallowed hard before he dropped the knife. It fell into the river below, and I tried not to think how far it had to go before it hit the water.

I didn't want that to be Aria.

Nor did I want it to be Travis because as much as I hated the man, I didn't want that. Because Aria would never forgive herself. And I didn't want her to see that.

"Let's talk."

"I'm done talking!" Travis cried out.

"Then talk to me," I blurted, afraid because Travis had just put his hand on Aria's arm.

Travis jerked slightly, and Aria's foot fell off the side of the bridge, and she let out a soft squeak before clinging to the side again, her foot finding purchase.

"What are you doing here?" Travis shouted, his eyes wide.

"I'm just here to talk, Travis. You don't have to do this."

"Yes, I do. Don't you see everything is ruined? Everything I touch turns to ash. It drowns itself in sorrows. I thought Aria understood. But she doesn't. Nobody understands."

Aria faced the bridge, her gaze darting between me and Travis. I saw fear on her face, etched in the lines beside her eyes, the furrowed brows. But there was nothing I could do other than try to talk him down. If he moved too quickly, he could pull her down with him. With the way that he was holding her, unless she kicked out and released his grip for him to fall, she was stuck where she was.

In Travis's hold.

Or beneath the bridge itself.

"I just want it to stop," Travis said, tears streaming down his face. "Why can't it just stop?"

"Let's just get you both to safety and then we can talk it out. Find a way to make it stop." I swallowed hard, one hand outstretched, the other holding the railing as I continued to move toward them. I hadn't bothered getting on the safe side of the bridge, instead walking on the minuscule piece of metal that they were standing on. I wouldn't be able to help Aria if I had to climb over the damn railing as well. Travis hadn't moved with each of my steps, so I kept going, hoping I could reach Aria in time.

"I don't want your help. I just wanted her to do what she promised."

Aria cleared her throat. "I'm here, Travis. Please, let's just talk. I'll do it. All of my promises."

"I don't want to talk anymore," Travis whispered, and everything went in slow motion.

The finality in his tone ripped through me, and I moved quickly, my feet nearly tripping over themselves as I grabbed for Aria.

She had one arm on the railing, the other pulled back as Travis tried to tug her down. She clamped onto his arm, trying to keep him up, even as her feet began to slide off the railing. I angled forward, one hand on the railing next to Aria's, the other wrapping around her hip.

In that moment, Travis met my gaze, eyes wide as he let go of the railing, still holding on to Aria.

"No!" I tugged on Aria, pulling her to me even as she reached for Travis.

But everything happened at once. I pushed Aria into the side of the bridge, her grip firm, but then Travis reached for me. I didn't know if he had second thoughts, or if he wanted me to be hurt right beside him, but he gripped my leg, and I slipped.

The water from the previous night's rain beneath my shoe couldn't keep me steady. I slid back, Travis's weight pulling me down. For some reason the water felt as if it were much farther down than it had been when I had been looking at it.

Or maybe, it all happened in a split second.

Because as Travis hit the water first, I followed right behind, a sharp pain slicing up my arm, and then there was only shadow.

Darkness, and Aria's voice, screaming.

"Crew!"

Chapter Sixteen

Aria

Travis's body hit the water first, and Crew followed him. There was a curse, a shout. And I didn't know if it was them or me. But they sank underneath the water below, and neither one came up.

People were shouting, bystanders making noises I couldn't decipher in my panic, and out of the corner of my eye I thought I saw Noah.

But I couldn't focus on them. I could only focus on the river below.

On the fact that Crew wasn't coming up.

"Crew! Crew!"

I knew I was screaming, and it wasn't helping anything. If he had hit his head, or worse, he wouldn't be able to come up.

"Crew!"

And standing on this bridge screaming for him wouldn't help.

So I did the one thing I could do. Most likely the most idiotic thing I could ever do, and I jumped.

This time it was Noah screaming my name as I jumped into the ice-cold water. The jump wasn't as far as I thought it was going to be, and the impact slammed into my feet then my knees, but thankfully the river was deep enough. Just the day before I had seen people jump in and be perfectly fine. And the river was deeper than it had been yesterday thanks to the rain. I knew the fall wouldn't have killed me, but I was damn lucky I hadn't hit anything beneath the surface. Only I was so fucking terrified that Crew had since he hadn't surfaced yet. I dove down, holding my breath, and reached out for anyone.

My first pass didn't touch anything, just rocks and wood. I was forced to go for breath again, and then dove back under, ignoring the shouts telling me to stop.

I needed to find him.

He needed to be okay.

And just as my lungs screamed and I was ready to try to break the surface, my hand caught on flesh. I didn't know if it was Crew or Travis, but in that moment, I needed to get them above the top of the water. So I pushed on the bottom of the riverbed and pulled whoever it was to the surface.

I sucked in a deep breath as I broke through the water, and looked at Crew, unconscious in my arms.

Tears fell down my cheeks as strangers and my family began to swim toward me. Teeth chattering, I looked around for Travis, but I could only focus on Crew.

Because there was blood on his arm, and he wasn't waking up.

Someone cursed beside me, and I kicked out trying to get closer to the side of the river. "We've got you. Never do that again," Noah spat as he wrapped his arms around me, and Ford and Daisy took Crew from my arms. We swam to the bank, Noah keeping me upright and above the water.

"Is he okay? Is he okay?" I asked through chattering teeth.

"Let's get to the bank," Noah answered without actually answering.

I looked past him and realized that strangers had pulled Travis out of the river, and the man who had tried to kill me and Crew was awake, blood on his fore-head, as he shook in the stranger's arms. I would deal with that later. Travis, the adrenaline, and emotions running in my veins. I'd face it. Face him. But not now.

I just needed Crew to be okay.

We made it to the bank and I couldn't fully track what was happening, my body shaking.

"He's breathing," Daisy said as the authorities came forward, taking over.

And at those words, I leaned into my cousin and burst into the tears I had been holding back since I had woken up in Travis's hold with a knife to my throat.

"He has to be okay," I choked through tears against Noah's chest.

My cousin didn't say anything. Instead he held me close before the paramedics took me away.

And Crew didn't wake up.

* * *

"Should we call his family?" somebody asked but I didn't know who. It was hard to think through the fog as I waited to hear that the person I loved more than anyone in the world would wake up. He had to be okay. He had risked everything to protect me. To save the person who had hurt him countless times. And there was nothing I could do.

"No," Lexington said from my side. He had shown up after I had been admitted into my room, complete with stitches in my forehead, and worried because I had been in the river for long enough it was an issue. I had a few new shots in my arm and they were keeping me warm, watching me in case of infection or shock.

My family was in and out of my room, and I knew others would be doing the same later. All while we waited to hear about Crew. Daisy, Noah, and the others wore scrubs, their hair finally dry, and all looked worse for wear.

"Don't call them," I repeated. "We are his family. *I'm* his family."

Lex squeezed my hand but didn't say anything.

We were waiting for the doctor to tell us when Crew would wake up. Not *if*. I refused to hear that word. It would be *when*.

Sebastian took Lex's place soon after and glared at me. "Never do that again."

I'd already gotten this lecture and while my choices were stupid, I wasn't going to regret them. I didn't want to think about how much longer Crew could have been in the water while we waited for others to wade to the center. I'd made the only choice I could, and I'd do it again. "He could've died. Of course I was going to follow him to make sure I could save him."

"I can't lose my twin. You understand that?"

I swallowed hard, his words hitting hard because I knew it wasn't just because of this moment. "I'm sorry that you're here. In this hospital." This hospital was where everything had changed for him, but he didn't react other than squeezing my hand tightly for a moment, before letting out a breath.

"I'm here because I love you, twin of mine. Stop worrying about me."

"I'm sorry for scaring you. For scaring everyone," I said as I looked over at my parents and my two other siblings.

My mother moved forward and fluffed my pillows. "I'm just happy you're okay. And Crew will be fine soon, and then I'm forcing you both to stay with us for a little while so I can pamper you and put you in bubble wrap."

My lips twitched even as I looked at my mom's watery eyes. "I don't think Crew would like that."

"Crew is going to have to deal with me as his new mom." She held up her hand. "I'm not talking about your relationship. I mean yes, I love you both, but Crew needs a mom and dad right now, and he is stuck with us."

"That gets a little incestuous," Gus mumbled.

"Gus Montgomery," my dad growled.

"I'm just saying."

"I'm not talking literally." My mom shook her head in exasperation. "I'm talking about the fact that I love you, daughter of mine. And I love that man who risked everything for you. So I am going to pamper him and show him exactly what a mother should be. Because I want to have words with that woman who calls herself a mother."

"Your mom is about to curse. Beware," Dad said softly, and I knew he was trying to keep the banter light.

"Fuck off, Alexander Montgomery. My babies are hurt." My mother immediately broke into tears as my father held her and I had to look away for a moment before they broke apart and stood next to my bed.

"I just need to see him." I let out a breath and leaned into my mother's hold.

"We will make that happen," she said so fiercely, that I knew if anybody could make it happen, it would be Tabitha Montgomery.

It took another three hours before I was able to see the man I loved.

I had never seen Crew so still before. Even when he slept, he constantly moved as if to protect me. That was just who he was. He boxed, he drove too quickly around curves, he hiked, painted, ran multimillion dollar businesses, and did countless things to keep busy. But he was never still.

Lex came with me first, because we were his family, and reached out to hold Crew's hand.

"He's not out of the woods yet," the doctor spoke softly. "He has much better chances when he wakes up. We just need him to wake up on his own, because he was underwater for a long time, and the river was just cold enough that hypothermia was an issue. But I have all the faith that he will make a full recovery as long as he wakes up soon."

He continued to say other things, but that ominous warning still echoed throughout my mind after he left.

"I need you to wake up, Crew. I love you so much. I want to see the world with you. I want you to get mad at me when I use the last of the milk and don't put it on the list. I want you to roll your eyes when I mix your socks with mine because I took over your dresser. I want to watch you paint and make the others laugh because you pretend you aren't a pretentious artist like the rest of us. We wasted so much time bickering. Now I'm going to keep yelling at you until you wake up. I love you, Crew. Please. You have to wake up."

Lex, who had returned, let out a sound by my side, but just held my other hand as I looked down at Crew and hoped that the love of my life would wake up.

Because he was my forever.

I wasn't going to take any other option.

Chapter Seventeen

Crew

Loud beeping echoed through the room, and I kept my eyes closed, holding back a moan. It felt as if I were trying to crawl through mud, my body far too heavy, my limbs not doing what I needed them to do.

"Crew. Crew I need you to open your eyes. You're so close. But I need you to open your eyes for me. Please, baby. Open your eyes for me."

I didn't know why Aria sounded so scared. And I wanted to do what she asked. Hell, I would do everything for her. Anything she asked, I was hers. But the thought of opening my eyes felt insurmountable.

Instead I let the quicksand take me under once more, the beeping growing distant, everything feeling far heavier.

The next time the beeping returned, it was slightly louder, a sharp staccato against my temple. Although I didn't know if it was a machine making noise, or the sound of my pulse.

What an odd thing to wonder, considering it felt like something I should know.

"Aria. You need to get some sleep. At least take a shower."

"You might be my twin, but you don't get to physically haul me out of here again."

"I am your twin, and though we don't have that psychic twin thing that people always say we should have, I know you're in pain."

"I always thought it was weird that Dara and Gus got that so-called psychic thing and we didn't."

"They were just messing with us."

"Were they? Maybe. I can't leave his side, Sebastian. What if I leave him, and he's afraid he can't open his eyes again? Because he opened his eyes that one time. I wasn't making it up."

There was a rustle of fabric, the sound of a chair squeaking. "I know you weren't. He's going to wake up."

"They keep telling me it's going to happen. But they also say the longer it takes, the worse it could be. And I don't want it to be worst case scenario. But if it is, I'll be there. Right by his side. I don't want to let him go."

There was a shuddering sigh and another squeak of the chair. "I'm sorry. I know being in this hospital probably isn't the best place for you."

"We already talked about that. I'm always here for you. But you need to shower. You really stink."

I wanted to growl. How dare Sebastian be so mean to Aria when she was clearly not feeling well. But I couldn't get the energy to move. Aria wanted me to open my eyes, and I was going to do it. I just couldn't.

I sank back into the quicksand, but perhaps not as deeply as I had the first time.

The next time sounds echoed through me, it was a deeper voice at my bedside.

"You're really starting to scare us. You're not one for dramatics. But then again, I didn't realize my best friend was going to jump from the bridge. I know you loved that one show from back in the day, but you didn't have to reenact that teenybopper crap. And don't tell me you didn't love it. Because you knew exactly who the characters were when Aria was talking about it with Daisy. So instead of reenacting it, wake up and tell me I'm an idiot. Just wake up, please."

"Did Aria really jump into the river?" I croaked, and immediately regretted saying the words. It felt as if fire licked up my throat, and my parched lips parted.

"Holy hell," Lexington barked before he scrambled up, and I realized my eyes were opened.

The lights were dimmed thankfully, so I didn't feel as if I were being blinded, but from what I could tell, Lexington hadn't slept for shit, and Aria wasn't there. My best friend had dark circles under his eyes, his clothes rumpled. He looked like he had spent hours running his hands through his hair so it stood on end. I could only imagine what I looked like.

"Did she?" I asked, wondering exactly what I was talking about.

Lexington just smiled at me, his eyes filling with tears. "Aria did. Haley was wearing that wedding dress, remember? She would have sunk. But Aria jumped into the damn thing after you. Don't scare me like that again, Crew. I should go to the doctors. The nurses. The National Guard. Hell, the Montgomerys. I will go tell the Montgomerys you are awake, and they will handle it."

I had never seen Lex so discombobulated, that I just lay there, my limbs still too heavy, and tried to get into the present.

"I will be right back."

I tried to reach out for him, but my hand was too slow, and my fingers nearly brushed his skin.

Lex froze before turning to me. "You are going to be

okay, Crew. They're going to explain everything. But Aria is going to kick my ass because I was here, and she wasn't."

"Water?" I rasped.

Lex cursed under his breath before he scrambled to a plastic cup and pitcher next to the bed. That's when I realized I was in a private hospital room, with oxygen filling my nostrils and an IV in one arm. There was a pulse ox meter on my finger, and probably a dozen other things that I couldn't quite figure out. There were also flowers, a couple of bags, a makeshift bed on the couch underneath the window, and photos that had to be from Aria. Still a little dizzy, I couldn't quite make them out, but I knew I would one day trace my fingers over all of them. Because those were Aria's. What she saw. What she wanted me to see.

Below them were hand drawn colorful pictures I knew had to have come from the kids. All of the Montgomery children who were starting to multiply.

My damn family had left their mark on this room, and I had no idea how long I had been here. I didn't even know if my blood family had visited me. But they didn't matter.

It had taken me a long time to realize that—almost too long—but in the end, my family was here. Including the man who was practically my brother in a twisted way. Lex stood over me, plastic cup of water in his hand.

"It hasn't been that long, really. We just threw the photos and things up an hour ago or so because we needed something to do with our hands. Okay, I'm going to get you some more water, and then I'm going to get the others. Because if I don't, I'm going to have to deal with all of the Montgomerys. And they may be my family, but I'm frightened of them."

A tear fell down his cheek, and I smiled before nearly dropping the cup. Lex took it away from me and shook his head.

"I think I saw in one of those TV shows if you have too much you could throw it up. I'm not sure. This is why I need a professional."

"Who the hell are you talking to?" Sebastian asked as he walked into the room. He froze as he looked down at me, before a wide smile covered his face, and he clicked his tongue ring against his teeth. "Well damn. You're a sight for sore eyes. I'm going to go get my sister before she escapes our parents' clutches. They're trying to feed her right now after we hosed her down in the shower that the hospital let us borrow after she checked out. That girl would not leave your side. Not that I blame her. If Raven was the one in that bed, hell, I would have done the same." Sebastian shuddered, and I knew exactly what he was thinking of. Marley. The woman that he had loved and who had died in child-birth. No wonder Aria had been so worried about Sebastian being there. Aria's twin tilted his head. "So, you were awake for that."

I hadn't even realized I'd said that out loud. I clearly wasn't all here yet. I shook my head and immediately regretted the action. "Not really. But I thought I heard voices."

"Those are always the best voices to hear," Lex rambled. "I am so fucking glad you're awake. Don't scare us again."

"I'll try not to."

Sebastian left then, Lex following him, and before I could wonder why they left me alone, the room was filled with nurses, staff, and people I assumed were doctors. They shined bright lights in my eyes, took readings, and asked how I felt.

I thought I answered, I couldn't quite remember or care. All that mattered was the woman who finally walked through the doorway, her wet hair pulled from her face, wearing clothes I knew her mother or another family member had brought for her from home.

She was so pale, her face clear of makeup. She was the most beautiful person I'd ever seen.

"Hey, baby," I said softly.

"If you ever think about jumping near that bridge again, or being somewhere where you can trip near it, I'm going to do something like burn down your house. Don't make me an arsonist."

I chuckled roughly, and then reached up to grip my side, the pain shocking me.

"Okay, now that you're really listening, let's go over exactly what happened," the doctor said. And then Aria was by my side, holding my hand, as a couple other Montgomerys stood in the corner, and I listened to the doctor explain what had gone on.

"You've been unconscious for the past two days."

"Two?"

"Two of the longest days of my life," Aria muttered.

I pulled her closer, trying to get her into bed with me. However, she wouldn't budge, and I was pretty sure the nurses weren't going to allow it. At least for now. I was going to get what I wanted soon.

"Yes, two days. You were underwater for long enough that we were worried about brain damage. However, from what we can tell all looks good. We are going to keep you a few more days to monitor you, and we're going to want you to come back to do more tests, but you should recover completely. You did break one rib, and bruise three more. You also have eighteen stitches on your arm from where you sliced it as you fell.

However, Ms. Montgomery here got you out of the water in time."

I glared at the woman I loved more than anything. "I can't believe you jumped in after me. What the hell were you thinking?"

"See, this is exactly how I thought things would go," Lex whispered.

"Can we have some privacy, please?" Aria asked as she lifted her chin, glaring at me.

"We will be back soon for more tests, but yes, let's clear the room so Mr. McTavish can rest."

I didn't know exactly who said that, and I didn't care at the moment. Because all I had eyes for was Aria. And I was damn angry.

"You could have died."

"Excuse me? That's where you're going? You fell off the bridge and were bleeding and you didn't come back up. Of course I was going to go in after you." Her whole body shuddered, and I sucked in a breath as I leaned over, shivering slightly.

"Get in bed."

"I'm going to hurt you. You have a broken rib."

"It's going to be broken no matter what. You can't fix that. I've done it before, remember?" I met her gaze, and I knew she remembered exactly what happened. When my mother had pushed me down the stairs when I had been a teenager, I had broken ribs then. Then again when I was rock climbing with Lex and had tripped. This wasn't my first time around a broken rib. "Get in bed with me. I need to feel you by my side."

With that, she let out a breath and carefully slid onto the hospital bed next to me. It was a tight fit since I wasn't a small man and it hurt to move, but that just meant I could feel her warmth completely.

"I am still so fucking pissed off you jumped after me."

"You think you were angry? You fell off a bridge saving my life and trying to make sure Travis didn't truly hurt himself. After all he did, you still tried to talk him down."

I pushed her hair from her face, the strand that had fallen from her ponytail, and finally asked what I hadn't. What I had been avoiding.

"Did Travis make it?"

Her eyes went dark, a solemn expression covering her face. "Yes. The other bystanders were able to get him. I don't know what's going to happen to him. What charges still need to be made. But right now he's on an involuntary hold, and hopefully he'll get some help. I'm so sorry I didn't walk away. That I didn't push him out of my life completely. You could've died."

"Fuck that."

Her eyes widened. "Crew."

"Fuck that. If you had iced him out completely and blocked his number, he still would've found a way to you. I was wrong. You are the kindest person I know, and you still held your space. You kept people that you loved safe. This is Travis. As much as I hate the fact, I have to say that. Because I know he's hurting. But I'm fucking angry with him right now so I'm going to remain angry for a little while longer. Yet I also feel sorry for him. Something is wrong with him. Something that we can't fix. But hopefully he figures it out. I'm just glad that he's still alive. Because if he would've died..." I let my voice trail off, knowing I didn't have any good way to finish that sentence.

I didn't know what I would feel in the future toward Travis. But in those last moments, he had looked so scared, and I was never going to get that out of my mind. I would forever picture the absolute terror in his eyes. So yes, he did some horrible things, and he had a long way to go, but I think he had enough to deal with without my anger in his face.

"He'll be okay. I have to believe that. But I'm honestly just so happy that you're going to be okay. I never want to even think about that again, although I know that it's going to be on constant rotation in my dreams."

"Same here." I cupped her face, my thumb sliding over her bottom lip. "I love you. I love you so damn much. And sometimes it's hard to imagine where we were all those months ago."

"I can't believe we tried to hide this. It turns out a few more people than we thought knew what we felt for each other before we did."

My lips twitched as I continued to study her face. Her face would've been the last thing I had seen if I hadn't made it to the top of the water. And while part of me knew that would've been a blessing, not having the years in front of us would've been the opposite.

"I wasn't very good about hiding that it seems."

"You do growl."

"I'm going to continue to do so. Just making sure you understand that."

She smiled then, and it finally reached her eyes. "I would love that as a promise." And then she leaned forward, brushing her lips against mine. "Now, you have a hundred Montgomerys and adjacent waiting for you. Would you like the sign in sheet now?"

I grinned, leaning back on my pillow as Aria snuggled into my un-bruised side. "I take it my mother is not one of them."

She stiffened, but I squeezed her shoulders.

"I'm not upset about. She would have made a scene.

I have my family here. It just took me a little too long to realize that."

"That's good. Because we're never letting you go."

"Deal."

One month later

"Should you really be lifting that?"

I resisted the urge to glare at the woman that I loved as I shifted the airtight container toward Lexington. My best friend took it from my hands and pressed his lips together so he wouldn't laugh.

"I see that laughter, Lexington Montgomery," Aria snapped.

"I'm sorry for trying to hide it. But seriously, the container is empty. He's fine." Lex shook his head, his shoulders shaking with laughter, before leaving me alone with Aria.

"Baby, I'm okay. It's been a month. And I'm not lifting anything really."

"You just tossed Nora on your back as you ran around the backyard and pretended you were her pony."

"And it didn't hurt me." Much. "She's your niece.

And she has had me wrapped around her little finger since she was an infant."

"That is true," Aria said with a smile. "Honestly, she's had all of us wrapped around her finger. I mean, the rest of the cousins as well, but Nora? It's like she realizes because her dad is my twin, our shared DNA means that I will drop everything for her."

"I think you would do that even if you weren't Sebastian's twin. And that little girl doesn't take advantage of it. She's just too damn nice."

"Seriously. My brother is so lucky."

She smiled wide and leaned forward, brushing my lips with hers. "You know, kids really scare me. I have never said that out loud before."

Aria's eyes widened, before she threw her head back and laughed. "Same. I love being an aunt. And with how many cousins are starting to go in that direction, it's going to be an endless number of babies for us to be aunts and uncles too. But I'm terrified of children of my own. I hope that's okay. I mean, we haven't had this talk though maybe we should at some point."

She was speaking so rapidly, I couldn't help but stop her ramble with my mouth. I deepened the kiss as she moaned into me, ignoring the way that her brothers flipped me off.

"Let's just have time for ourselves, okay? It took us long enough to get here. I'm not in any rush."

"Good. Because we have the world to travel. I mean, some duke wants your painting. You're kind of a big deal."

"I am. But that's also what you told my dick last night," I whispered.

"Oh my God, I heard that. Please stop," Jamie, another one of the Montgomerys said as she rushed past.

I just laughed and wrapped my arm around Aria as I looked throughout the large yard where we were having a Montgomery barbecue. Because of course we were. It was a day that ended in y, so there needed to be food, drinks, and extra cheese when the Montgomerys created a crowd.

This time it was for Colin's birthday, so I leaned back against the pillar, Aria in my arms, as we watched everybody set up food, drinks, and all of the materials that went with that over a few tables. There was even a table just for cheese. Yes, it was a small table, and yes, the family leaned into it, but I was pretty sure this particular one was to test to see if the person Colin was currently dating could handle the Montgomerys en masse. They were a rowdy bunch. Loyal to a fault. And I counted myself lucky for being adopted into them so many years ago. And for the moments I needed to steal one for my own.

Not that I would put it like that to Aria's father.

I did value my future after all.

"So, what do you say? I know we have to go to Berlin for your show, but I've always wanted to go to Florence. I know they're not side by side, or in the same country, but pretty sure it's easier to drive between the two than it is for us to drive down and meet the other cousins in Texas."

"I think the math holds up on that. And it sounds amazing. I've never been."

Her eyes widened. "What? I thought you had."

"I've never been outside the US. I travel all over the country, but it never really appealed to me to leave."

"How did I not know that?" she asked, her eyes wide.

I shrugged. "Lex and I were planning, and then that opening at his internship started early, so plans fell through. And I don't want to go alone."

"Well, you're stuck with me then. Because I want to see the world. And I just happen to be dating a Sugar Daddy."

"I can't wait to see the world through your eyes. And your lens. And I can't wait for your payment for this trip of ours." My thumb brushed the underside of her breast, and she rolled her eyes before kissing me hard on the mouth.

"Well then, I'll start working on our savings tonight. Promise. Now, let's go party with the Montgomerys. Because I'm pretty sure you are fully assimilated now."

"I'm just glad that I accidentally bumped into Lexington that one day."

"If that was an accident, does that mean you accidentally fell in love with me?" she asked, fluttering her eyelashes.

"Of course. Who would want to fall in love with a woman connected to such an insanely large family on purpose? I mean, you are a lot of work."

She rolled her eyes at me, before taking me toward the cheese station, the others all laughing and playing games and living their lives.

Because, indeed, I hadn't meant to fall for Aria Montgomery. I had always known it would be a mistake. That I would end up heartbroken or left behind.

And I was so glad to be wrong. I hadn't expected forever, but it turned out when you asked for what you wanted, and took it from fate, sometimes fate let you keep the girl you promised never to fall for.

And I was keeping Aria Montgomery.

Chapter Eighteen

Lexington

2 Years Ago

"I can't believe I'm getting married tomorrow."

I leaned back in my seat, one leg propped on the chair beside me, my arm draped over the back of it, and raised my brow at Justin. The man had said that a few times over the past couple of hours and while it should bother me, it didn't. I had been through enough family weddings to know that nerves were *always* an issue. Even if they pretended they weren't.

Of course, this wasn't a Montgomery wedding. Meaning there was a distinct lack of cheese and dairy jokes at this rehearsal dinner. However, I wasn't about to complain to Nina, the wedding planner who had been running from one side of the room to the other all night.

I didn't know how the woman did that in stilettos that seemed to be so tiny they could break at any moment. That's why I stood clear of heels.

There had been that one time at the family barbecue when we had needed some way to pass the time during a random obstacle course. My mom had laughed at all of us, though we had broken two of her shoes. Dad ended up getting her the fancy red soled ones as an apology, considering it was his idea.

"Why are you smiling like that?" Justin asked, pulling me out of my thoughts.

I sipped my whiskey and shrugged. "I was just thinking about a family story. Nothing important."

"I don't know how you can even think with so many family members around you all the time. I'm an only kid. And sometimes even my parents are too much."

My lips quirked. Not everybody understood our family. My father had five brothers, and my mother had six. My mother also had four male cousins on one side, and a few others on the other side, while my dad had sixteen cousins, plus the countless people who had married in or just became family versus friends.

That meant my family was slightly boisterous. In fact, compared to the rest of my cousins, my brother and I had the most members. It was a little ridiculous.

"You do realize I only have one sibling, right? Silas and I were rather quiet."

Justin snorted before downing the rest of his scotch. He tapped the bar with two fingers, and the bartender poured another shot.

I was a little worried how much he was drinking the night before his wedding, but I knew Justin could hold his liquor. Plus he was staying at my house, so I would make sure he had enough water and caffeine to get through the evening.

Justin scoffed. "You say that, but you hang out with your cousins more than any other person I know. It's nice, but it's a lot."

"True. It can be a lot. But you're not marrying me. So you don't need to know everybody's name."

Justin narrowed his gaze at me. "Does Gia hate your family?"

I winced. "No. But she's an only child like you and didn't really understand family dinners."

In fact, Gia nearly ran in the other direction when the loud and boisterous Montgomerys and Wilders had showed up. It wasn't as if my family circled her and tried to induct her into a cult. They just wanted to get to know her.

I drained the rest of my glass, not really in the mood to talk about that memory.

"She'll get used to my family." I hoped. "But this is your wedding. Let's not talk about my girlfriend." Who wasn't even coming to the wedding since she had another event. I'd have thought she'd want to come to this one because there wouldn't be any of my family here, but I'd been wrong. And that was probably not a healthy way to think considering I loved my family and liked spending time with them.

"Yes. Because I'm getting married tomorrow. To Mercy." He gave me that faraway look, and I just smiled at the man.

"You are. And we just finished your lovely rehearsal dinner. Let's get back to my place so that we can sleep this off, and make sure you have your vows written."

Justin's eyes widened. "Shit. Was I supposed to write those?"

I froze, blinking at my friend. "What?"

"Kidding. You know Mercy, like she'd ever let me not have my vows perfectly done."

I studied his face, wondering where that tone came from, but smiled as Mercy, the bride herself, walked forward.

Her long dark blonde hair was piled up in a weird bun thing, and she'd painted her lips bright red. She had on a dark gray dress that matched the bridesmaids in some form of theme, and I lifted my water glass in a toast.

"Hello there, Bride."

She rolled her eyes at me. "Oh, Lexington. Are you getting my betrothed in trouble?" She wrapped her arm around Justin's shoulder, and he leaned against her. The two looked so comfortable with each other, completely in love. And I was only a little jealous. Not of either one of them, but the fact that they'd found someone. Much like many of my cousins had. Maybe Gia would be the one. It could happen.

Maybe.

"I thought you were heading out?" Justin asked, as he set down his empty glass.

"I am. I just wanted to say goodbye." She looked over at me and winked. "Cover your eyes, Lexington. There's about to be PDA."

I laughed, and then jokingly covered my eyes.

There was a wet sound, and a little bit of moaning, and I groaned. "Are you two serious right now?"

Mercy threw her head back and laughed. "Okay, take this man home. Get him sobered up. We have a wedding to attend."

"You got it. Where's your ride?" I asked, looking around the emptying rehearsal hall.

Another woman with dark brown hair and pink colored lips came walking forward and stood at my side. Emily grinned before wiping her forehead with her arm. She'd been tired all day but I knew she worked long hours. "Don't worry. I got her. I mean, my twin sister is getting married tomorrow. We have to do our ritual."

"Do I want to know what this ritual is?" Justin asked with a snort.

"Is it a sexy ritual?" I teased, wiggling my brows.

Emily gagged, while Mercy just beamed. "You know it. I might be getting married tomorrow, but we do have to throw some herbs into a cauldron and dance around naked."

"Well, why can't we come to that?" I asked, as I stood up to hug both of them goodbye. "I got this one, you guys take care of yourselves. We have to be here at eleven tomorrow, right?"

The twins laughed, but Nina came running up, panic etched on her features. "That's when the wedding begins. I thought we went over the schedule today."

I held up both hands, feeling bad that the frazzled wedding planner had overheard me joking. "I'm just teasing them. We had everything written down. You're doing great, Nina."

"Thank you, now everybody go get some sleep. We

do not want dark circles tomorrow." She squeezed everybody's hands tightly, before running back to do something else.

"She scares me," I whispered.

"One of our friends used her before. I kind of wish we would have used Claire, your friend, since Nina stresses lots, but my mother loved her. So this is where we are."

"I will mention that to Claire," I teased.

"Good, because one day I will get married, and I will need someone who doesn't stress me out," Emily whispered.

We laughed, parted ways, and I dragged the groom back to my place. The night went off without a hitch, with Justin passed out in my guestroom, and me alone in bed while I went through what seemed like a thousand emails on my phone for the business, and the constant group chats for the family.

I muted them often because there were so many. With dozens of cousins, let alone friends and other family, subgroup chats and big group chats were always there. And yet, nobody cared if we went on mute. Yes, we were always in each other's business, but it was because we loved each other. We were *needy*, as my other girlfriend Carly had once said. I shook my head, pushing her out of my mind before I plugged in my phone and went to sleep.

The alarm came far too early the next morning, but I rolled out of bed with a pep in my step. Justin and I had coffee, ate breakfast, and then headed out to meet the groomsmen. Today was going to be a big day, and Justin looked nervous as hell.

"Are you doing okay?" I asked as we got ready in the groom's suite.

Justin's hands shook as he tried to tie his tie but nodded. "Is it wrong that I just want to get this over with?"

"No, because that means you get to the wedding night," one of other groomsmen said with a sneer, and I glared at the other man.

Before I could say anything though, Nina was there to tie Justin's tie for him, and then she patted his chest. "You've got this."

"I do. Thanks, Nina." Justin smiled at her, before the wedding planner turned to all of us and held up both hands. "You look amazing, let's get this done." Then she clapped her hands twice and led us out.

The place was all done up in golds and grays, which I wouldn't have thought would look nice together, but somehow it was classy and soft at the same time. I stood up next to Justin, rings in my pocket, and went through exactly what I was supposed to do thanks to the rehearsals. My job was easy. I got to see one of my good friends get married to one of my childhood friends. I couldn't ask for better.

Bridesmaids made their way down the aisle, with Emily last as the maid of honor. She winked at me, and I did the same to her, trying not to smirk.

And then Mercy was there, no veil because she would never hide her face, and she grinned over at Justin. She walked herself down the aisle, because of course she did, and I knew she was holding herself back from running.

Justin's hands were shaking as he reached out for Mercy.

"Are you ready?" she asked, all smiles.

Justin nodded in answer, and then the two of them were standing at the altar.

"Friends and family, we are here to celebrate the love and promise of two wonderful individuals," the man began.

"Wait," Justin called out.

I froze as Mercy blinked up at the man she loved, and Emily went pale, the color draining from her face.

"Is something wrong?" Mercy asked, her voice soft, tentative.

"I can't do this."

There were gasps and murmurs in the pews, and I tugged at Justin's shoulder. "Is this really the time?" I bit out.

"Now or never." Justin shook his head, pushed off my grip, and looked at Mercy. "I'm sorry. I'll explain later." And then he looked toward the back of the long room and tugged at his tie.

"Nina. I can't do this anymore."

And then the wedding planner burst into tears as the groom ran from his bride down the aisle. As the two left, the silence was so thick you could cut it with a knife. And I felt as though I was having an out of body experience.

"Mercy," I whispered as I looked over at her.

But she just shook her head at me. "Did you know?"

"No!" I practically shouted. "Shit. Let's get you out of here."

"Mercy?" a soft voice said from behind her, and we both looked to see Emily staggering toward us. Alarmed, I nearly cursed again at the gray pallor of her skin.

I was moving toward her without even thinking, arms outstretched. Because there was blood seeping from her nose, and when she coughed, blood sprayed over the white of Mercy's dress.

"Emily!" Mercy cried out.

And as I caught Emily in my arms, taking her to the ground, the bride knelt beside me. We shouted for an ambulance, and people started screaming, pulling out their phones to call for someone or to record because that's what people did.

But it was all I could do to hold the mirrored copy of the bride in my arms, as tears slid down Mercy's cheeks.

All thoughts of a runaway groom and broken promises gone.

And I knew the nightmare was only just beginning.

Next in the Montgomery Ink Legacy series: Lexington is finally gets his turn in Last Chance Seduction.

IF YOU'D LIKE TO READ A BONUS SCENE: CHECK OUT THIS SPECIAL EPILOGUE!

Want more Montgomerys? Start the Montgomery Ink Legacy series with: Leif and Brooke in Bittersweet Promises.

Want to read Alex and Tabby's heartbreaking romance? Check out Ink Exposed!

And to read another romance between two fiery characters check out The Forever Rule!

And if you want to see what's going on with Livvy and why I needed to write her story, read Always a Fake Bridesmaid!

Bonus Epilogue

Crew

"When you said we were going on a nice vacation on the ocean, I thought you meant a boat rental or even a surprise cruise. Not a freaking yacht you *own*."

I pulled my attention from the tan of Aria's shoulders and did my best not to reach out to pull down the straps of her sundress. Truly, her skin begged for my lips at this moment, and it had been at least a good hour since I'd been balls deep inside her. That was far too long.

"Crew. Eyes off my boobs and on my face, please."

I blinked and forced my gaze off her tits since, yes, I had been staring at the way her nipples pressed against her dress. "Huh?"

Aria rolled her eyes at me before going to her tiptoes and kissing my chin. "Perv."

"Your perv." I shrugged as I said it before leaning down to brush my lips along hers. "And it's not my yacht. We're borrowing it. And before you call me a rich boy, in order to borrow it, you not only have to pay for the time, but you have to donate to a local charity."

"I'm sorry that you're 'borrowing' a yacht. I'm sure one day you'll be all grown up and get your own."

I pinched her side and laughed as she wiggled into my hold. "Brat. And no, I don't need to own a yacht since we live in a freaking land-locked state. In case you forgot."

"Of course I haven't forgotten. We live in the best state in the world. I mean...have you *seen* the Rocky Mountains?"

I blinked. "I might have. They're the sharp pointy things that don't actually look real in the distance, right? But you always know where west is when you're driving in Denver."

"I think that sounds right. But, Crew? I did not expect this."

"We were going for expecting the unexpected. I don't own a boat, though I thought about it for the week. However, I like going hiking with you more. If this boat thing isn't for you, we can find something else."

I'd do anything for her, and I hoped she knew that by now.

"I love it, Crew, but I'm just saying. I love you. And I'm having the best time, but this is so not you."

I shrugged, knowing she was right. "You do realize that the family trust owns the private plane that got us here, right?"

"I do. And while I'm forever grateful that now we are part of the mile high club, I still don't understand how this is us."

I took a seat on one of the long comfort benches on the top portion of the yacht and pulled her into my lap. "It's not us. We're doing something ridiculous because we can, and because it's about time we got away from the one thousand Montgomerys that are watching my every move. I mean seriously, they won't stop asking when the wedding is."

"They only ask because they know they're not actually pressing. We can get married whenever we want, or we could just not get married at all. I mean, it's whatever we feel like. We don't have to be traditional."

I heard the hesitancy in her tone, and I knew she was thinking along the same lines as I did. I would propose when it was time. When I knew Aria was ready for a big wedding and all the trimmings. Hell, she was on the damn yacht with me. She was going to get everything she deserved and more.

She shook her head, leaned forward, and kissed me softly. "I love you."

"I love you too. I'm never going to get tired of saying that."

"Me either. Which is weird because it feels as if I've loved you for all of my life. Which would've been pretty weird when you were dating my cousin."

I let out a groan. "You're never going to let me off the hook with that, are you?"

"Of course not. I mean, we made you sing the *Frozen* song so you could be your own Disney Prince at our last karaoke night. You did amazing."

"I am no Jonathan Groff. Though, 'Lost in the Woods' is pretty catchy."

"I knew you wanted your boy band ballad."

"If you keep teasing me, I'm going to put you over my knee."

Her breath caught slightly, and as she stood between my legs, I slid my fingers along her upper thigh, below her dress, and around her hips.

I paused in the action, narrowing my gaze. "Are you not wearing panties on this boat?"

"I'm not wearing any underwear under this dress. I

mean, if I were to stand in front of that sunset light bar, you'd be able to see everything."

I growled. "And so would everyone else on this yacht."

She kissed my jaw again, and I pulled her onto my lap once more.

"Tease."

I crushed my mouth to hers, as I slid my fingers between her legs, loving the fact that she was already wet for me. She panted into my mouth, my fingers working in and out of her, my thumb on her clit. And when she perched in my hold, moaning my name, I couldn't help but stare down at the woman that I love, coming so beautifully.

"Crew," she breathed.

I slid my fingers out of her, and then sucked them clean, my gaze on her. "Well, you come on a boat, a plane, I guess I'm going to need a train next. Maybe an air balloon after that."

"Are we writing our own travel book now?"

"If that's what you want." I kissed her again, lingering as I took her in. She was so damn beautiful that sometimes it was hard to breathe.

And hell, I never thought I'd be that guy to sit here and make those statements. I didn't think in poetry. I was an asshole who fought in my gym, boxed when I felt like it, painted when the mood hit, let the art flow through me when I could get it to work, and tried to just be me.

I didn't sing Disney songs and wax lyrical poetry about the woman I loved.

But here I was.

Maybe there was a reason I was so damn nervous tonight. Then again, sometimes Aria just made me nervous. She could be my calm in the storm and my hurricane all at once.

Aria slid off my lap, a little wobbly on her heels since I knew her knees had to be at least a little weak, and leaned over for her camera.

I reached out and slid my hand over her hip to keep her steady. She looked over her shoulder and winked at me before standing straight and turning toward me, camera in hand.

"How many photos are you going to take of me on this trip? I thought you didn't do portraits."

I said the words for a reason and I was grateful when she answered in that vein.

"I only avoided portraits for so long because they were Dad's first. But I always want to take photos of you." A click of a shutter. "Makes me feel like a stalker."

I leaned back on the love seat as the sun began to set

and put my hands behind my head. "Snap away. But I'll require payment."

She rolled her eyes behind the lens. "Like you didn't already do that earlier. I'm still walking a bit sore from our christening of this boat."

My dick hardened at the memory of her bent over in front of me, my cock sliding in between the swollen folds of her pussy as I worked the vibrator in and out of her ass. She was so damn beautiful and I couldn't help but want her each and every day. It was hard to concentrate when she was around, but then again, I never wanted her to go.

"And we're not even finished yet."

Her teeth bit into her delectable lip and I reached down to adjust myself. Her gaze caught the motion and she snapped another photo.

Snorting, I reached for her. "Oh no. I'm not going to model for those kinds of photos. Your family already knows *way* too much about our sex life."

She rolled her eyes but kept snapping photos—though not just of me. As we slowly made our way down the coast, she continued to take in the scenery, the camera a connection to the view in a way I could appreciate. As it was, I knew I'd paint this.

A camera in her hand, the backdrop of the sun, and the water surrounding us. Wind in her hair and a *very* satisfied smile on her face. Like her, I didn't always include people in my art, but she was mine no matter what. And I couldn't help but want her on canvas.

"You tell Lex everything. I tell the girls everything. But no, I won't be taking any naked photos of you. Those images are all for me." She looked over her shoulder and narrowed her gaze. "And you better not paint me naked."

"And if I do?" I asked, brow raised.

"Then I get to do an entire black and white study of your form. Every. Inch." She gave a pointed look to my tented pants and I barked out a laugh.

"Deal. Plus, your body is mine." A slow blink. "And yours of course. You know what I mean."

"As long as you're mine."

"Equality in our dual ownership. I don't mind." I swallowed hard, knowing it was nearly time. And yet I couldn't help but be nervous. Things with Aria never worked out the way one thought they would so I had to wing it most days. But that was Aria—my chaos.

She beamed at me before leaning down once again to put her camera in her bag. She rustled around inside for a bit as I swallowed hard, knowing I was running out of time to make this right. I sat up, looking around the deck to see if doing this right now would be the best place, but when I looked forward, I froze.

Aria, my sweet, fucking sexy, fucking unpredictable Aria knelt on one knee in front of me, her eyes watery, and a bright smile on her face.

"What the fuck are you doing?" I snapped, then realized me yelling at her right now probably wasn't the best thing.

She merely rolled her eyes at my tone, her smile widening. "I'm doing something that will annoy you to no end but will bring me immense joy."

"You can't propose to me," I blurted.

Instead of looking as if I'd slapped her—because that's how I thought it sounded in that moment—she shook her head. "I love you, asshole. I love you more with each passing day. I think I loved you when the two of us bickered over coffee while I was waiting on Leif to finish his client so I could get my tattoo. You remember the day? It was right after you and Daisy broke up and you were all surly and angry but you bought me a muffin because I was scared and you made me laugh. I knew I shouldn't want you that day but I totally fell for you. And I want to fall for you for all the rest of my days. I also know that you probably wanted to do this yourself, but I'm going to be the terrible person and do it first."

"Aria. You are...I have no words."

"Well, you better find words for our vows because I *really* hope you say yes in a moment when I finish the longest proposal ever. Plus my knee is starting to hurt so I have no idea how guys do this."

I shook my head, laughing as I knelt down in front of her and brought her closer so she was forced to kneel on *both* knees, but still be in my arms. "You're taking my moment, Montgomery."

"This is *our* moment, so get over it, hopefully-soon-to-be-Montgomery. Marry me, Crew. Let me make you a Montgomery so you can be the prince and I'll be the princess and we can fight and make up and figure out this thing called life together. I want to be your wife. I want to claim you and be all alpha and I don't care who knows. But I want to wear your ring and your ink and your everything. And I want you to do the same. So let me be possessive and marry me."

Tears streamed down her face and I just knelt there, throat tight as I wiped them away with my thumbs. "You are the most perfect crazy person I have ever known."

"The romance, Crew. The romance with you is bursting right now," she said through her laughter.

I looked down between us at the black wedding band she held and let out a sigh. "Yes, Aria Montgomery. I'll marry you. But only if you do one thing."

She blinked at me, her smile falling. "If it's that I take your name, sure. But you get to take mine too. Sorry, but you wanted to marry a Montgomery so that means you get the name. You know the rules. Plus, you love us. You're already part of the cult."

A rough chuckle escaped my lips as I kissed her softly. "Crew Montgomery has a nice ring to it. I'll take it. But...you have to do this." I reached into my pocket and pulled out the jewelry box. Her eyes widened and I couldn't help but keep laughing. "You are the queen of the unexpected so I should have known you'd make this the best most unpredictable day of my fucking life. Wear my ring, Aria. Let's make it full circle. Because I love you so much it hurts to breathe. I want to see the world with you. I love seeing it through your eyes— through the lens and on canvas. I just want to be with you. Your family is a bonus, but I'd take you without them. Know that. I'd take every bit of you in any way I can. Marry me as I marry you. Let's be the most ridiculous end of a Disney movie yet."

And while she didn't say yes—as her mouth was too busy with mine—she did wear my ring. Just as I wore hers.

This was the woman I had accidentally fallen for— the woman I would love until the end of my days. And I knew there could be no other ending than this.

"My Montgomery," I whispered.

"I knew you'd catch one of us at some point," she teased.

And I kissed her again, claiming her as she claimed me—and there was nothing else I could ask for.

Next in the Montgomery Ink Legacy series: Lexington is finally gets his turn in Last Chance Seduction.

Want more Montgomerys? Start the Montgomery Ink Legacy series with: Leif and Brooke in Bittersweet Promises.

Want to read Alex and Tabby's heartbreaking romance? Check out Ink Exposed!

And to read another romance between two fiery characters check out The Forever Rule!

And if you want to see what's going on with Livvy and why I needed to write her story, read Always a Fake Bridesmaid!

A Note from Carrie Ann Ryan

Thank you so much for reading **Accidentally Forever.**

I loved, loved this book. I also fought this book. I knew Aria's romance wasn't going to be easy, but I hadn't realized Crew would be the one to break my heart.

I never meant to write this book to be honest. Aria was for the next Montgomery Ink series. (Spoilers!). But I needed tow rite her romance.

And now this might be my favorite of the series so far.

And Lexington? OOF. Just you wait. Last Chance Seduction will be...well...just you see.

Loved Aria and Crew and their dynamic? Read the first chapter of this second chance, small town, contemporary suspense romance: **The Forever Rule.**

The Montgomery Ink Legacy Series:

Next in the Montgomery Ink Legacy series: Lexington is finally gets his turn in Last Chance Seduction.

IF YOU'D LIKE TO READ A BONUS SCENE: CHECK OUT THIS SPECIAL EPILOGUE!

If you want to make sure you know what's coming next from me, you can sign up for my newsletter at www. CarrieAnnRyan.com; follow me on twitter at @CarrieAnnRyan, or like my Facebook page. I also have a Facebook Fan Club where we have trivia, chats, and other goodies. You guys are the reason I get to do what I do and I thank you.

Make sure you're signed up for my MAILING LIST so you can know when the next releases are available as well as find giveaways and FREE READS.

Happy Reading!

The Forever Rule: Chapter 1
Aston

The Cages are the most prestigious family in Denver—at least according to the patriarch of the Cage Family.
And the Cages have rules.
Rules only they know.

I always knew that one day my father would die. I hadn't realized that day would come so soon. Or that the last words I would say to him would've been in anger.

I had been having one of the best nights of my life, a beautiful woman in my arms, and a smile on my face when I received the phone call that had changed my family's life.

The fact that I had been smiling had been a shock,

because according to my brothers, I didn't smile much. I was far too busy being *The Cage* of Cage Enterprises.

We were a dominant force in the city of Denver when it came to certain real estate ventures, as well as being one of the only ethical and environmentally friendly ones who tried to keep up with that. We had our hands in countless different pots around the world, but mostly we gravitated in the state of Colorado—our home.

I had not created the company, no, that honor had gone to my grandfather, and then my father. The Cage Enterprises were and would always be a family endeavor. And when my father had stepped away a few years ago, stating he had wanted to see the world, and also see if his sons could actually take up the mantle, I had stepped in—not that the man believed we could.

My brothers were in various roles within the company, at least those who had wanted to be part of it. But I was the face of Cage Enterprises.

So no, I hadn't smiled often. There wasn't time. We weren't billionaires with mega yachts. We worked seventy-hour weeks to make sure *all* our employees had a livable wage while wining and dining with those who looked down at us for not being on their level. And others thought we were the high and mighty anyway since they didn't understand us. So, I didn't smile.

But I had smiled that night.

It had been a gala for some charity, one I couldn't even remember off the top of my head. We had donated between the company and my own finances—we always did. But I couldn't even remember anything about why we were there.

Yet I could remember her smile. The heat in her eyes when she had looked up at me, the feel of her body pressed against mine as we had danced along the dance floor, and then when we ended up in the hallway, bodies pressed against one another, needing each other, wanting each other.

And I had put aside all my usual concepts of business and life to have this woman in my arms.

And then my mother had called and had shattered that illusion.

"Your father is dead."

She hadn't even braced me for the blow. A heart attack on a vacation on a beach in Majorca, and he was dead. She hadn't cried, hadn't said anything, just told me that I had to be the one to tell my brothers.

And so, I had, all six of them. Because of course Loren Cage would have seven sons. He couldn't do things just once, he had to make sure he left his legacy, his destiny.

And that was why we were here today, in a high-rise

in Centennial, waiting on my father's lawyer to show up with the reading of the will.

"Hey, when is Winstone going to get here?" Dorian asked, his typical high energy playing on his face, and how he tapped his fingers along the hand-carved wooden table.

I stared at my brother, at those piercing blue eyes that matched my own, and frowned. He should be here soon. He did call us all here after all."

"I still don't know why we all had to be here for the reading of the will," Hudson whispered as he stared off into the distance. Neither Dorian nor Hudson worked for Cage Enterprises. They had stock with the company, and a few other connections because that's what family did, but they didn't work on the same floors as some of us and hadn't been elbow to elbow with our father before he had retired. Though dear old dad had worked in our small town more often than not in the end. In fact, Hudson didn't even live in Denver anymore. He had moved to the town we owned in the mountains.

Because of course we Cages owned a damned town. Part of me wasn't sure if the concept of having our name on everything within the town had been on purpose or had occurred organically. Though knowing my grandfather, perhaps it had been exactly what he'd wanted. He had bought up a few buildings, built a few more, and now we owned three-quarters of the town, including the major resort which brought in tourists and income.

And that was why we were here.

"You have to be here because you're evidently in the will," I said softly, trying not to get annoyed that we were waiting for our father's lawyer. Again.

"You would think he would be able to just send us a memo. I mean, it should be clear right? We all know what stakes we have in, we should just be able to do things evenly," Theo said, his gaze off into the distance. My younger brother also didn't work for the company, instead he had decided to go to culinary school, something my father had hated. But you couldn't control a Cage, that was sort of our deal.

"Why would you be cut out of the will?" I asked, honestly curious.

"Because I married a man and a woman," he drawled out. "You know he hasn't spoken to me since before the wedding," Ford said, and I saw the hurt in his gaze even though I knew he was probably trying to hide it.

"Well, he was an asshole, what do you expect?" James asked.

I looked behind Ford to see my brother and co-chair of Cage Enterprises standing with his hands in his pockets, staring out the window.

With Flynn, our vice president, standing beside him, they looked like the heads of businesses they were. While they wore suits and so did I, we were the only ones.

Dorian and Hudson were both in jeans, Hudson's having a hole at the knee. And probably not as a fashion statement, most likely because it had torn at some point, and he hadn't bothered to buy another pair. Theo was in slacks, but a Henley with his sleeves pushed up, tapping his finger just like Hudson, clearly wanting to get out of here as well. Ford had on cargo pants, and a tight black T-shirt, and looked like he had just gotten off his shift. He owned a security company with his husband and a few other friends, and did security for the Cages when he could, though I knew he didn't like to work with family often. And I knew it wasn't because of us. No, it was Father—even if he had officially *retired*. It was always Father.

And he was gone.

"Can't believe the asshole's gone," I whispered.

Ford's brows rose. "Look at that, you calling him an asshole. I'm proud."

"You should show him respect," Mother said as she came inside the room, her high heels tapping against the marble floors. I didn't bother standing up like I normally would have, because Melanie Cage looked to be in a *mood.*

She didn't look sad that Dad was gone, more like angry that he would dare go against their plans. What plans? I didn't know, but that was my mother.

She came right up to Dorian and leaned down to kiss his cheek. She didn't even bother to look at the rest of us. Dorian was Mother's favorite. Which I knew Dorian resented, but I didn't have to deal with mommy issues at this moment.

No, we had to deal with father issues at this point.

"I'm going to go get him," Flynn replied, turning toward the door. "I'm really not in the mood to wait any longer, especially since he's being so secretive about this meeting."

As I had been thinking just the same, I nodded at Flynn though he didn't need my permission. However, just then, the door opened, and I frowned when it wasn't just Mr. Winstone walking into the conference room.

I stared as an older woman walked through the door following Mr. Winstone, and four women and another man with messy hair and tattered cut-up jeans that matched Hudson's walked behind them.

The guy looked familiar, as if I'd seen him somewhere, or maybe it was just his eyes.

Where had I seen those eyes before?

"Phoebe? What are you doing here?" Ford asked as he moved forward and gripped the hands of one of the women.

"I was going to ask the same question," Phoebe asked as she looked at Ford, then around the room.

Those of us sitting stood up, confused about why this other family—because they were clearly a family—had decided to enter the room.

"We're here to meet the lawyer about my father's death, Ford. Why would you and the Cages be here?" she asked, and I wondered how the hell Mr. Winstone had fucked up so badly? Why the hell was he letting another family that clearly seemed to be in shock come into our room? This wasn't how he normally handled things.

Ford was the one who answered though—thankfully —because I had no idea what the hell was going on.

"Phoebe, we're here for my dad's will reading. What the hell is going on?" he asked. Phoebe looked around, as well as the others.

I stared at them, at the tall willowy one with wide eyes, at the smaller one with tears still in her eyes as if she was the only one truly mourning, and at the woman who seemed to be in charge, not the mother. Instead she had shrewd eyes and was glaring at all of us. The man stood back, hands in pockets, and looked just as shell-shocked as Ford.

But before Mr. Winstone or anyone else could say anything, my mother spoke in such a crisp, icy tone that I froze.

"I don't know why you're acting so dramatic. You knew your father was an asshole. He just liked creating drama," she snapped.

As I tried to catch up with her words, the older woman answered. "Melanie, stop."

This couldn't be happening. Because things started to click into place. The fact that the man at the other end of this table had our eyes, and that everybody looked so fucking shocked. I didn't know how Ford knew this Phoebe, and I would be getting answers.

"We had a deal," my mother continued, as it seemed that the rest of us were just now catching on. "You would keep your family away from mine. We would share Loren, but I got the name, I got the family. You got whatever else. But now it looks like Loren decided to be an asshole again."

"What are you talking about?" the shrewd sister asked as she came forward, her hands fisted at her side.

"Excuse me," I said, clearing my throat. I was going to be damned if I let anyone else handle this meeting. I was The Cage now. "Will someone please explain?"

"Well, I wasn't quite sure how this was going to work out," Mr. Winstone began, and we all quieted, while I wanted to strangle the man. What did he mean how *the hell this would work out?* What was this?

This seemed like a big fucking mistake.

"Loren Cage had certain provisions in his will for both of his families. And one of the many requirements that I will go over today is that this meeting must take place." He paused and I hoped it wasn't for effect, because I was going to throttle him if it was. "Loren Cage had two families. Seven sons with his wife Melanie, and four daughters and a son with his mistress, Constance."

"We went by partner," the other mother corrected.

I blinked, counting the adults in the room. "Twelve?" I asked, my voice slightly high-pitched.

"Busy fucking man," Dorian whispered.

Hudson snorted, while we just stood and stared at each other.

This could not be happening. A secret family? No, we were not that cliché.

"I can't do this," Phoebe blurted, her eyes wide.

"Oh, stop overreacting," my mother scorned.

"Do not talk to my daughter that way." The other mother glared.

"It was always going to be an issue," Mother continued. "All the secrets and the lies. And now the kids will have to deal with it. Because God forbid Loren ever deal with anything other than his own dick."

"That's enough," I snapped.

"Don't you dare talk to us like that," the shrewd sister snapped right back.

"I will talk however I damn well please. I am going to need to know exactly how this happened," I shouted over everyone else's words.

Out of the corner of my eye I saw Phoebe run through the door. Ford followed and then the tall willowy one joined.

"Shit," I snapped.

"Language," Mother bit out.

I laughed. "Really? You are going to talk to me about language."

I looked over at James, who shrugged, before he put two fingers in his mouth and whistled that high-pitched whistle that only he could do.

Everyone froze as Theo rubbed his ear and glared at me.

"Winstone," I said through gritted teeth. "I take it we all have to be here in order for this to happen?"

He cleared his throat. "At least a majority. But you all had to at least step into the room."

"Excuse me then," I said.

"You're just going to leave? Just like that?" my mother asked.

I whirled on her. "I'm going to go see if my apparent *family* is okay. Then I'm going to come back and we're going to get answers. Because there is no way that I'm going to leave here without them."

I stormed out the door, and thankfully nobody followed me.

Of course, though, I shouldn't have been too swift with that, as the woman who had to be the eldest sister practically ran to my side, her heels tapping against the marble.

"I'm coming with you."

"That's just fine." I paused, knowing that I wasn't angry at these people. No, my father and apparently our mothers were the ones that had to deal with this. I looked over at the woman who Mr. Winstone and the mothers had claimed was my sister and cleared my throat.

"I'm Aston."

"Is this really the time for introductions?" she asked.

"I'm about to go see your sister and my brother to make sure that they're fine, so sure. I would like to know the name of the woman that is running next to me right now."

"I'm running, you're walking quickly because you have such long legs."

I snorted, surprised I could even do that.

"I'm Isabella," she replied after a moment.

"I would say nice to meet you Isabella..." I let my voice trail off.

She let out a sharp laugh before shaking her head. "I'm going to need a moment to wrap my head around this, but not now."

"Same."

We stormed out of the building, and I lagged behind since Ford was standing in front of Phoebe who was in the arms of another man with dark hair and everybody seemed to be talking all at once.

"I just. I can't deal with this right now," Phoebe said, and I realized that something else must have been going on with her right then. She looked tired, and far more emotional than the rest of us.

I looked over at the man holding her and blinked. "Kane?" I asked.

Kane stared at me and let out a breath. "Wow," he said with a laugh.

"We'll handle it," Isabella put in, completely ignoring us. "And if we need to meet again later, we will." Then she looked over at Ford and I, with such menace in her gaze, I nearly took a step back. "Is that a problem?"

I raised my chin, glaring right back at her. "Not at all. However I want answers, so I'd rather not have the meeting canceled right now. But I'm also not going to force any of my," I paused, realization hitting far too hard, "*family* to stay if they don't want to."

And with that, I turned on my heel and went back into the building, with Isabella and Ford following me. Everyone was still yelling in the interim, and I cleared my throat. As Isabella had done it at the same time, everyone paused to look at me.

"Read the damn will. Because we need answers," I ordered Winstone, and he shook like a leaf before nodding.

"Okay. We can do that." He cleared his throat, then he began going over trusts and incomes and buildings and things that I would care about soon, but what I wanted to know was what the hell our father had been thinking about.

"Here's the tricky part," Winstone began, as we all leaned forward, eager to hear what the hell he had to say.

"The family money, not of the business, not of each of your inheritance from other family members, but the bulk of Loren Cage's assets will be split between all twelve kids."

"Are you kidding me?" Isabella asked. "What money? We weren't exactly poor, but we were solidly middle class."

"We did just fine," the other mother pleaded.

My mother snorted, clearly not believing the words.

I glared at the woman who raised me, willing her to say *anything*. She would probably be pushed out of the window at that point. Not by me, by someone else, but she probably would've earned it.

The lawyer continued. "However to retain the majority of current assets and to keep Cage Lake and all of its subsidiaries you will have to meet as a family once a month for three years. If this does not happen, Cage Enterprises will be broken into multiple parts and sold." He went on into the legalese that I ignored as I tried to hear over the blood pounding in my ears.

"You own a town?" the other man asked.

I looked over at the one man in the room I didn't know the name of. "Not exactly."

"Kyler," Isabella whispered.

In that moment, I realized that I had a brother named Kyler—if this was all to be believed.

"This can't be legal right?" the tall willowy person said.

"Yes Sophia, it can," their mother put in.

Oh good, another sister named Sophia.

Only one name to go. What the hell was wrong with me?

I forced my jaw to relax. "Are you telling us that we need to have all twelve of us at dinner once a month for three years in order to keep what is rightly inherited to us? To keep people in business and keep their jobs?"

"We don't need the money, but everyone else in our employ does," James snapped. "As do those we work with."

"Damn straight," Dorian growled.

"How are we supposed to believe this?" I asked, asking the obvious question.

"First, only five must attend, and two must be of a different family." The lawyer continued as if I hadn't spoken. "Of course you are *all* family..."

"Again, how are we supposed to believe this?" I asked.

"Here are the DNA tests already done."

"Are you fucking kidding me?" Isabella asked.

I looked at her, as she had literally taken the words out of my mouth.

"Isn't that sort of like a violation?" Kyler asked, his face pale.

"We need to get our own lawyers on this," James whispered.

I nodded tightly, knowing we had much more to say on this.

"There's no way this is legal," the youngest said, and I looked over at her.

"What's your name?" I asked.

"Emily. Emily Cage Dixon," she said softly, and we all froze.

"Your middle name is Cage?" I asked, biting out the words.

"All of our middle names are Cage," Sophia said, shaking her head. "I hated it but Dad wanted to be cute because our father's name was Cage Dixon, or maybe it wasn't. Is he also a bigamist?" she asked.

Her mother lifted her chin. "We never married. And no, your father's name was not Dixon, that was my maiden name."

"What?" Sophia asked. "All this time...are our grandparents even dead?"

"Yes, my parents are dead. The same with Loren's." The other mother's eyes filled with tears. "I'm sorry we lied."

"We'll get to that later," Isabella put in, and I was grateful.

I let out a breath. "In order to keep our assets, in

order to keep the family name intact, we need to have *dinner*. For three years."

The small lawyer nodded, his glasses falling down his nose. "At least five of you. And it can start three months after the funeral, which we can plan after this."

"This is ridiculous," Hudson murmured under his breath, before he got up and walked out.

I watched him go, knowing he had his own demons, and tried to understand what the hell was going on. "Why did he do this?" I asked, more to myself than anyone else.

"I never really knew the man, but apparently none of us did," Isabella said, staring off into the distance.

"Leave the paperwork and go," I ordered Winstone, and he didn't even mutter a peep. Instead, he practically ran out of the room. James and Flynn immediately went to the paperwork, and I knew they were scouring it. But from the way that their jaws tightened, I had a feeling that my father had found a way to make this legal. Because we would always have a choice to lose everything. That was the man.

"It's true," my mother put in. "You all share the same father. That was the deal when we got married, and when he decided to bring this other woman into our lives."

"I'm pretty sure you were the other woman," the other mom said.

I pinched the bridge of my nose.

"Stop. All of you." I stared at the group and realized that I was probably the eldest Cage here, other than the moms. I would deal with this. We didn't have a choice. "Whatever happens, we'll deal with it."

"You're in charge now?" Isabella asked, but Sophia shushed her.

I was grateful for that, because I had a feeling Isabella and I were going to butt heads more often than not.

I shrugged, trying to act as if my world hadn't been rocked. "I would say welcome to the Cages, because DNA evidence seems to point that way, however perhaps you were already one of us all along."

Kyler muttered something under his breath I couldn't hear before speaking up. "You have my eyes," he said.

I nodded. "Noticed that too."

The other man tilted his head. "So what, we do dinners and we make nice?"

I sighed. "We don't have to be adversaries."

"You say that as if you're the one in charge," Isabella said again.

"Because he is," Theo said, and they all stared at him.

I tried to tamp down the pride swelling at those words—along with the overwhelming pressure.

Theo continued. "He's the eldest. He's the one that takes care of us. And he's the CEO of Cage Enterprises. He's going to be the one that deals with the paperwork fallout."

"Because family is just paperwork?" Emily asked, her voice lost.

I shook my head. "No, family is insane, and apparently, it's been secret all along. And it looks like we have a few introductions to make, and a few tests to redo. But if it turns out it's true, we're Cages, and we don't back down."

"And what does that mean?" Isabella asked, her tone far too careful.

Theo was the one who finally answered. "It means we're going to have to figure shit out."

And for just an instant, the thought of that beautiful woman with that gorgeous smile came to mind, and I pushed those thoughts away. My family was breaking, or perhaps breaking open. And I didn't have time to worry about things like a woman who had made me smile.

The Cages needed me and after today's meeting there would be no going back to sanity.

Ever.

Finish reading The Forever Rule and get to know the Cage Family!

Also from Carrie Ann Ryan

The Montgomery Ink Legacy Series:

Book 1: Bittersweet Promises (Leif & Brooke)

Book 2: At First Meet (Nick & Lake)

Book 2.5: Happily Ever Never (May & Leo)

Book 3: Longtime Crush (Sebastian & Raven)

Book 4: Best Friend Temptation (Noah, Ford, and Greer)

Book 4.5: Happily Ever Maybe (Jennifer & Gus)

Book 5: Last First Kiss (Daisy & Hugh)

Book 6: His Second Chance (Kane & Phoebe)

Book 7: One Night with You (Kingston & Claire)

Book 8: Accidentally Forever (Crew & Aria)

Book 9: Last Chance Seduction (Lexington & Mercy)

The Wilder Brothers Series:

Book 1: One Way Back to Me (Eli & Alexis)

Book 2: Always the One for Me (Evan & Kendall)

Book 3: The Path to You (Everett & Bethany)

Book 4: Coming Home for Us (Elijah & Maddie)

Book 5: Stay Here With Me (East & Lark)

Book 6: Finding the Road to Us (Elliot, Trace, and Sidney)

Book 7: Moments for You (Ridge & Aurora)

Book 7.5: A Wilder Wedding (Amos & Naomi)

Book 8: Forever For Us (Wyatt & Ava)

Book 9: Pieces of Me (Gabriel & Briar)

Book 10: Endlessly Yours (Brooks & Rory)

The Cage Family

Book 1: The Forever Rule (Aston & Blakely)

Book 2: An Unexpected Everything (Isabella & Weston)

Book 3: If You Were Mine (Dorian & Harper)

Clover Lake

Book 1: Always a Fake Bridesmaid (Livvy & Ewan)

The First Time Series:

Book 1: Good Time Boyfriend (Heath & Devney)

Book 2: Last Minute Fiancé (Luca & Addison)

Book 3: Second Chance Husband (August & Paisley)

Montgomery Ink Denver:

Book 0.5: Ink Inspired (Shep & Shea)

Book 0.6: Ink Reunited (Sassy, Rare, and Ian)

Book 1: Delicate Ink (Austin & Sierra)

Book 1.5: Forever Ink (Callie & Morgan)

Book 2: Tempting Boundaries (Decker and Miranda)

Book 3: Harder than Words (Meghan & Luc)

Book 3.5: Finally Found You (Mason & Presley)

Book 4: Written in Ink (Griffin & Autumn)

Book 4.5: Hidden Ink (Hailey & Sloane)

Book 5: Ink Enduring (Maya, Jake, and Border)

Book 6: Ink Exposed (Alex & Tabby)

Book 6.5: Adoring Ink (Holly & Brody)

Book 6.6: Love, Honor, & Ink (Arianna & Harper)

Book 7: Inked Expressions (Storm & Everly)

Book 7.3: Dropout (Grayson & Kate)

Book 7.5: Executive Ink (Jax & Ashlynn)

Book 8: Inked Memories (Wes & Jillian)

Book 8.5: Inked Nights (Derek & Olivia)

Book 8.7: Second Chance Ink (Brandon & Lauren)

Book 8.5: Montgomery Midnight Kisses (Alex & Tabby Bonus(

Bonus: Inked Kingdom (Stone & Sarina)

Montgomery Ink: Colorado Springs

Book 1: Fallen Ink (Adrienne & Mace)

Book 2: Restless Ink (Thea & Dimitri)

Book 2.5: Ashes to Ink (Abby & Ryan)

Book 3: Jagged Ink (Roxie & Carter)

Book 3.5: Ink by Numbers (Landon & Kaylee)

The Montgomery Ink: Boulder Series:

Book 1: Wrapped in Ink (Liam & Arden)

Book 2: Sated in Ink (Ethan, Lincoln, and Holland)

Book 3: Embraced in Ink (Bristol & Marcus)

Book 3: Moments in Ink (Zia & Meredith)

Book 4: Seduced in Ink (Aaron & Madison)

Book 4.5: Captured in Ink (Julia, Ronin, & Kincaid)

Book 4.7: Inked Fantasy (Secret ??)

Book 4.8: A Very Montgomery Christmas (The Entire Boulder Family)

The Montgomery Ink: Fort Collins Series:

Book 1: Inked Persuasion (Jacob & Annabelle)

Book 2: Inked Obsession (Beckett & Eliza)

Book 3: Inked Devotion (Benjamin & Brenna)
Book 3.5: Nothing But Ink (Clay & Riggs)
Book 4: Inked Craving (Lee & Paige)
Book 5: Inked Temptation (Archer & Killian)

The Promise Me Series:

Book 1: Forever Only Once (Cross & Hazel)
Book 2: From That Moment (Prior & Paris)
Book 3: Far From Destined (Macon & Dakota)
Book 4: From Our First (Nate & Myra)

The Whiskey and Lies Series:

Book 1: Whiskey Secrets (Dare & Kenzie)
Book 2: Whiskey Reveals (Fox & Melody)
Book 3: Whiskey Undone (Loch & Ainsley)

The Gallagher Brothers Series:

Book 1: Love Restored (Graham & Blake)
Book 2: Passion Restored (Owen & Liz)
Book 3: Hope Restored (Murphy & Tessa)

The Less Than Series:

Book 1: Breathless With Her (Devin & Erin)
Book 2: Reckless With You (Tucker & Amelia)
Book 3: Shameless With Him (Caleb & Zoey)

The Fractured Connections Series:

Book 1: Breaking Without You (Cameron & Violet)
Book 2: Shouldn't Have You (Brendon & Harmony)
Book 3: Falling With You (Aiden & Sienna)
Book 4: Taken With You (Beckham & Meadow)

The On My Own Series:

Book 0.5: My First Glance
Book 1: My One Night (Dillon & Elise)
Book 2: My Rebound (Pacey & Mackenzie)
Book 3: My Next Play (Miles & Nessa)
Book 4: My Bad Decisions (Tanner & Natalie)

The Ravenwood Coven Series:

Book 1: Dawn Unearthed
Book 2: Dusk Unveiled
Book 3: Evernight Unleashed

The Aspen Pack Series:

Book 1: Etched in Honor
Book 2: Hunted in Darkness
Book 3: Mated in Chaos
Book 4: Harbored in Silence
Book 5: Marked in Flames

The Talon Pack:

Book 1: <u>Tattered Loyalties</u>
Book 2: <u>An Alpha's Choice</u>
Book 3: <u>Mated in Mist</u>
Book 4: <u>Wolf Betrayed</u>
Book 5: <u>Fractured Silence</u>
Book 6: <u>Destiny Disgraced</u>
Book 7: <u>Eternal Mourning</u>
Book 8: <u>Strength Enduring</u>
Book 9: <u>Forever Broken</u>
Book 10: Mated in Darkness
Book 11: Fated in Winter

Redwood Pack Series:

Book 1: <u>An Alpha's Path</u>
Book 2: <u>A Taste for a Mate</u>
Book 3: <u>Trinity Bound</u>
Book 3.5: <u>A Night Away</u>
Book 4: <u>Enforcer's Redemption</u>
Book 4.5: <u>Blurred Expectations</u>
Book 4.7: <u>Forgiveness</u>
Book 5: <u>Shattered Emotions</u>
Book 6: <u>Hidden Destiny</u>
Book 6.5: <u>A Beta's Haven</u>
Book 7: <u>Fighting Fate</u>
Book 7.5: <u>Loving the Omega</u>
Book 7.7: <u>The Hunted Heart</u>

Book 8: Wicked Wolf

The Elements of Five Series:

Book 1: From Breath and Ruin

Book 2: From Flame and Ash

Book 3: From Spirit and Binding

Book 4: From Shadow and Silence

Dante's Circle Series:

Book 1: Dust of My Wings

Book 2: Her Warriors' Three Wishes

Book 3: An Unlucky Moon

Book 3.5: His Choice

Book 4: Tangled Innocence

Book 5: Fierce Enchantment

Book 6: An Immortal's Song

Book 7: Prowled Darkness

Book 8: Dante's Circle Reborn

Holiday, Montana Series:

Book 1: Charmed Spirits

Book 2: Santa's Executive

Book 3: Finding Abigail

Book 4: Her Lucky Love

Book 5: Dreams of Ivory

The Branded Pack Series:
(Written with Alexandra Ivy)

Book 1: <u>Stolen and Forgiven</u>

Book 2: <u>Abandoned and Unseen</u>

Book 3: <u>Buried and Shadowed</u>

Acknowledgments

I never write a book alone. Over time, my team and help line has truly grown.

Thank you Brandi for all you do. You truly saved this book in more ways than one. We deserve our travel day because no amount of growling will be able to erase the path of getting this book published.

Lauren, Ann, Classy, Brianna, Ashley, and Ann Marie—thank you for teaching me that I'm allowed to ask for help. I'm so grateful to be able to work on Aria and Crew and focus on what they needed, knowing other things were being handled.

Emily and Tina — Your group chats are seriously the only way I get through the day.

Sarina, Kyla, Lauren, Kate, Jess, Gwyn, Eric, Christine, Echo, Meghan, Hailey, Maria, Claire, Dakota, Kat, and crew — thank you for all of the pep talks, plot help, and author crew needs that remind me we aren't alone in this author world.

Jaycee, Wander, T, and I - Thank you for your craft in graphics, photos, and art!

Lasheera - I'm so honored you're my agent! Thank you for working so hard to get the Montgomerys in so many parts of the world. You work like no one I know and I'm in awe of your talent.

Thank you Wesley, M, Honor, and Rose. Thank you for trusting me with your stories and research as I did my best to bring Aria and Crew to life. I hope I did y'all proud.

Farrah Rochon, thank you for reaching me about Souper Cubes so I cold freeze my meals and work late nights on this book. Seriously, you changed the game. Plus I love your books!

Thank you to R,S,K, and R for being there for me during this book. Crew was grumpy, therefore I was. (Haha. That's my excuse!) So thank you for dealing with me!

Maxie, Bingo, Cane, and Sundae - thank you for laying on my hands, trying to break my computer, and sitting on me for most of this book. Yes. I'm thanking my cats for being annoying. But seriously. Knowing I wasn't alone truly helped in some parts of this book!

Thank last, but certainly not least, thank you dear readers. You've been with me for years, months, or days, and I appreciate you so much. I never thought this would be my career and I couldn't keep going without you.

Happy Reading, My Irises!

~Carrie Ann

About the Author

Carrie Ann Ryan is the New York Times and USA Today bestselling author of contemporary, paranormal, and young adult romance. Her works include the Montgomery Ink, Redwood Pack, Fractured Connections, and Elements of Five series, which have sold over 3.0 million books worldwide. She started writing while in graduate school for her advanced degree in chemistry and hasn't stopped since. Carrie Ann has written over seventy-five novels and novellas with more in the works. When she's not losing herself in her emotional and action-packed worlds, she's reading as much as she can while wrangling her clowder of cats who have more followers than she does.

www.CarrieAnnRyan.com

Made in United States
North Haven, CT
24 August 2025

72106444R00232